# Veiled

## in D

A
Wedding
Planner
Mystery

Lacy and lethal . . .

# Stephanie Blackmoore

**KENSINGTON**
U.S. $8.99
CAN $11.99

## SAY "I DO" TO THE
## WEDDING PLANNER MYSTERIES!

EAN

ISBN-13: 978-1-4967-1755-9
ISBN-10: 1-4967-1755-4

Tabitha picked at her newly arrived razzleberry pie. The server had placed the pies on the table with a warmed dollop of French vanilla ice cream running in rivulets through the red-and-blue baked fruit.

"Mallory." Her voice grew even more serious. "I love history. I love material culture. But I saw a man die over it. That veil is trouble. I want you to get it out of your possession."

"I couldn't agree more." The veil was seeming more like a curse at this point than a boon. I thought of the psychological damage keeping such a secret had wrought on my friend. I recalled how the Pierces' machinations and power had ruined good people's lives. I didn't want to get messed up in that. I gave my friend's hand another squeeze.

Tabitha took in a restorative, if shaky breath, and tried to drink some coffee, but only succeeded in spilling several sloshes on the table. "What I can't figure out now was how the veil, missing these twenty-five years, got in our shop."

"Your store is the perfect hiding spot," I mused. "Or someone could be trying to frame you guys. But it looked like that hatbox had been in the basement of the Antique Emporium for a long time." I stared into space, feeling good enough to eat most of my pie. "What I can't get is whether what happened at Cordials and Cannonballs had something to do with this."

"Just promise you won't go all Nancy Drew and try to solve this, Mallory." She held out her pinky and made me swear not to intervene. I joined in her laughter. No way would I touch this . . .

Books by Stephanie Blackmoore

ENGAGED IN DEATH

MURDER WEARS WHITE

MURDER BORROWED, MURDER BLUE

GOWN WITH THE WIND

MARRY CHRISTMAS MURDER

VEILED IN DEATH

Published by Kensington Publishing Corp.

# Veiled in Death

## Stephanie Blackmoore

KENSINGTON BOOKS
www.kensingtonbooks.com

KENSINGTON BOOKS are published by

Kensington Publishing Corp.
119 West 40th Street
New York, NY 10018

All Kensington titles, imprints, and distributed lines are available at special quantity discounts for bulk purchases for sales promotion, premiums, fund-raising, and educational or institutional use.

Special book excerpts or customized printings can also be created to fit specific needs. For details, write or phone the office of the Kensington Sales Manager: Kensington Publishing Corp., 119 West 40th Street, New York, NY 10018. Attn. Sales Department. Phone: 1-800-221-2647.

Kensington and the K logo Reg. U.S. Pat. & TM Off.

First Kensington Books Mass Market Paperback Printing: October 2020

ISBN-13: 978-1-4967-1755-9
ISBN-10: 1-4967-1755-4

ISBN-13: 978-1-4967-1756-6 (ebook)
ISBN-10: 1-4967-1756-2 (ebook)

10 9 8 7 6 5 4 3 2 1

Printed in the United States of America

For my mom and dad

# CHAPTER ONE

"So, are you going to get hitched or not?" My dear friend Bev Mitchell raised one artfully plucked blond brow above her purple cat's-eye glasses. The rhinestones adorning the frames twinkled as merrily as the mirth in her eyes. Her basset hound, Elvis, opened one droopy eye to regard his mistress. His floppy ears barely moved as he swiveled his gaze from Bev to me. Then he placed one smooth paw over his eyes and returned to his nap. Apparently, he wasn't interested in having this conversation.

*That makes two of us, buddy.*

"Of course!" I tried to tamp down the frisson of annoyance I heard escape my lips. I took a measured breath. Although we were dear friends, today Bev was also technically a client. I wanted to focus on the business at hand and help her plan her upcoming wedding. Meddling in my love life was not on my to-do list for today. I pasted a serene smile

on my face and answered Bev in a more modulated tone. "We're just deciding some last-minute
things. Like whether to get married at work or not."

It was true. Most brides wouldn't give a fleeting
thought about getting hitched at the place where
they earned their living. It simply wouldn't make
sense. But as a wedding planner, my biggest hesitation was whether or not to get married at my home
and also my place of business, the mansion where
I regularly held weekend weddings.

"Oh, hogwash. I know a professional procrasti-
nator when I see one." Bev gave my arm a warm
squeeze and returned to the task at hand, foraging
for antique pieces to gussy up her own wedding.
Bev and her lucky beau were due to wed in less
than three weeks. Bev bestowed me with a gentle
smile and amended her statement. "But you've
only been hesitant when it comes to planning your
very *own* wedding. You've been pitch-perfect planning my big day! I can't wait!" Bev forgot her haranguing and held up her find, a daisy-themed
brooch made of citrines and pearls. Her eyes grew
wide with excitement as she held the bauble up to
the light. She nodded and placed the brooch into
an already overflowing rattan basket of wares with a
contented smile. Bev was no doubt imagining her
own nuptials and how the brooch tied in seamlessly
with her theme. I breathed an inward sigh of relief.

*I'm off the hook. For now.*

Bev and I had spent the last hour pouring over
the wares in the Antique Emporium. Bev showed
no signs of slowing down, and I gave myself an

imaginary pat on the back. We'd begun this planning session even earlier in the day, starting out with mugs of coffee in the garden behind my mansion B and B. We'd spent a contemplative and productive hour on the swath of land anchored with its very own hulking mansion, a place with its very own name, Thistle Park. Bev was set on having an outdoor wedding, and we'd strolled around the garden in the early morning sunlight, the June sunrise evaporating the fine dusting of dew glinting off each petal and blade of grass. Bev had nearly dropped her mug of steaming French roast when she alighted on a backdrop of lush and cheery daisies.

"That's it! The perfect spot. This is where I want the trellis placed, and where I want to exchange my vows with Jesse."

Her decree several hours ago had sealed the deal and finally given me a definitive theme for her ceremony and reception. Bev's wedding to Jesse would be lush and sophisticatedly simple, drawing largely on elements from both the garden and the Fourth of July. I would design the wedding around the aforementioned daisies in the fields, as well as star-patterned tablecloths, and my sister would make Bev and Jesse a cake featuring red accents and sparklers.

"Is this too cheesy?" Bev furrowed her blond brows behind the frames of her bedazzled spectacles. She struggled as she held aloft a rather large oil painting of a field of daisies.

"Ooh, not at all. We could put this on an easel

in the front hall, right next to the guest book. Bring a little of the magic and wonder of the outdoors inside." I smiled as Bev placed a small green sticker on the back of the painting's frame, claiming it for her own. I took a step back and nearly grew dizzy taking in all of the Antique Emporium's wares. We were in a small room, one of many that made up the rabbit warren of spaces that occupied the deceptively small-looking store. It featured a narrow storefront but spanned the length of two city blocks as its depth made up for the lack of width. The store teetered on the edge of being categorized as carefully cluttered, and barely resisted sliding into chaos. The labyrinthine layout of a marching succession of small rooms kept the whole visit from becoming overwhelming. The proprietress of the store, June Battles, knew her way around the knickknack chaos. She could famously find an item in thirty seconds flat, seemingly having catalogued her wares by memory.

I cradled a small set of ceramic leaves arranged in a crystal vase. The leaves made a pleasant plink against the cut crystal.

"Looking for inspiration for your own big day, hmm?" Bev couldn't tamp down her grin. Her cessation in nagging me about setting a wedding date of my own had been annoyingly short.

I set the pretty display down and stifled a rueful smile. "Maybe I am."

It was time to stop being annoyed at the well-meaning friends and family in my life who could never stop haranguing me about picking a wedding date. I glanced at the pretty champagne antique diamond ring on my finger, a vintage estate piece my fiancé, Garrett, had procured from this very store.

"At least we've narrowed our wedding down to one season," I added wryly. I abandoned the promise I made mere minutes ago not to take Bev's bait, as I couldn't resist defending myself against the gossip about my refusal to seal the deal on my fiancé's proposal.

"Let me guess." Bev cocked her head, her highly teased platinum beehive teetering as if she'd designed her hair to replicate the Leaning Tower of Pisa. But the beehive stayed put. Her gravity-defying do always remained artfully atop her head, with nary a spritz of hair spray, and today was no exception. A slow smile graced Bev's face. "Fall!"

I rewarded Bev with a smile of my own. "You know my tastes well."

My beau and I had indeed decided on an autumn ceremony and reception. The light in Port Quincy, Pennsylvania, would be mellow and cozy. The lovely tree-lined streets would be adorned with leaves in a riot of color. The orange, topaz, rich red maple, and vibrant yellow leaves would set the tone. I could picture a banquet chock-full of sweet and savory foods, seamlessly melding comfort and sophistication.

*But it's so far away.*

I brushed away that nagging thought and told myself at least it was still happening, albeit months later than I'd prefer. After some crazy events had befallen me, my family, and my business, I was secretly itching to get hitched. When I joked about eloping to Vegas, my fiancé, Garrett, was all for it. But my secret rush to wed was not what everyone else saw. They saw a bride who was continually stalling and delaying and waiting for the perfect time to wed. But I was no Goldilocks bride. I just simply didn't have the time and space in my schedule to throw my own wedding. Not just yet. Which was good, because my mother, Carole, was pushing to occupy *the* starring role planning my wedding, and I didn't want the impending drama.

My phone vibrated with an angry buzz, like a taunted yellow jacket. Bev raised one brow as I let out a sigh. "It's my mother."

It was as if thinking of her had conjured her from the cell-phone-wave ether. I squinted to read the text in the somewhat muted light.

**Sorry I can't make it, sweetie.**

I breathed a sigh of relief. My mom was well-meaning, and an expert steamroller to boot. She would have no misgivings about riding roughshod over my very own plans for my very own wedding if she disagreed stylistically. And she'd been dying to be here to help me start looking for inspiration for my wedding. But Mom's decorating and staging business was booming. She had her own business meetings scheduled today. She had initially expressed guilt over missing a chance to go antiquing. Until she'd heard the purpose of today's visit was to help Bev plan her wedding.

Many moons ago, after my father had left, Mom briefly dated Bev's fiancé, Jesse. Although Mom and

Jesse's relationship was long in the past, Mom and Bev still performed a tetchy little dance each time their paths crossed in the small town of Port Quincy. While the two women weren't outwardly hostile, unfortunately and understandably, I predicted they'd never truly feel comfortable in each other's company.

My phone buzzed again with another text.

**I did come across this today. I couldn't help myself!**

Attached to my mother's text was a grainy photo of a cream layette set for an infant.

"Oh, c'mon, Mom!" I dropped my phone into the depths of my bag, refusing to engage and take the bait. Bev gave me an amused and quizzical look.

"You might tease me too much about how long it's taking me to tie the knot, but at least you're not nagging me about grandchildren. My mom really needs to slow her roll."

A knowing look lit up Bev's face, and I regretted my little outburst immediately. Bev was a dear friend but also the biggest gossip this side of the Monongahela River.

"Not that I'm even thinking about that yet," I backtracked hastily. "I need to focus on your wedding, and mine!" I heard the panicked cheeriness in my voice and hastily wheeled around to hide the blush I felt warming my neck. The truth was, I'd been thinking a lot about my mom's constant nagging to give her a grandchild.

My fiancé had been maddeningly unspecific about whether we should have a child. Up until my mother's constant hints and nudges, I'd been ambivalent, too. I'd always thought of it as a someday thing. The door wasn't closed and there was certainly no deadline. But lately my mother's needling was getting to me. She'd set my biological clock a-ticking and a-tocking. And I'd realized with a start that I hadn't had a real discussion about the matter with Garrett. Just bringing up the matter would be a big deal. It would no doubt cause seismic shocks to the little family we were about to create with the two of us and his fourteen-year-old daughter, Summer.

"Holy tamale." I stopped pacing from Bev and stood still. Before me was a dress that was nothing short of a vision. I took it as a sign that I could push my weightier concerns away for the moment and concentrate on the present.

Bev joined me and let out a low whistle. Elvis briefly raised his head from his paw, then went back to sleep. "That dress is lovely, Mallory."

I couldn't tear my eyes from the pretty lace sundress silhouetted in the window. It was a deep mellow color reminiscent of French vanilla ice cream. The fit would be barely off the shoulder, with a simple yet slightly daring deep V-neck top. The bodice was fitted with subtle pleats, and the barely flared bell skirt with its whimsical lace overlay nearly floated in the soft ceiling-fan breeze. The dress was a kind of a country-chic version of Jackie Kennedy's gown, if such a thing were possible. It was probably meant to be tea length, but if I tried it on, I bet it would skim my ankles. It would look equally stunning with low-heeled sandals, wedges, or flats. I'd come to favor wearing chic flats during big events as I bustled around making sure everything was going well. It had been difficult to return to sky-high heels the few times I'd tried. Comfort reigned in my job, but the flats I chose weren't boring. I always advised my own brides to tuck away a comfy but pretty pair of sandals or ballet shoes for their reception. I could picture wearing stunning, but still comfortable shoes with this dress for the whole day in order to accent and accommodate the ankle-skimming and train-less length.

I couldn't suppress a grin. This dress was some kind of lightning-bolt muse.

I was just getting started with ideas percolating rapid fire in my brain as I reached out to touch the creamy lace. I'd been excited to marry Garrett, of course, but hadn't been too enthused about planning the wedding. I was suffering from a strong case of wedding burnout, an occupational hazard of being a wedding planner. But this dress was the spark. A catalyst to get me out of my funk and inspire my mind with hundreds of ideas.

*This is it.*

And I had accompanying me today the best person to consult about the dress. Bev was the owner of Port Quincy's only bridal shop, Silver Bells, and an excellent seamstress as well.

"Can you work your magic on this dress?" I turned eagerly to Bev and rushed on in my excitement. "What would be most appropriate? A backyard wedding? Or perhaps something small in the greenhouse?" I took in Bev's amusement and prattled on. "This is definitely a summer wedding dress. Dare I move things up?" I felt a slow, sly smile steal over my face. A moved-up summer wedding would quell the rumors of my supposed cold feet. And I'd owe it all to the unlikely inspiration from this sweet and sophisticated gem of a dress.

Port Quincy's resident wedding-dress expert tsked and stared down her button nose at the pretty lace on the dress form in the window. Two frown lines marred the smooth expanse of her forehead beneath the beehive.

*Uh-oh.*

I didn't like where Bev's initial silent opinion was going.

"But I thought you had your heart set on fall." Bev's reminder sent me spiraling back to earth from the heady orbit the dress had sent me to.

"I guess so." I felt the magic glow of the dress fade and rallied to preserve it. "But this dress could still work, right?" I turned beseechingly to my friend. "I could tweak the accessories to make it work for fall."

Bev's blue eyes took on a kind cast behind her outrageous glasses. "I think this dress is lovely, too, Mallory. But it's a little informal, don't you think? This dress is much more suited for rehearsal dinner fare. It's far from an actual gown."

I felt Bev's pronouncement with a visceral stab, as if it were a long pin popping and deflating my wedding balloon hopes. Hopes I wasn't even aware I'd had minutes ago.

Bev seemed to realize her words had wounded me and rushed on. "You could pair it with a chocolate velvet jacket or a butternut scarf for your fall wedding. It would be perfect for the rehearsal dinner, before the big day when you don a gown befitting of your prowess as a wedding planner."

I felt my head numbly bob up and down in shocked agreement. I had indeed just revealed to Bev that Garrett and I had chosen a fall palette. Bev did know my style, but also what made the most impact, from collaborating with me on dozens of weddings. I dimly wondered if Bev's resistance to this pretty dress stemmed from a not-so-hidden motive. I bet Bev wanted me to purchase my dress from her store. Not for any crass reasons, like earning a sale, but for the experience of helping a dear friend choose her own special dress. Bev seemed to read my mind, confirming my hunch.

"Of course I will dress you!" Bev clapped her hands together at the prospect.

I laughed and found myself reluctantly joining in Bev's enthusiasm. I remembered trying on wedding gowns as a stunt double for my friend Olivia's wedding. Bev had hundreds of sample gowns in her shop, and I was sure to find the perfect attire for the cozy fall wedding I'd envisioned.

"Yes, of course I will get a dress from your shop, Bev. The sundress is lovely, but maybe not for a wedding. Especially since a fall ceremony will need a slightly more dramatic dress to compete with the foliage."

I reluctantly made up my mind and turned my

back firmly against the ethereal sundress. My fingers were drawn to a display of vintage earrings hanging from wicker birdcage bars. The heavy, crystal stalactites seemed to help anchor me back in reality after I'd gone gaga over the impractical sundress.

Bev let out a squeal of delight. "Yes, *this* is your style, Mallory. We'll find a gown befitting these beauties. Satin for fall, or maybe even a rich brocade if you stray into November." She wiggled her eyebrows impatiently, the neat blond arches dancing above her rhinestone cat's-eye purple spectacles. "We'll know exactly the right look to go for, if you ever nail down the darn wedding date!"

A pretty trill of baby laughter announced June's arrival. The owner of the Antique Emporium was a foster mom, and today a delightfully cooing infant peered at us from her perch in the front-facing baby carrier. June carefully approached us, weaving expertly among her room of things, giving some items a loving pat. June Battles had an affinity for history, just like her daughter Tabitha, who ran the historical society. While Tabitha curated items for posterity and the public good, June just happened to sell them and match them up with new owners.

"Hello, Bev and Mallory." June swooped in for a hug, treating me to the sweet smell of baby lotion. The baby made a swipe for one of the crystal earrings I held in my hand.

"That's the only occupational hazard to contend with when I bring Miri to work with me." June chuckled as she extricated the crystal prism from the baby's grasping hand. "Everything in this store looks like a shiny toy to a six-month-old." The infant's visage dimmed for a moment, before June expertly replaced the earring with a buzzing rattle. Miri laughed and turned her attention to the toy.

"I couldn't help but see how taken you were with this item, Mallory." June gestured toward the ethereal sundress, and gently turned me around when I refused to follow her gaze. I did, however, take in the momentary scowl on Bev's face.

"I'm not certain this dress will work for the fall wedding I've tentatively planned," I murmured to June. I shouldn't have turned back around. I found myself falling in love all over again with the sundress, practicality be damned. It would be ridiculous to plan a whole wedding around this budget find. But I realized with a start I encouraged the couples I worked with to do just that.

"And I think the crystal earrings would actually work quite well with the sundress." June nimbly plucked an earring from the birdcage and held it up in the air above the sundress, where the earring would hang when worn by the woman lucky enough to purchase the pretty garment.

"Hm. It's eclectic, but it would work!" I felt my excitement growing and kindled all over again. Bev wasn't so subtle this time. Her groan caused Elvis to wake again, his doggie head swiveling back and forth between gazing at his owner and at June and me.

"Yes, Mallory." June shared in my excitement. "The sundress is casual, and the crystal earrings are formal. The two would be an unlikely pairing,

but the juxtaposition would be interesting and unexpected." June's eyes quickly took me in before she
turned her keen gaze to the dress. "You wouldn't
even need to alter it, I bet. It's vintage, from the
early 1960s. It would complement your figure perfectly." June deftly unzipped the dress from the
dress form. She swiveled around quickly to hand
me the garment just out of baby Miri's sticky grasp.

"Thank you." I heard a certain note of rever-
ence in my voice. I held the dress against my even
more informal coral skirt and striped tank top and
peered into a gilt mirror affixed to the wall.

It was truly a magical dress. I performed an impetuous, joyful spin and my doppelganger in the
mirror broke out in an infectious grin. I recalled
the not-quite-right ball gown my would-be mother-
in-law Helene had once strong-armed me into
choosing.

*This dress was made for you.*

I finally took in Bev's terse smile hovering just
behind me in the mirror.

"Or this could be a perfect rehearsal look for
Mallory," Bev put in flatly. "Or the starting inspiration for Mallory's eventual gown choice. But not
for the main event."

June shrugged, seeming to wish to avoid a fight
over a sundress. "Maybe you're right. This pretty
little thing might not have enough stature for a big
autumn wedding. And you are Port Quincy's dress
expert, my dear." June gave Bev's arm a knowing
pat without a hint of condescension.

I felt a bubble of annoyance drift up just as Bev relaxed. My friend's wedding-gown expertise was duly noted, and territory over my dress choice was ceded. Before I could protest, June sent me a subtle wink. I felt my bubble of annoyance burst and gave a relieved laugh. June had an impressive and well-honed emotional IQ and had defused the situation expertly. As much as I adored Bev and usually sought out her wedding-gown expertise, I wasn't giving up my dream dress without a fight. A diplomatic, well-meaning fight.

I smiled at both women. "I'll think about the dress, June. It would certainly work well as a rehearsal dinner look, or even a second reception dress. I'll talk it over with Garrett, and probably be back." A wave of relief washed over me as we all pondered the dress. I instantly felt better after announcing my intentions to purchase the dress soon. As a wedding planner, I was used to making quick and decisive recommendations for my brides. But I needed a smidge more time for myself. I'd purchase the dress after chatting with my fiancé and decide later how I'd incorporate it into my wedding celebrations, whether as the starring centerpiece of my look, or merely a bit player. A shiver stole down my spine as I recalled the wedding I'd called off several summers ago. Unbeknownst to me at the time, the experience had kicked off my wedding-planner career. I wasn't going to be strong-armed into making decisions about this wedding, the only one I planned on ever having.

"Anything else for you?" June glanced at Bev's overflowing basket of flower-themed wares with keen approval.

"These earrings, too." I reached beyond June to pluck a pair of heavy crystal earrings that had remained on the birdcage. These ones were faceted briolettes in the shape of fat teardrops, clear yet carved enough to throw off some subtle sparkle.

June's eyes went wide as she took in the set. "I didn't think I'd put these out. Pia must have found them." She looked as if she wanted to make a grab for the jewelry, and I wondered if I'd be able to purchase them after all.

June confirmed my suspicions. She leaned in closer for a better look and rewarded me with another baby-powder whiff from Miri. "There's supposed to be a necklace that matches this very pair." She tut-tutted and shook her head. "I promise to find the missing crystal necklace that goes with these beauties. For now, I'll hold on to them for safekeeping and eventually sell it to you as a set!" Before I could stop her, June grabbed the pretty baubles as if she were a magpie alighting on a particularly glittery find.

I followed June to the front of the store, exchanging a shrug with Bev. Elvis finally woke up for good, and trotted dutifully behind his mistress, his droopy basset ears nearly skimming the rose-patterned carpet of the antiques store. His short little legs needed to churn to keep up. Maybe June really was holding back on the sale of the earrings until she found the matching necklace. The pieces would look stunning on my big day, whether I ended up pairing them with the sundress or not.

And before I could give the incident of snatching back the earrings another thought, a pint-sized version of June arrived on the scene.

"There. This is the last heap of stuff from the northwest corner of the basement." The girl before me set a stack of ancient luggage down on a wide oak table in the center of the store. A pillar of dust rose from her column of suitcases. June wheeled around to cover baby Miri until the dust had literally settled.

June leaned over to plant a kiss on the dirt-smudged cheek of the pretty girl wearing an incongruous crown of dust bunnies. "Pia, my little ragamuffin." She spoke the term with much love.

"You need to get a little dirty working in an antique store, Mom." The pretty redhead smiled up at her mom. Both women sported auburn locks, but June's were cropped short and threaded with silver. The young woman's tresses were bound in a low ponytail.

"I'll have you know I run a tight ship around here," June protested, gesturing to the almost-cluttered but also orderly store. "My mother, Claudia, is in charge of inventory in the basement, and let's just say I didn't inherit my organizing genes from her."

I realized with a start that Pia must be my good friend Tabitha's younger sister. Tabitha, the town historian, chose to dye her hair a striking Ariel-the-mermaid red, while Pia's looked like her natural color, a subtler shade of auburn. Tabitha was a whole head taller than Pia, just like my sister, Rachel, who towered over me.

"Let's see what you found." June bounced a now-fussy Miri as she anxiously awaited the opening of the luggage.

"They were pretty heavy." Pia started with a pretty pink leather hatbox. The pale-shell shade of the leather and smooth grain of the luggage made it look like a giant makeup compact. "Hm." Inside the box was another hatbox, this one a more daring magenta. Pia let out a laugh as she found yet another, smaller hatbox within, this one a light pink with magenta polka dots, marrying the colors of the two larger pieces encasing them.

"They're like girly luggage Russian nesting dolls." I blurted out my assessment as Pia opened the last hatbox.

"Nada." Pia's expectant look deflated as she patted the inside of the hatbox.

"The set is gorgeous, though," Bev cooed. "I would love to purchase this, too! All cleaned up, these three hatboxes would make a darling addition to my wedding trousseau."

I knew Bev and Jesse were headed to Williamsburg, Virginia, with Bev's teenage son, Preston, for her honeymoon.

June blushed again. "They're all yours. But please don't pick them up until tomorrow, when I've had a chance to scrub off all of the accumulated grime." She made to swipe a finger through the dust adorning the bright luggage, then stopped herself at the last second. She couldn't suppress a shudder, though.

I realized that though the store was chockablock full of antiques, everything was meticulously polished and pristine with nary a speck of dust anywhere. Well, until Pia had brought up the luggage.

"Claudia promised me she'd get the basement under control." June rolled her eyes and gestured below her. "My mom doesn't keep the most meticulous records. The upstairs of the Antique Emporium is *my* domain. I like to think of this floor as carefully ordered chaos. But Claudia's basement? *Pfft.*" June shook her head. "That's *true* chaos."

A small frown stole over Pia's pretty face. She had a chameleon look, sometimes recalling the sharper features of her sister, Tabitha. At other angles, she favored her mother's slightly softer features. "Grandma Claudia finds the neatest stuff, though, Mom. She has the best eye of the three of us. You can't argue with that."

June seemed to melt at the defense of her mother given by her daughter. "Fair enough, sweetie. The three of us make a great team."

I beamed at her admission. It was fun to imagine three generations of women working together in this store. Though I'd never set eyes on Pia until this very day. I knew she'd been away at college in Washington, D.C.

"Hold up." Pia bit her lower lip as she patted the inside of the last hatbox. "Do you feel something?" Her slim fingers hovered over a slight split in the top panel of the luggage. There seemed to be a barely perceptible rent in the now faded, but once-lurid red satin lining the hatbox.

"Ooh, let me see." Bev ran her plump and capable fingers over the torn fabric. "I can fix this right up. But I think I know what you mean, Pia. Maybe there's something in there?"

The nested hatboxes seemed to contain even more surprises.

"This is like a little treasure hunt." Pia ran her hands over the interior of the hatbox once more, her eyes lighting up. Bev took her turn, trying to smoosh her rather plump fingers into the tiny slit in the fabric. She gave up a moment later. "Mallory, can you get in there? I don't want to tear the fabric any more."

I slid my ring and pinky fingers into the tear in the faded satin.

*Pay dirt.*

My fingers connected with some kind of soft fabric, smooshed down at the bottom of the hatbox's top panel. I felt a thrill of excitement ripple through me, heralding what seemed like a portentous occasion.

*Don't be silly.*

"What is it?" The three other women crowded around me as I worked on extricating what felt like a soft bundle of flattened fabric. Even baby Miri looked mildly curious as she gummed her silicone rattle.

"I almost have it." In a final whoosh I pulled out a swath of stunning and ancient-looking lace. The fabric kept coming and coming, much like a silk tie produced by a magician performing a trick.

"It's just gorgeous." Bev stood back reverently as

I spread the swath of antique lace out on a second, pristinely clean table. "It's the perfect length to serve as a long bridal veil." Bev appeared just as smitten with the fabric as I was.

"Is this for sale?" I heard the catch in my voice as I stated my query. The pretty sundress was long forgotten now that I was smoothing out this lovely and intricate piece of lace.

"Yes!" Pia gave her blessing and promptly gave way to a sneezing fit. "I mean, is that okay, Mom?"

June handed her daughter a tissue and paused for a second as she turned her keen eyes on the runner of lace. "Of course, honey."

"It's a bit aged," Bev mused as she traced a delicate star pattern around the edge of the fabric. The pretty lace was largely intact, with only a few snags in the delicate pattern. But the fabric had mellowed over who knew how many years into a deep champagne color. "Nothing a little OxiClean won't gussy up!"

"No!" This time both June and Pia yelped at the same time. Baby Miri gave a little jump in her carrier.

"It's too delicate for that," June clarified, a bit more gently.

"I guess we could take it to a fabric restorer," I chimed in. I knew such a person existed since I'd had some work done on the turn-of-the-century tapestries in my inherited mansion.

"We?" Bev turned to me with a hopeful gleam in her eyes.

"Of course! I can see how much you love it,

too." I cocked my head and regarded the veil. "Is this something you'd want to wear on your big day? You could wear it in July, and I could wear it in the fall. It's even long enough to ask the fabric restorer about dividing it in half." Bev nodded enthusiastically at my ideas. But I caught June's wince at my suggestion to divvy up the lace into two pieces.

June recovered nicely. "I'd be honored if you two ladies wore this veil at your weddings." She pivoted and reached an arm around Pia, who had succeeded in brushing much of the dust from her sleeves and hair. "My Pia knows a thing or two about weddings."

Pia blushed and wriggled out from under her mother's embrace. "That was my part-time job in D.C., but this summer is dedicated to helping you make sense of all the inventory Grandma Claudia has stashed in the basement. Until I get a full-time job, that is." She smiled. "Hopefully back in D.C."

"You have event-planning experience?" My spidey senses perked up. My sister, Rachel, and I were looking for a new assistant to help us with our ever-burgeoning slate of weddings, parties, and events. We were thrilled to expand our business, but we'd reached the point of turning away new gigs because we didn't have enough hands on deck.

"Just a bit. I've assisted eight weddings, a few retirements, and planned two baby showers on my own." Pia grew less bashful as she described the work she'd done as an assistant in D.C. on the weekends.

"She even has a digital portfolio of her work," June gushed. She dashed behind the front counter rife with glittering estate jewelry pieces and emerged triumphant with a slim tablet. "Look!"

Pia narrowed her eyes at her mother, then burst out laughing. "I see what you're doing, Mom." She included Bev and me in her amused gaze. "Now that I've graduated college, I'm here for the summer to help out. But then back to D.C. I go. Not that you'd have any openings in your wedding planning business anyway."

"As it so happens, I do have an opening for an assistant." I murmured this as I flicked through Pia's extensive résumé and accompanying photos in her digital portfolio. "You have a wonderful eye." The photos displayed nuanced and fresh table settings and layouts.

"I taught her well." June beamed.

"Your personal website is lovely, too. You made all of this?" I gestured to the tablet.

Pia blushed prettily again and rightfully claimed the praise. "Yes. And I do adore event planning. Weddings are my favorite," she added. "But Mom needs my help."

June shook her head. The mama bird seemed to be gently pushing her daughter out of the nest, whether she liked it or not. "While business is doing well, Pia, you know I can't take you on as a permanent employee. Even with Claudia retiring." June sighed and took in her large store overflowing with wares. "Cataloguing and making each item here available online has stemmed some of the slowdown in antique sales. But it hasn't cured everything."

I sympathized with June's sharing of her business woes. With nearly every physical good also available to shoppers online, one had to be nimble.

"And while I love helping out, I'm not sure I'd want to join the family business full-time." Pia laughed at her mother's mock shock at her pronouncement. The young woman was very pretty, even with a streak of dust marring her rosy cheeks.

"I don't want to force you to apply, but we are holding interviews tomorrow to fill the full-time wedding assistant position," I tentatively offered. "I know it's quite last-minute."

Pia cocked her head and seemed to ponder the invitation. Then she nodded with a serene smile. "I'd love to interview. Thank you for the invitation."

I scheduled Pia's interview for the next day to occur just after the other three candidates my sister and I would be meeting. As far as I was concerned, Pia was all but hired. This impromptu process was a little rushed, but sometimes the universe presented you with an opportunity. I just hoped my sister would be okay with my on-the-spot interview invitation. I gave an inward shrug. I knew Pia would be excellent, and I bet Rachel would think so, too.

June gently clapped her hands, causing baby Miri to squeal with delight. I gave the shop owner an appraising look. It seemed as if June had art-

fully nudged her daughter into working for me.
June was a slick one. I'd let her know earlier this
week that Bev and I would be stopping by. Maybe
Pia just happened to be in the store, or perhaps
June had arranged our chance encounter. I decided I didn't care. Good employees were hard to
find, and I had a feeling Pia would be a perfect fit.

"Now that that's settled, let's ring up this veil."
Pia would be a good businesswoman. She crisply
changed the subject back to the sale at hand. "What
do you think, Mom? Twenty dollars?"

June was contemplative as she considered the
long swath of lace laid out on the table.

"Mom? Are you sure you're okay selling it?" Pia
seemed to call her mother back from somewhere
far away.

"Of course! It certainly is a pretty lace veil." June
looked up and graced Bev and me with a warm
smile. "I'm glad it's found a good home. Twenty is
a fine price, Pia. After all, this lace will need a bit
of repairing, even though it's mainly intact." June
observed her daughter carefully folding up the
veil. "Ladies, you'll spend a pretty penny with a
fabric restorer if you choose to go that route."

Bev and I produced ten dollars each and solemnly handed the bills over to Pia. She rang us up
and handed me the receipt and the veil ensconced
in a clear plastic bag, the brick red curlicue script
logo of the Port Quincy Antique Emporium printed
on the front. It was a done deal.

"You know what this veil is?" Bev pointed to the
bag with a jab of excitement. "A sign!"

*Uh-oh.*

Bev was beginning to sound like Delilah, her fiancé's tarot-card-reading mother.

"We should have a double wedding! Look at this fabric, it screams summertime, with the flowers and the trim of embroidered stars. It'll be a perfect tie-in for my wedding a few days before the Fourth of July. And if you're going to wear this veil, too, and divide it up, you may as well coordinate your look!"

"I love the idea of getting hitched this summer, and there's no one I'd want to share a wedding with more than you." I beamed at my close friend. "But I'm enjoying my engagement to Garrett, and if there's one thing I've learned as a wedding planner, it's not to rush things."

I watched Bev deflate before me. I did wonder if today's events were some kind of sign. First, I recalled the enchanting sundress at the back of the store, which I'd just pledged to buy. It was really suited to a casual summer wedding, just the kind Bev was having. I could almost see it. A double wedding with one of my best friends would be both silly and wonderful. I had promised in a weak moment, after I'd gotten engaged, to have my own wedding featured in a glossy bridal magazine. This would be a good hook. But more importantly, it would be good fun.

June seemed to pick up on my wordless considerations. "If you marry this summer, the sundress would work, Mallory. I could remove it from the dress form and have it sent over."

Bev frowned at the idea of me wearing a dress that didn't come from her shop, but seemed to like her double-wedding idea more. "I'd be happy to do alterations on the sundress." She sighed. "Though I thought we all agreed it would be better as a rehearsal dress."

But I couldn't get the vision of myself standing in the garden at Thistle Park, my inherited mansion-turned-B-and-B, out of my head. I could picture my sandy curls peeking out from half of the swath of that gorgeous lace, a champagne-colored chiffon wrap adorning my shoulders to tie the aged lace and retro sundress look together. And I'd be married to the love of my life sooner, in the summertime, no less.

*Darn it. I knew I'd end up marrying at my house. Maybe I'm destined for no separation of life and work after all.*

A nagging voice in the back of my head cautioned me from following the whims driven by serendipitous finds at the Antique Emporium. I loved working as a wedding planner, marrying the analytical with the creative. I always encouraged brides and grooms to find inspiration around them and from their personal histories and to build new memories and celebrations around those experiences. But I also advised them to be practical with the funds and the logistics of planning a wedding and reception. This practicality part seemed to be missing for me, as I was changing up plans fast and furious based on the things I'd found in this very antique store one random June morning.

"I need to run this all by Garrett." I felt a rueful smile tick up the corners of my mouth. "Contrary to popular opinion, the other half actually does have a say." Some brides and families assumed it was their show, with no input needed from their partners.

June sagged, perhaps seeing the sale of the sundress slip away. But Bev was triumphant, no doubt thinking she could dazzle me with some dress in her store's stock. I guess she wasn't as invested in her momentary plan for a double wedding as she initially appeared. It was probably better this way. It had still been a productive day shoring up the details of Bev's wedding theme, and we'd found the lovely veil to boot.

"Ready, friend?" I gave Bev a warm smile. There was still time to sort out all the details.

Bev nodded, and we bade the Battles women goodbye. And were nearly taken out by a human cannonball barreling through the storefront door.

"Out of my way!"

In rushed Claudia Battles, dressed head-to-toe in colonial-era soldier's garb. June's mother, the matriarch of the Battles family, sported a tricorn hat knocked askew and a brown homespun outfit. She flew through the door as if being pursued by the British. She carried what looked like some kind of ancient gun, perhaps a rifle. Claudia's wispy bun was disheveled and about to unravel, with strands of snow-white hair peeking out, probably once the same red as the other women in her family. She must have just come from the practice battlefield. My event-planning duties for this sum-

mer included a new gala celebrating Port Quincy's
founding as a town. We'd christened the event
Cordials and Cannonballs. The big day would feature a reenactment of a Revolutionary War battle
waged over two hundred years ago right here in
Port Quincy. It appeared that Claudia had been
practicing in earnest.

Before we could ooh and aah, the look of consternation on Claudia's face was suddenly understandable. She slammed the glass door behind
her, and it snapped shut on the silhouette of my
nemesis and once-upon-a-time almost mother-in-
law. Hurricane Helene Pierce pushed the heavy
glass door open with her bony hands dripping in
rubies and pearls and made a nimble beeline after
Claudia with her kitten heels striking hard on the
wooden floor.

June quickly unsnapped the baby carrier and
handed baby Miri to me. The little infant seemed
to instinctively cling to my front and I shielded her
from the wrath of Helene. I drank in her baby
smell and gently bounced her up and down as I
planned a quick exit if necessary.

Bev leaned over with a conspiratorial smile.
"You're a natural, Mallory."

*Good grief. Not with the baby talk again.*

And in that moment, I realized why all of the
seemingly good-natured comments about hurry-
ing up and finally getting hitched and growing a
family were getting to me. I confronted the issue
that Garrett and I hadn't discussed the possibility
of kids. I hadn't had the heart to bring it up, partly

because I was so busy and partly because it would change the dynamic between Garrett, his daughter Summer, and myself. And mainly because I was scared of what his answer would be, either way. I gulped and held baby Miri closer.

"Women are absolutely not allowed to participate in the Revolutionary War reenactment." Helene punctuated her decree with a little stamp of her kitten-heeled foot. Her vicious tap made her ubiquitous nude pantyhose pool a bit around her bony ankles.

"Fiddle-faddle." Claudia righted her tricorn hat and dismissed Helene's statement with a wave of her hand. Her nonchalance only made Helene even more furious. "I will be participating as a soldier this weekend, and nothing you can do will stop me."

"I took a vote!" Helene sputtered, her usual command of the situation faltering.

*Interesting.*

"A vote that the town council agreed did not count." Claudia's lined face took on a particularly sour cast. She rolled her eyes in consternation. "Did you really think you could pull off making up some tale about a fire alarm and canceling the meeting, then holding it at your house with the only other two misogynists left on the historical planning commission board? It doesn't count if you jury-rig the vote. You violated the sunshine law!" Claudia jabbed the air with this claim and succeeded in making Helene flinch. "Thankfully, the other members are more forward thinking and voted the correct way. Four to three, women can participate in the reenactment battle." Claudia drew herself up to the impressive full height that June and my friend Tabitha had inherited, but Pia had not. "Now get the heck out of my store. You're not wanted at our establishment."

Helene was ever ready with a stinging volley, the kind I'd been on the receiving end of quite frequently several years ago when I'd almost married her son. "This old collection of junk? I haven't set foot in this abomination of a business since the 1990s."

I snickered. Coincidentally, the early 1990s is when Helene's fashion awareness seemed to stop, as well. Helene favored pantyhose, shoulder pads, Chanel bouclé jackets, and Bill Blass and Halston suits. Being in her proximity was as much a time-capsule experience as being in the Antique Emporium or planning Cordials and Cannonballs.

Claudia said not a word but let her actions do the talking for her. She took one step toward Helene. She coolly rested her hand on her waist-high replica rifle.

*That had better not be a working gun. Of course not, she wouldn't.*

Claudia put that idea to rest and simultaneously skyrocketed my hackles into the stratosphere. "This baby is full of fresh gunpowder. And I know how to use it."

I took an involuntary step back with the infant in my arms, and Helene flinched, but held her own. The resident dowager-empress of Port Quincy,

Pennsylvania, turned her steely powder-blue eyes on me at last.

"Hello, Mallory."

I should have been cheered that it had taken all of this time for Helene to acknowledge my presence. Miri whimpered as I held her ever closer.

Claudia seemed to come to her senses seeing her daughter's foster child. She leaned her rifle against a puffy ottoman and squared off against Helene with folded arms. "I mean it, Helene. Out. Now."

It was Helene's turn to dismiss Claudia with a flick of her heavily jeweled hand. "Not until you listen to reason, Claudia." And she couldn't resist a dig at yours truly. "I'm not surprised you're consorting with this riffraff, Mallory dear." Her term of affection slapped on at the end was as cozy and sweet as a cup of battery acid.

"Why, you . . ." Bev made a step toward Helene, bouncing on her heels like a pugilist. It was no easy feat holding back Bev while cradling Miri.

But June rescued us. "You're free to go, ladies." It was a compassionate command to leave, not really a request. She seemed to want to rescue Bev and me from Helene's shenanigans. I reluctantly handed over the baby, but not before taking one more whiff of her sweet smell. I was rewarded with an adorable coo.

"I can't believe we left them in there." Bev nearly collapsed as she leaned against the maroon brick front of the Antique Emporium.

"We needed to get the heck out of there as soon as we could."

It was night and day, breathing in deep gulps of fresh summer air on the sidewalk. We were a safe distance from Helene and her irrational demands. Outside the store, Bev and I exclaimed over the veil. It felt good to examine our find in the clear, bright June sunlight.

"Ooh, it's more gorgeous than ever." I traced the outline of delicate stars smattered around the edge of the floral pattern. The veil's lace was even more intricate and lovely in the bright summer sunlight. "I'll call the fabric restorer," I promised Bev. "I suppose she can give good advice about whether we can divvy up the veil or if it's better to keep it intact."

Bev gave an excited nod, her eyes sparkling behind the cat's-eye frames. "This will somewhat change the look I decided on for my big day, but it's worth it. This is meant to be."

*Or perhaps not.*

A whoosh of cold air bathed us as the door to the Antique Emporium hurtled open.

*Uh-oh.*

Helene wasn't done with us. Claudia and June must have finally kicked her out of the store. Helene flounced onto the sidewalk in her red Bill Blass suit, her pageboy teased out over her ears so she resembled a king cobra. Her shoulder pads were as tall as ever, padded enough to land her a guest role as a linebacker for the Pittsburgh Steel-

ers. The metal spikes of her suede kitten heels
struck the mica-studded concrete sidewalk with
considerable force. Her still-sharp, eagle-eyed gaze
landed on the delicate length of fabric held in my
hands. Her eyes nearly bugged out of her head.

I rolled my eyes. Helene didn't faze me. Now, if
I hadn't serendipitously jettisoned my engagement to her son a few years ago, I'd be in a heap of
trouble. But my better senses had saved me from
that debacle. That and my ex, Keith's, wandering
eye.

"Where did you get this?" Helene's voice was so
enraged, it was nearly an inaudible hiss.

I instinctively swiveled around to protect the veil
as if I were still holding baby Miri.

"I don't need to talk to you, Helene." There.
Boundaries. I wouldn't consort with this maniac,
not today.

"That veil is a long-lost family heirloom! It be-
longs to me. And I will take it back." Helene's bony
talons gripped my shoulder and spun me around
with surprising force. A small group of walkers at
the nearby corner paused to sip their coffee and
take in the show.

"Take your hands off of me, you loon!" I barely
had time to extricate myself from her clutches. But
Helene was just getting started. The audience at
the corner grew by three more people, and Helene didn't disappoint. She lunged forward and
grabbed the lace from my hand. I held tight to my
end.

In a single, sickening second of time, the veil ripped in two.

I didn't even hear the primal gasp that slipped from my lips. Instead I heard the collective inhalation of the small crowd now watching it all go down.

"You idiot! Look what you did!" Helene was incandescent with rage. The septuagenarian leapt like a cat and lunged for the remaining, now jagged, piece of veil in my hands.

"Catch!" I sidestepped Helene and flung the fabric at Bev, who, in her finest hour, caught the piece of lace as it pirouetted through the air like a delicate, oversized snowflake.

"Not so fast." Like a ninja, Helene plucked the other piece from a surprised Bev and hightailed it down the street. I was too stunned to follow the purloined veil.

"What the heck just happened?" Bev buried her distraught face in her plump hands.

"Beats the heck out of me."

The melee only grew in intensity, as we were treated to a show of flashing lights and wailing sirens. I'd never welcomed the squeal of tires from a Port Quincy police vehicle more than in this moment. The crowd on the corner, and the steady thrum of traffic sliding down Main Street, blocked Helene's exit. The police car could barely drown out Helene's indignant caterwaul.

# CHAPTER TWO

Not one, but two police cars executed screeching stops in front of the Antique Emporium. Port Quincy's chief of police, Truman Davies, who happened to also be my fiancé's father, exited his car and surveyed the scene. His partner Faith Hendricks, several decades his junior, got out of her own police car. Her blond ponytail swung back and forth as she hurried over. Her aviator glasses were in full effect.

*Great. Helene really knows how to bring out the whole cavalry.*

I was used to Helene's shenanigans, which up until now had not included grand theft veil on Main Street, Port Quincy, Pennsylvania.

Truman finished observing the mess before him. At first, he seemed concerned, then irritated, and finally his crinkled eyes rested at mildly amused. I watched him cycle through those emotions as he took in the lay of the land and made his own decisions about what was probably happening. He gave a rueful chuckle and a barely perceptible shake of his head. I watched Helene lock her icy-blue eyes with Truman's, and her heavily padded shoulders seemed to sag in defeat. It wasn't a sight I'd had the pleasure to witness before. Soon we'd have this sorted out and Bev and I would have our pieces of the lovely veil. I inwardly cringed as I replayed the sickening shred of the delicate fabric when Helene viciously ripped the lace from my grip. Helene still had the veil clutched to her chest, a strange and rare air of defeat cloaking her more closely than her ancient designer duds.

But my celebration was premature. A moment later, Helene seemed to spot a small opening in the crowd before her and made a final run for it with the veil. Truman's amusement slid right off his face.

"Stop her!" He hefted his frame in an impressively quick fashion and motored off after Helene. He sprinted half a block and stopped when Faith rounded the corner from the other direction, her hands on her hips. Faith thankfully did not reach for her holstered gun, but she still meant business. She may have been young, but she exuded authority. Her youthful appearance didn't take away from her stature as a policewoman. Faith gave one short, disapproving shake of her head, her blond ponytail swishing against her black policewoman's uniform in apparent disapproval.

Faith slipped her sunglasses down her nose and delivered a scathing gaze at Helene. Then she marched Helene back to us with her hand firmly clamped on the collar of Helene's jacket, as if Faith were a scolding mama cat. But Helene was no cute kitten. She was the spitting image of an angry, bedraggled show cat sputtering in her Bill Blass suit.

"What's all this about?" Truman's voice was stern. His previous mirth at this improbable situation had evaporated in the June sun.

Bev, Helene, and I began talking all at once. Our voices grew louder and incomprehensible.

"Whoa. One at a time." Truman couldn't suppress an eye roll as he delivered his order. I was a bit miffed at being scolded like a toddler. No way did I want to be lumped into the same category as Helene. I wasn't the one to rip a rightfully purchased item from someone's hands in broad daylight and try to abscond with it.

Helene took a step forward, her defeated posture gone. She clutched the purloined veil to her middle with one hand, and puffed out her king-cobra pageboy hairdo with the other.

"I was just liberating my long-lost family heirloom from these hooligans." Her thin lips swathed in pearlescent coral lipstick settled into a smug, if not terse and triumphant, grimace.

"What?!" Bev took offense to Helene's name-calling and reached for the veil.

"Bev." Truman flashed a warning glance at the seamstress. Bev dejectedly took a step back.

"We just bought that veil a minute ago!" Bev

managed to restrain herself from manhandling Helene, but her voice was shrill.

"That's right. Bev and I bought this piece of lace right here at the Antique Emporium." I gestured toward the brick storefront, willing any of the Battles women to emerge and corroborate my story. "I have the receipt and everything."

"Okay. Let's see it." Truman held out his large palm, now barely suppressing a smile. He sensed this kerfuffle would soon be solved and the spectacle on Main Street would go away.

*Let's get this charade over with.*

I reached into the clear shopping bag from the Antique Emporium and stifled a cry.

"It's gone." I held up the bag. It fluttered in the slight breeze, the plastic now in tatters. I'd been holding the thin receptacle in the same hand as the veil, and Helene's barbaric swipe with her peach French tips had ripped the bag open with the precision of a velociraptor. My eyes tore up and down the sidewalk, seeking the slim white slip of paper receipt that had once nestled safely within the bag.

"How convenient, Mallory, *dear*." Helene gave a toss of her head, her icy eyes positively dancing with mirth.

This time it was Bev who laid a steadying hand on my arm. I swallowed and urged myself to stay cool. The only thing keeping me from losing it was sending up a silent prayer of thanks that I'd had the good fortune and sense to not marry Helene's son, Keith. I finally noticed the growing chatter around me. The crowd of early morning shoppers and walkers had grown. They clutched their iced coffees, scones, and donuts as if waiting for us to deliver a reality-show-worthy cat fight.

"Truman, we have a copy of the receipt." Claudia's bell-like voice cut through the whispers as she emerged from the Antique Emporium with a restorative whoosh of cold air.

I couldn't suppress a giggle as I took in her get-up. She must have started changing out of her reenactment gear when this melee went down. She wore bright turquoise capris with an embroidered pineapple pattern atop pretty melon-colored espadrilles. But her top half was still cloaked in a homespun shirt and rough-woven brown jacket, her tricorn hat still pinned on, but knocked askew. She looked like a time traveler caught in a comical mid-change back to the future. Claudia was Helene's adversary, and now my knight in shining armor.

*Er, make that colonial-era garb.*

"See? We sold it to Mallory and Bev." Claudia stopped to draw in a breath. She was feisty and in good health, but this kerfuffle seemed to have rattled the septuagenarian. "Excuse me, I'm a bit out of breath. I haven't run out that door this fast in years. But it'll be good practice for when I rush the field this weekend." She couldn't resist shooting Helene a little smile with her dig. Then she nearly doubled over and stifled a wheeze. She finally righted herself and laid a slip of yellow paper into

Truman's still-outstretched palm. "I gave them the top copy of the receipt."

The chief scanned the paper with keen hazel eyes. I blinked and realized with a start that Garrett was a near carbon-copy of his father, just twenty-five years his junior.

"She just made that up!" Helene's composure dissolved in a screech.

"Oh, give me a break." I was glad I hadn't had a chance to don my sunglasses, the better for Helene to see my displeasure with her with a mighty eye roll.

"It's time-stamped seven minutes ago." Truman glanced at the crowd and sighed. "I really don't think this is a tough one to solve. This seems to be the end of the matter." He handed the store-keeper's yellow copy of the receipt to Claudia and laid his upturned hand out again, this time before Helene.

"Relinquish the veil."

Helene's eyes nearly bugged out of her skull at Truman's demand. "I. Will. *Not.* And you of all people, Truman, should understand why." Helene jammed the delicate lace into Truman's face. He took a protective step back. But he couldn't hide the flinch that slipped out when he got a closer look at the veil.

*Huh?*

Before I had time to process that puzzling exchange, the door to the Antique Emporium flew open again. Out streamed Pia and June, the latter expertly wielding a mint-condition Louisville Slugger. She'd no doubt nabbed the baseball bat from her stock.

"Easy there, June," Truman cautioned.

June ignored the chief and directed her ire at Helene. "I was captain and the best hitter for the Quincy College softball team, class of 1978." Her voice carried down the sidewalk as the small crowd of curious onlookers grew. I was more shocked at her outburst than anything. June was expertly persuasive in her store, but never pushy. If anything, the reedy redhead was serene and calm as she moved through her kingdom of antique treasures. This was a side of her I never expected to see. Her assertiveness mixed with her normally willowy, patrician air was strange to see.

Truman cleared his throat to stifle a laugh. "That won't be necessary, but thank you, June."

I saw Pia relax by a degree. She had been hovering behind her mother, looking ready to spring into action and restrain her if necessary.

"We found the veil in the store this morning." June seemed to come to her senses and let the thick wooden bat drop to her side. She'd win Truman over with reason instead of subduing Helene with threatened force.

A dawning look of realization seemed to steal over Truman's face, but it was fleeting. I began to doubt I'd even seen it.

"This is ludicrous. Mallory and I bought this veil, fair and square. We found it in a—"

But Bev was cut off by a nearly frantic Pia, who I now realized had baby Miri strapped to her front in the carrier.

"You're saying too much, Bev." Pia's gimlet green eyes, so like her sister Tabitha's, were wide with caution.

"Pia, she's just setting the record straight." June was a bit exasperated with her daughter.

"Mom, you need to stop talking, too." Pia was firm, issuing her mother a demand.

June was shocked enough to be quiet. She seemed to realize her mistake and instead sent her daughter a grateful look.

I gave the young woman a shrewd glance. She'd make a fair attorney, in addition to her event-planning skills. Her instincts to keep our facts and case close to the vest in front of Helene were savvy and sound. No one should give Helene anything that she could later use to claim the veil was hers. June clammed up for good, but not before she mouthed a silent thank-you to her daughter.

All was still under the now oppressive sun. The small crowd began to buzz again with pent-up energy. Truman once more held out his hand.

"The veil, Helene."

The reigning queen bee of Port Quincy looked up and down the street in thought. She took in the gaggle of looky-loos and shuddered. She mounted one last attempt to keep the veil in her possession. "I think you need to keep it at headquarters, Truman, or better yet, neutral grounds." She fluttered her thin lashes. "A place like my bank safe-deposit box. Just until this matter is cleared up." Her plea came out in a desperate sputter.

Truman raised an eyebrow and looked irritated. He waited a beat and instead chose to laugh at her gall. "The idea that our police headquarters is not neutral is hysterical."

Helene went for the jugular. Her icy gaze swept over me. I suppressed an incongruous shiver in the now-glaring sunlight.

"It appears we're witnessing some regrettable, but predictable favoritism." Helene's spine grew ramrod straight for this speech. The crowd quieted. "Mallory here is engaged to Chief Truman's son, as you all know." Helene gave a pitiful and staged sigh. "I think the town of Port Quincy should know you can never get a fair shake if you go against Truman Davies's near and dear." She sent a sinister smile my way.

*You wretched woman.*

This time I felt the steadying touch of both Bev and Claudia on either arm. Their presence barely kept me from lashing out at Helene. Truman was used to such claims and better able to brush them off. He seemed genuinely amused.

"That's so preposterous, I can't even get riled up, Helene." Truman almost patted her arm, then retracted at the last second as Helene recoiled and took a stumbling step back in her kitten heels.

"Don't patronize me!"

Truman's eyes filled with kindness. "I wouldn't do anything of the sort, Helene. If you have an issue with what happened today, you can file a report." But as he said it, his face took on a worried cast.

Helene shook her head, finally capitulating. "There doesn't need to be an investigation, Truman. I know the truth now." Her usually haughty expression dimmed belying an emotion I'd never seen her reveal.

*It's almost like she's going to cry.*

I wanted the icky twilight-zone feeling to go. Because I was feeling something I'd never felt. A genuine flash of sympathy for Helene Pierce, my mortal enemy.

Now that she couldn't command Truman to give her the veil, the weight of defeat wilted Helene more than the intensity of the midday June sun. Her narrow shoulders sagged in capitulation. A trickle of sweat marred her carefully powdered countenance. Her lips actually puckered, the coral lipstick bleeding into her frown lines. Her dowager-empress façade frizzled in the heat. She usually looked so composed, icy, and mean.

She was still impeccably dressed; that is, if the time machine that looked like it brought Claudia back from the late 1700s made a pit stop in the 1980s and picked up Helene. But all her shoulder-padded elegance and imperiousness had wilted. Also, she bore a second expression that belied something I realized I'd never seen before, in addition to her sadness.

*Helene looks downright scared.*

The might and main of being the biggest mover

and shaker in our little corner of the world was turned upside down. I couldn't help but feel a smidge of compassion for the woman who had once been slated to be my mother-in-law, even though she rarely sent a speck of kindness my way.

But it was short-lived. Helene seemed to stiffen and change course.

"My business here is done. But Claudia, I'll have you know, you will not be setting foot on that reenactment field." Helene had lost the battle over the veil and resumed her original fight with Claudia over women participating in the mock battle at Cordials and Cannonballs.

"Oh yeah? I'd like to see you try to stop me." Claudia stepped forward and pushed her sleeves up and readied her fists.

"Over my dead body." Helene issued her threat as a hiss, and the crowd audibly gasped. But Helene wasn't done. "I will get you fired, Mallory Shepard, from your event-planning duties at Cordials and Cannonballs if a single woman sets foot on that field."

I snorted at her threat. This was the Helene I was used to. I was even able to tamp down a flash of worry that Helene would get me fired. Helene hadn't been happy I'd been appointed to do the event, but she'd played nice. Well, nice for her, which translated to icy indifference and well-timed sighs and eye rolls about my planning choices. Which was downright cordial considering our past feuds. I'd offered my event-planning services to the town at a steep discount and was happy to do it. Helene had tried to meddle with my past events, but it wouldn't work.

Elvis the basset hound had been napping a comfortable distance from Bev. His long leash allowed him to doze in a patch of shade under a nearby store's awning. I wished I could have snoozed during this whole show, too. Elvis chose this moment to awaken like a doggie Sleeping Beauty, execute a magnificent stretch, and settle down at Bev's feet with a luxurious yawn.

The crowd laughed at his seeming dismissal of Helene, and I couldn't help but join in. Maybe this was the bit of levity we needed to end this charade. The laughter seemed to snap Helene out of her funk. She stormed off without the veil, her suede kitten heels striking the sidewalk with angry force. The crowd parted around her like the Red Sea, no one eager to get in her way.

I felt the defensive energy that was racking my body flow out in a whoosh.

"That was intense." I turned to Bev and witnessed her shoulders sag, too.

"Not what I expected after the lovely morning we'd had planning my wedding." Bev gave a shiver.

I turned to Pia. I needed to salvage what we'd set up inside the Antique Emporium. "Are you still interested in interviewing for the assistant position tomorrow? I promise my interactions usually aren't as fraught."

Pia laughed, then toned down her voice to avoid the now-napping baby Miri. The little one had been surprisingly unfazed throughout this whole ordeal. The sweet baby had slipped into a blissful snooze midway. "Those were some crazy fireworks we just witnessed. We need to keep those for the festivities surrounding Founder's Day and the Fourth of July."

Bev's eyes twinkled merrily. My friend seemed to have recovered somewhat from the last half hour. "Or save those fireworks for a joint wedding with me!"

I groaned at my friend once more pushing me to move up my wedding.

Truman happily took Bev's bait. "When are you two finally tying the knot?" The few passersby laughed and finally moved along. It was the town joke apparently that the wedding planner couldn't seal the deal on her own wedding. I thought this dramatic melee would finally get people's minds off of my lack of a finalized date with Garrett. I sent my soon-to-be father-in-law a withering sigh and an arched brow as my answer.

Bev and Truman roared with laughter, and I found myself joining in. It was a lovely, if now too-hot day, the sky a vivid and cloudless periwinkle. The little crowd had finally completely dispersed. Pia and Miri, Claudia and June returned to their store, with firm plans for Pia to interview for the assistant's position the next day. All was well.

*For now.*

I couldn't shake the incongruous look of fear in Helene's eyes.

"Here." Truman motioned me over and gently

and reverently divvied up the two jagged halves of the veil to Bev and me.

I glanced down at the swath of lace. It was still lovely, except for the violently ragged edge where it had been torn asunder.

"Is this even possible to mend?" Bev moaned. She sent a glance down the sidewalk, seeming to expect Helene to reappear out of the ether. "Why don't you keep my half with yours in your safe?" She reunited her piece of the veil with mine, seemingly happy to offload the veil we'd both desperately wanted just a bit ago.

I wrapped the scraps of ancient, delicate fabric in what was left of the ripped plastic Antique Emporium bag and deposited the lot into my own bag. The light lace veil seemed to weigh heavily within. The coveted fabric had not been rent carefully with Bev's capable seamstress's shears, but by the hands of Helene, administered with her white-hot anger. I couldn't suppress a shiver.


"Truman's right, you know." My mother whirled around from her stance at my kitchen sink and sent me a smirk. She dried her hands on a pretty floral apron embossed with cheery sunflowers and daisies. The apron occluded her more formal business look beneath. Today she'd donned a purple sheath dress with matching jelly sandals and a poplin headband. Her temporary look with the summer floral apron echoed Bev's wedding style.

"You need to hurry up and get hitched, missy. What in the world is keeping you two from following through?!"

*Out of the frying pan and into the fire.*

I didn't suppress my eye roll as I took the delft blue pitcher from my mother's hands. I was rewarded with the tart, pleasant scent of freshly squeezed lemonade. I was hoping to quench my thirst and relax after the crazy happenings earlier in the day. Instead, it felt like every denizen in Port Quincy was poking fun at me. My mom's not-so-subtle nagging usually rolled right off my back. But not today. I wanted my home and B and B to be a den of calm. I ignored her barb and carefully poured the lemonade into two cut crystal glasses. I plastered what I hoped was a serene smile on my face and gestured for my mom to sit down. She seemed irritated I wouldn't take the bait.

Still, it was nice to hang out with my mom. She and her business partner, Justine, were busier than ever with their less-than-a-year-old staging and decorating venture. It was a real joy to catch my mom making herself at home in my B and B kitchen for a respite from her own busy day. She must've ferreted out the hidden key under the back porch and let herself in. I didn't mind the boundary smashing since she'd whipped up this batch of lemonade for us. I was ready for a calm rejoinder.

"I just got engaged on New Year's Day. It's only June. I told you Garrett and I are aiming for fall. That's a quicker timeline than most people getting hitched."

"You aim for the bull's-eye in a dart game, Mallory, not a wedding date. Just set the darn thing and be done with it!" My mom attempted to blow her bangs from her forehead in frustration. She seemed to have forgotten she'd pushed them back today with the purple gingham headband.

My tiny calico cat, Whiskey, appeared at my mom's feet. She blinked her impressively large ochre eyes and let out a delicate but insistent *meow*. I nearly thanked the thoughtful feline for seeming to sense my need for rescue. My mom tsked and blushed. She seemed to realize her outburst went a bit too far. She produced a cat treat from the pantry and was rewarded by a happy, purring kitty twining around her ankles.

"I am worried that I won't be able to properly attend to your wedding as mother of the bride and chief wedding designer. When the time does finally come, that is." She softened her tone with a sprinkling of the fretfulness I was used to. "You're a professional wedding planner. But I want to relieve you of that role for your own big day. You should just sit back and enjoy."

"That's so thoughtful, Mom." My heart warmed toward my mother, Carole. Her sentiments were in the right place, even though *pushy* could have easily been her middle name. I also couldn't help but compare my mom's offer to Bev's. My dear seamstress friend had made the same offer of wedding planning help just this morning. It would make sense for my mom and Bev to team up to design my wedding. Garrett and I would happily hand over the reins in that arena. It was totally enticing to imagine myself as a regular blushing bride, instead of managing my own wedding as my very own client.

It was too bad pigs flying had a better chance of happening than those two special women in my life working together. Carole and Bev were more alike than their strikingly different appearances belied. My mom favored preppy outfits all in one hue, and her persona was persnickety and careful. She was always admonishing me to watch my figure and to keep propriety in mind. Bev, in contrast, favored loud prints and patterns to cloak her own ample, apple-shaped short frame, and as many sparkly hair accoutrements as her impressive blond beehive would hold. But like my mom, Bev was a whizz at her business. She dressed nearly every bride in Port Quincy, as well as their attendants, in addition to being a skilled seamstress. Her renown had grown, and brides frequently traveled from Pittsburgh, western Maryland, and West Virginia to check out her special shop, Silver Bells. I wished Carole and Bev could be friends. And in another universe, where my mom hadn't once dated Bev's fiancé, Jesse, maybe they would have been.

It was a different story for my stepfather, Doug, and Bev's Jesse. The two had made nice at one of my winter events, Paws and Poinsettias, and were becoming fast friends. The men had bonded over their shared love for the Pittsburgh Penguins and American history. It wasn't a rare sight to see the two men catching dinner together in downtown Port Quincy. I just wished their other halves would have been willing to bury their hatchets, too, or the similar sketch pads they both used in their work as a stager and decorator and a bridal-store owner and seamstress. But I wasn't holding out hope for that. The two women did an uncomfortable and tetchy little dance each time they were unfortunate enough for their paths to cross in Port Quincy. Which in a town this small, was pretty darn frequent.

Mom let out a thoughtful sigh. "I never thought I'd complain about my business doing so well. But I can just see how this is going to go. I won't be able to be your wedding planner despite being the perfect person for the job. After all, I can see where you got your natural design eye from." She fluffed out her hair, carefully dyed the same shade as my sister Rachel's beachy, caramel tresses.

And almost as if being summoned, my gorgeous, Amazonian sister strolled through the back door. My mom bestowed a quick kiss on my sister's cheek.

Rachel grinned. She must've caught my mom's last utterance as she trailed in the door. "Don't worry about being Mallory's wedding planner, Mom. Bev can do it." Rachel didn't seem aware of the dagger blow she'd just delivered to our mom. Carole recoiled and leaned against the kitchen counter. My oblivious sister poured a healthy goblet of lemonade and drained it in ten seconds flat, making the hurried action somehow seem like an audition for a Country Time lemonade commercial. But Rachel had that effect. She was eight inches taller than yours truly, with a daring sense of style and a magnetism that left nearly every unattached man in Port Quincy drooling in her wake. It was too bad for them that my sister seemed to be permanently off the market, having fallen head over heels in love with her boyfriend and our event-planning business's part-time chef, Miles.

"C'mon, Mom. I'm just joking." Rachel set her sweaty goblet of drained lemonade on the counter and sent our mom a more caring gaze. "Mallory is a control freak, just like you. I'm sure she'll manage to plan her own wedding herself somehow."

I burst out laughing at my sister's prediction. "I don't mind being a control freak if it leads to gorgeous and thoughtful ceremonies and receptions for my clients. And maybe you're right, Rach. My instincts will be to plan my big day with Garrett. But I'd also be happy to relinquish that control."

Rachel's pretty green eyes lit up at my offer. "Just say the word, and I'll do it."

I gulped on a swig of tart and sweet lemonade and sputtered as the liquid went down the wrong pipe. "Thanks, Rach." I took in my sister's outfit of the day and regretted making the offer to plan my wedding, even though it had been half in jest. She wore a daringly short romper of gold and green dots, the pattern like a zoomed-in pointillist painting. She tied in the colors with a swath of metallic bronze glitter eyeshadow, her hair in a jaunty side ponytail to reveal the giant gold hoops swinging in her ears. The big earrings matched her pretty hair, a sun-kissed shade between blond and brown. And she towered even higher than ever above me in a pair of cut-out, high-heeled gold lamé basketball shoes, a Frankenstein-matchup of Converse All Stars and stilettos. And to top it all off, that zany getup somehow looked amazing on Rachel. It was as if Anna Wintour had personally designed this look and my sister was ready to grace a fashion magazine. I think if I donned the same getup, I'd be asked about where the costume party was being held. You could definitely see the resemblance between us, but my sister was all flash and sparkling green eyes and prodigious height and curves, and I was shorter, with sandy curls and eyes a more subdued shade of brown.

My sister reined in her personal style when it came to working with me, planning weddings. Her daring suggestions were incorporated in small increments that really made the designs pop. But left unbridled, I wondered if my tentative fall wedding would turn into a mix of Malibu Barbie and fall harvest glitter-bomb.

"I'd love your help, Rach," I reiterated, careful not to choke on my second swig of lemonade. Rachel beamed her assent, and I felt so much love toward my sister. Of course, she could help design my wedding, even if it did turn into a spectacle. I was touched that so many lovely people in my life wanted me to have a nice, carefree wedding, and take over my professional planning role. It was just too bad there was no chance for a Carole-Bev-Rachel trifecta of a collaboration.

Rachel and I both seemed to remember our mother and turned to take her in at the counter. She hadn't recovered from Rachel's suggestion several minutes ago that Bev plan my wedding. She narrowed her eyes from her station and stripped off the sunny apron. She glowered at us in a purple-hued low-boil rage, refusing to treat Rachel's joke as a mere flippant comment.

"Mom, Rachel was just joking." I attempted to soothe my mother and took out ingredients to make some cold salads for dinner to accompany our oven-fried chicken. I wordlessly handed my mom a head of broccoli and bowl of shredded cabbage. I rustled around in the pantry for a jar of mayo and some golden raisins to complete the broccoli salad.

My mother gave up her protestations and started washing the veggies, but not before she sent Rachel a haughty look. My sister shrugged and grabbed a washed floret and popped it in her mouth.

Carole suddenly wheeled around, an arc of water spraying us from the head of broccoli she held in a murderous grip. "This really is all moot, Mallory, until you and Garrett stop stalling and set the darn date."

I opened my mouth to soothe my mom rather than lay down some kind of gauntlet. She obviously was more perturbed than I would have guessed at the prospect of Bev having any kind of hand in planning my wedding. But then she had to step way out of line.

"I think it's time for me to intervene, Mallory."

*Say what?*

I braced myself for the undoubtedly amusing and probably preposterous thing my mom would say. But nothing prepared me for her next decree.

"I think you should get married this summer. I took the liberty of peeking at your schedule in your office. You have a few Friday and Sunday dates left in July and August. Just set the darn date!"

I opened my mouth to jump in, but Carole wasn't done. Her green eyes flicked up and down my figure. "You'll need to shed a few pounds, and fast." She narrowed her gaze at the jar of mayo, momentarily sparing me. "Swap this out for some low-cal Miracle Whip."

"Mom. You've officially gone too far." I held up my hand like a traffic attendant. "I happen to like the way I look. I don't appreciate comments about my weight." I didn't have the bombshell looks of my sister, but I tried to make time for exercise and good food choices, even if that only translated to bike rides and long walks with my fiancé and his daughter Summer, and the occasional consumption of a salad. I wouldn't have my mom berate my appearance. But apparently, she wasn't finished.

"You'll be eating for two soon enough, Mallory." Carole waved a dismissive hand at what must have been my flummoxed and appalled face. "You need to give me some grandbabies, and you and Garrett may as well get the show on the road."

Rachel had appeared indignant at my mother's mixed weight-loss decree and pep talk, but Mom's latest demand made Rachel spit out her lemonade. She shook her head as she grabbed a napkin. I was glad that my sister was as stunned as I was. Her giant etched-gold hoops hit her shoulders as she glanced back and forth between our mother and me, wondering who would say what next. Whiskey the cat stood in rapt silence, watching Rachel's earrings like a pendulum.

"Your clock is ticking, Mallory." My mom chose to double down on her bold remarks rather than apologize.

I stood still in my kitchen, hoping the grip I used on the tea towel in my hands didn't give away my anger. But I thought of my role as unofficial therapist when I planned weddings. I often had to maneuver around potential and real emotional minefields and wounds exposed between family members when they attempted to come together to plan a big day. I cautioned my brides to stand up for themselves and not take the familial bait, and I would do the same with my mother.

I answered her evenly and truthfully. "Garrett and I haven't discussed it."

The gasp that reverberated around the room wasn't my mom's, but Rachel's. Mom was shocked into total silence.

*Whoops.*

Rachel finally found her voice. "You haven't talked about kids?" Rachel let out an alarmed yelp. "Mallory, that's not a good sign." Rachel shook her head, the gold hoops' dancing becoming increasingly agitatcd. "Miles and I have it all planned out. A long engagement, with him probably popping the question on Valentine's Day. Then a big winter wedding a year after that. Followed by several months of international travel. And our first of four kids a year after that."

I was happy to hear my sister's lavish life blueprint all laid out for my mom to hear. Somehow Rachel's declaration put Carole into more of a tizzy than my own dearth of procreation plans.

"It's time to put the brakes on all that, young lady." My mom turned her alarmed expression to Rachel. It was a running theme that I'd grown up a bit too fast, watching my sister, four years my junior, after school when we'd been latchkey kids. My dad had left one day and never returned, with nary a clue or trace. My mom had given up her suburban housewife role and launched an uber successful decorating business from nothing. But I'd looked out for Rachel, and my mom couldn't get it out of her head all these years later that I might not want to do things on some preapproved timeline, and that my wild-child sister might actually be ready to settle down. People's perceptions of each other could be hard to change.

I let them argue about Rachel's readiness to plan out her life, and retreated to my thoughts. My mom's rather crass demand for grandbabies had set my head spinning.

It had been on my mind. I spun back a few hours prior, when I held sweet Miri in my arms. I couldn't stop thinking about her baby-powder scent, the brief cuddles, and her joyous baby laughter. Not that I wanted all that tomorrow, either. My heart pulled.

*How in the heck do I bring this up with Garrett?*

The adorable six-month-old had reminded me yet again that Garrett and I hadn't broached the subject of kids in any formal way. The topic made me uneasy. Maybe because I wasn't sure what I wanted. And I was worried to discover what Garrett's thoughts were on the matter.

My fiancé had been maddeningly unspecific about whether we should have a child of our own. And until a few weeks ago, I'd been ambivalent, too. I was happy and excited for my friend Olivia's impending birth and had agreed to plan her baby shower. I realized my beau and I had just talked unnervingly and ambiguously about having another child. It was a someday thing, if a thing at all. I didn't think the door was closed, but I was alarmed that there was no deadline. And now my mom's needling was getting to me. A-ticking and a-tocking indeed.

And how would Summer feel? I loved my fiancé's daughter as my own, but I'd also never try to usurp her mother, Adrienne.

"I obviously do need to discuss this with Garrett." I threw my mom and Rachel a bone. "And Summer needs to weigh in on things too, it's only fair. She's fourteen and this would drastically change her life. If Garrett and I even consider it."

"Summer is the loveliest young woman, Mallory," my mother added. "But I also know you and Garrett will add to your family. The more the merrier!"

I gave my mother what felt like a thin-lipped smile and turned back to the broccoli salad, effectively ending this discussion.

But my mom wasn't finished. She bulldozed on with horrifying and admirable aplomb. "If you and Rachel hire an assistant tomorrow, you and Garrett could get things going and take a nice, long maternity leave. Why," she added slyly, "you could even hand the reins of the business over to Rachel for a while!"

*Oh no, she didn't.*

My power-hungry sister literally licked her glossy, glittery lips. "That's a brilliant idea, Mom. Mallory, you can take a well-deserved break and I'll show you what I can do."

I stifled a giggle at this ambush and couldn't even act mad. My mom and sister were being ridiculous. I was still inwardly reeling at my mother's allusion to Garrett and I "getting things going." But not worried, because it ultimately didn't concern her. It was more worrying that my mom was pushing this plan in a bid to award my sister with more responsibility. I felt like these two had colluded.

But Mom had already moved on to less weighty subjects. "I will be there when you get your dress, Mallory. Rachel and I are planning this wedding for you. We're family. Maybe it would be best if we skipped Bev's little shop." My mom spat out the seamstress and dress-store owner's name in a little sibilant hiss.

I suppressed my eye roll and answered in a calm tone. "Don't worry, Mom, you'll be there." No way was I going to mention the ethereal sundress Bev and I had stumbled upon in the Antique Emporium as a possible dress contender. The fact I'd discovered it with Bev instead of her would have sent my mom reeling over the edge.

"Well, I really must be going." Mom glanced at her plum-colored watch and gathered an equally hued leather bag. "I have a meeting with a client, but I'll be back for dinner."

Rachel and I gave our mother a cheery wave of a send-off, then collapsed into a gale of laughter.

"That was too intense," Rachel sputtered.

"Mom is too intense," I corrected. "The nerve of her demanding grandbabies!"

"She's right about our assistant search, though," Rachel cautiously began. "I'm not, um, pushing for you to get married and knocked up or anything, but you do work too hard in general. And with my cake business busier than ever, we need to hire someone who will see this as a long-term career rather than a part-time gig while they're finishing school."

I nodded and recalled the spreadsheets and reconfiguring my sister and I had done to make this a full-time position with good benefits and room to grow. The three candidates we'd be interviewing seemed like they'd be good fits, and it would be hard to make a hiring choice. Which reminded me.

"We have one more candidate, Rach."

My sister set down her second goblet of lemonade a bit too hard on the counter, sloshing the pale yellow nectar over the edge. Whiskey the calico rushed over to sniff the dripping puddle forming on the floor. The cat turned her nose up at the acidic drink and instead sauntered over to her water dish.

"You what? Without consulting me? No way. Cancel the interview." Rachel's pretty green eyes flashed with anger.

I sighed and placed a hand on my hip. Rachel wanted to be an equal partner in the business, but had increasingly been pulled in the direction of her baking side business and her relationship with Miles. "I'd hoped you wouldn't mind one more addition. She's slated to interview right after our first three candidates. I think you'll agree she's so promising that we couldn't let this opportunity pass."

But my ringing endorsement of Pia only riled Rachel further. "It sounds like this person is basically hired, Mallory. Mom is right. I need more of a say here."

I opened and closed my mouth like a beached fish while I gathered my thoughts and tempered my own annoyance. "I don't think that's exactly what Mom said. And since when are you taking advice from Mom?"

Rachel bristled. "So just who is this person?"

I sighed. "Pia Battles. There." I touched my cell phone's screen. "I just forwarded you her CV and a link to her web portfolio. She has ample event-planning experience, and she just moved back to Port Quincy for the foreseeable future."

But Rachel didn't appear to have heard anything beyond the surname *Battles.*

"Is she related to Tabitha?" Rachel spoke the name with icy disdain.

"Yes, she's Tabitha's little sister, just graduated from college in D.C."

"Absolutely not."

I shook my head at my sister's decree. A few summers ago, she'd dated Tabitha's ex, to disastrous results. Tabitha had tried to warn Rachel, and received an earful. The women were civil, but would never be friends.

*I guess the apple doesn't fall far from the tree.*

Rachel had learned her epic grudge-holding skills from our mom and was destined to detest Tabitha forever. Just as my mom would never be friends with Bev.

I sighed and turned from my sister to put the pitcher of lemonade into the refrigerator. "I'm sorry, Rach. I should have run this by you. But the interviews are tomorrow, and I just added Pia on. We don't have to hire her. But I want to do her the courtesy of keeping the interview. And I hope you will give her a chance. Whatever happened between you and Tabitha shouldn't poison your opinion of her little sister. They're different people, after all."

My sister placed a fist under her chin and sighed.

The chandelier reflected off of her sparkly bronze acrylics. She shrugged. "I'm a professional. I'll give her a shot."

Later that evening my mom, sister, stepdad, and I gathered around the table for an evening of chitchat and familial fun. While my parents had their own abode, it was always fun to host them for dinner. We had a good time, no doubt because we all carefully chose to avoid the landmine topics of earlier in the day. I regaled everyone with a more detailed version of my impromptu showdown with Helene. All seemed well. The pretty but ripped veil was tucked away in the safe in my office. I fell into bed that night with a full heart. My family was a bit crazy, but they loved me fiercely. Whatever happened with my wedding, and with the heart-pounding conversation I'd soon have with Garrett about having kids someday, everything would be fine.

At least that's what I told myself.


"Two down and one to go." My sister seemed to melt into the loveseat we were sharing as we interviewed candidates for the assistant wedding-planner position. I'd been impressed with my sister's professionalism this morning after her reaction yesterday to granting Pia an interview.

"Macy and Simon were incredible. It'll be hard to choose between them." My sister closed her eyes and seemed to shut down any discussion, too.

"Not so fast, sis." I realized Rachel's apparent acceptance of Pia's interview was anything but. She was just banking on our other candidates being so good we could bypass Tabitha's little sister altogether. Fine. I'd play my sister's game. For now. But she couldn't stop Pia walking in the door in T-minus-ten-minutes.

"Macy and Simon would both do a wonderful job." I acquiesced and played along. "I think we'll finally have a permanent assistant."

But Rachel seemed to catch on to my performance. "I'm still mad at you, Mallory. You're not off the hook just yet." Rachel's voice dropped to a low grumble. "I was in on selecting the other three candidates. I still can't believe you added a fourth based on an impromptu interview in the Antique Emporium! When you're out on maternity leave, this won't happen." She smirked after delivering her final barb.

"Whatever, Rach." I retaliated by lobbing a small decorative pillow, which I purposely sent wide. I wouldn't want to mess up my sister's interview look. Rachel giggled and expertly batted it away like the volleyball player she'd been back in high school. But I could tell that even though we had just made light of it, Rachel was ticked to her core that I'd unilaterally invited Pia to an in-person interview. Ticked enough to make a running and annoying joke about the parent-in-waiting gauntlet our mother had thrown down yesterday. I could remain amused as long as this all remained in the realm of jokes and giggles.

Rachel was usually the more easygoing person

in our business, but she had vetted our other three candidates with ruthless efficiency and an eagle eye. I could set aside my annoyance and understand why she wasn't too thrilled to have Pia sweep in during the eleventh hour. But fate had been kind to me. Our most promising candidate had canceled this morning. She'd been gracious and had not wanted to waste our time as she'd just accepted a job in Pittsburgh. Which left Macy and Simon, who had both aced their interviews. But Rachel couldn't be mad about Pia, who brought this round of interviews back to the three-candidate number we'd decided upon. I wasn't going to apologize any longer.

"Honestly, Rach, I hope Pia works out. Macy told us she plans to commute from Pittsburgh, and Simon seems bitten by the big city bug, too. They'd both do well here, but Pia has no illusions about sleepy small-town life since she grew up in Port Quincy."

Rachel batted away my list of reasons with a flick of her acrylics. "I can't believe you made me call Pia's references already. That's a bit premature, Mallory. Just promise, no more big decisions without consulting me." Rachel was as annoyed as I'd seen her in a long time. It was true we were formal business partners now. But her maudlin pout catapulted me back to when we were decades younger, arguing childishly about the fairness of this or that.

I rejoindered with an exasperated sigh. "But we called everyone else's references last week, Rachel.

We're just giving Pia an equal chance. The same as we granted the other candidates."

Rachel remained defiantly skeptical. "I'll withhold judgment until I meet this supposed event-planning Svengali. This job requires finesse and sophistication and excellent communication skills. The young man and the woman we just interviewed were both fantastic and would be immediately helpful to our business." She flounced back into the loveseat with an unprofessional harrumph and crossed her arms against any apparent rejoinder I'd have. Her sweeping tassel-chandelier earrings swished against her shoulders in silent censure as she shook her head once in my direction. Rachel had partially covered her curve-hugging black catsuit with a pretty khaki jacket and red sky-high heels. Her beachy, caramel waves piled high on top of her head were held in place with rose-gold chopsticks. She'd topped off her look with faux, round red reading glasses with powerless glass lenses. She looked amazing, true to her daring style, yet still professional.

It wasn't anything I could pull off, though. I was the more subdued version, my hair less golden, curlier and more unruly, too. I was still pleased with my interview outfit of a peach sundress with a smattering of green leaves, flat espadrilles, and a white linen jacket. Rachel and I were so different, but we complimented each other in every way. I didn't want to preface Pia's interview with a sisterly fight.

It was time to stop convincing Rachel. I was sure

Pia was our next assistant. I just hoped Pia could persuade my sister as well. I tried to suppress the smirk I felt forming at the corners of my mouth. "You'll see, Rach." I took a delicate swig of my tea.

The sonorous clang of the bell announced our final interview candidate. Rachel and I both jumped and laughed. It was a more fortunate sign, and I'd gladly take it. I hustled into the cavernous front hall of our mansion-turned-B-and-B and made my way to the heavy double front doors. Rachel lagged behind in silent protest. When she reached the doors, we smoothed our outfits and put on our interview game faces. I gestured toward the door, but Rachel shuffled me forward with a frown. "Let Ms. Battles in." She sounded pained.

*Behave, Rach.*

I ushered Pia into Thistle Park. Rachel coolly deigned to shake Pia's hand but refused to join in the banal chitchat I engaged in as I seated our interviewee.

I took in Pia's nervous gulp of the water we offered her. She was truly the youngest candidate. But so far, she was holding her own, her expression poised and calm. She'd dressed in a navy pantsuit with a lovely watercolor red and yellow scarf tied at her neck. On her petite feet were a pair of bright yellow flats bejeweled with red gems. I caught Rachel giving Pia's look a grudgingly approving appraisal. I in turn appreciated Pia's apparent seriousness in choosing to don professional attire but also admired her personalized touches showing some serious style.

As we made our way to our office and offered Pia a seat, Rachel slipped the prescription-less hipster reading glasses down her nose and it was all I could do to stifle a giggle. She next pulled a pencil officiously from behind her ear, but the writing utensil got caught in her huge tassel earrings. My sister was playing hardball with Pia, much more so than with our other two candidates.

"Shall we begin?" I shot Rachel a warning glance and we formally began the question portion of the interview. We pelted Pia with questions focused on eliciting experiential answers. Pia answered with aplomb. With each skilled answer anchored in her past event- and wedding-planning tasks, I could see my sister's attitude change right before my eyes.

*Pia is nailing this.*

She was magnificent. It was true she had less experience than the other candidates, but what she had done as a part-time assistant in D.C. sounded thorough and innovative. She was customer oriented but not afraid to take risks. I tried to suppress a grin for the sake of professionalism, but found myself failing.

And my formerly irritated sister was trying doubly hard to tamp down her enthusiasm. As we asked question after question and heard Pia's excellent answers and subtle promotion of her skills, I witnessed my sister smiling, nodding, and relaxing. I knew I was doing the same.

After an hour of interviewing, Rachel was positively dazzled. She squeezed my hand under cover of a decorative velvet pillow. I sent my sister a look that telegraphed, "I know! She's awesome."

"Ahem. Do you have any more questions for me?" Pia offered us a tentative smile, her mouth quivering a bit after having to be on for an hour of intense questions. Rachel and I answered Pia's questions about her role and our business and finally the formal interview portion came to a close.

"If you'll excuse me, I'd like to use your restroom." Pia's pretty green gimlet eyes darted to the door and into the hallway.

"Of course." This time my sister jumped up to personally escort Pia. She came back to our shared office with a giant grin.

"She's amazing!" Rachel pulled me to my feet and danced a little jig.

"I know!" I refrained from tacking on a smug *I told you so.* I was happy enough that Rachel also recognized Pia's amazing skills. "I really think she'll fit in well with the dynamic we have here."

Rachel nodded, her tassel earrings swishing and punctuating her enthusiasm. "She's just what we needed. She's a natural! I hope she accepts our offer!" My sister giggled as a slow blush climbed her face. "I guess you were right. I'm glad fate sent Pia our way yesterday."

I grinned at my sister. "She's perfect!" My sister and I uttered the words in unison and erupted in laughter. "Jinx." We crooked our pinkies together and turned toward the door.

*Oops.*

Pia was standing in the doorway with a goofy grin on her face. I wondered how long she'd been standing there unnoticed. It was her turn to blush. She took a deep breath and began in a timid tone, "I guess I got the job?"

Her question wasn't at all untoward after what she'd probably just overheard.

"Yes!" It was Rachel who affirmed the answer with unbridled glee. The three of us abandoned professionalism and gave high fives.

"Welcome aboard, Pia."

Rachel chatted animatedly with our new hire as I gathered a thick stack of paperwork for Pia to fill out. A half hour later we lingered over the treats I'd hidden behind a large stack of files on my desk. Another plate of goodies resided on my desk chair, obviously not appropriate for the interview. But Rachel and I had taken restorative breaks in between each candidate, since interviewing was draining for all parties involved.

Pia finished her snack and sank into a chintz chair with relief. She then seemed to remember herself and sat up straighter. She delicately dabbed at the corner of her mouth with her cloth napkin. Then she abandoned her daintiness and bit into a slice of cranberry banana bread with gusto, now that she'd been officially hired. I thought of how she somewhat resembled her sister and my friend, Tabitha, but not completely. Their resemblance was much like my own with Rachel.

Pia let out a contented giggle. "I was so nervous this morning that I didn't eat. My blood sugar was in the basement." She laughed as Rachel cut her another slice of fragrant bread. "And I'm sorry about the incident with the veil." She blushed prettily again. "Grandma Claudia usually puts on a tough front. She's one of the few women taking part in the reenactment this week." Pia's mirth dimmed a bit, and she turned pensive and solemn.

"It's not her fault." I jumped in. "We're dealing with Helene. She was just extra ornery because she didn't get her way."

Pia nodded. "Thank goodness Grandma Claudia isn't shaken up by Helene. She loves history and couldn't wait to take part in this inaugural reenactment. Who cares if our family is not descended from Revolutionary War participants?" Pia shook her head. "Did you know Helene wanted it initially limited to participants based on that silly distinction?"

I wrinkled my nose in disgust. "That's appalling. Each person, no matter how they got here, is part of our country. Immigrants have always made this country great, and we still celebrate that history. Helene is insane. Thank goodness the voting council doesn't share her reactionary views."

"And speaking of history." Rachel let out a pretty peal of laughter as our stepfather, Doug, walked into our office. He was dressed in full Revolutionary War regalia, his homespun outfit echoing Claudia's from yesterday.

Doug was a history buff and adjunct professor at Quincy College. We'd sought out his expertise to help organize Cordials and Cannonballs.

"Hello, Pia." Doug tipped his tricorn hat toward our guest and sent us into a fit of giggles. He spun around in a circle and showed off his patriot costume.

"I'm proud to wear this silly thing," he said with a laugh. "It was hard to get people to play British soldiers, but we have enough. Can you believe there'll be fifty people on that field tomorrow?" Doug shook his head in amazement and caught his hat from teetering off at the last second.

"It's a crazy good turnout," Rachel gushed. It certainly helped that the reenactment would be paired with one of the biggest bashes of the year, hosted by Rachel and yours truly. The town of Port Quincy had enjoyed great success in revenue and revelry with the yearly Founder's Day celebration. This year the council voted to expand the festivities to a full Founder's Week, kicked off with the inaugural Cordials and Cannonballs and ending with the traditional Founder's Day festivities and dance.

"Excuse my sorry state." Doug procured an incongruous bottle of neon-green Gatorade from his homespun fabric satchel, finally and truly breaking the spell of his Revolutionary War affect. "We've been practicing in the midday heat to replicate the actual skirmish that took place in Port Quincy. And also, because that's when the reenactment takes place, in a few days." Doug seemed positively tickled to align the reenactment time with the rumored actual time of the small Battle of Port Quincy.

"It's like being in a sauna outside," Pia added. "I was second-guessing my choice to wear a suit to this interview, but your air-conditioning cuts the humidity."

"I just hope the weather cooperates." Doug cast a worried gaze out the window at the cloudy but hot day. "I'd hate for the very first reenactment, and Cordials and Cannonballs, to be canceled." Doug finally unslung the long weapon he'd been carrying behind his back.

"Your costume gun looks a bit different from Claudia's weapon." I could get a closer look at the impossibly long gun leaned up against a striped mint ottoman. It was more out of place than the colonial-era militiaman before us with his fluorescent-green sports drink in hand.

Doug nodded. "Her weapon is a rifle. Back in the day, Claudia's weapon would have been more precise than this gun, which is technically a musket." Doug eyed the replica. "Plus, this uses a leaded shot."

I must have looked confused. Doug further explained. "A musket ball. Ah, muskets use rudimentary balls instead of bullets. I think you girls saw some when we took a trip to Williamsburg one summer. It was hard to get any accuracy when most of the men fighting for independence were using muskets. It was a sad war. The soldiers just lined up in a wall of men." He shook his head. "They shot their muskets, hoping to hit someone on the other side, with no precision." The musket loosened from its perch against the ottoman and slid to the ground. We all winced. "Don't worry, ladies, this replica is not loaded."

Doug carefully put away the weapon in the hall outside the office, as if he sensed it made me uneasy. I'd seen my share of the weapons, enough to last a lifetime. And I realized that Doug hadn't said his replica was inoperable, merely that it was unloaded.

Rachel must not have felt my unease, and piped up. "What other replica weapons will be on the battlefield?"

Doug took another swig of Gatorade. "There will be bayonets and tomahawks in addition to rifles and muskets. Some reenactors will have little hatchets. They're either super dull, or better yet, plastic. Some people are even bringing plastic swords. There'll be a few pistols, too." Doug rubbed his hands together in apparent excitement. It was odd to see my pacifist stepdad, who usually abhorred weapons, getting excited about them. But I knew it was the history draw for him rather than the arms themselves. "Quincy College has a small collection, and I like to take my students to the archives to see them. Handling the material items from the time period helps make history come alive." Doug was positively glowing.

I relaxed by a degree. "Especially when they've all been curated and deemed inoperable."

Doug nodded. "None of the weapons, including the cannons and muskets, will be armed with real ammunition during the reenactment." He fondly gestured toward his musket out of sight in the hallway. "Technically, that one could be used. But it doesn't have real gunpowder or musket balls in it at the moment, so don't worry." Doug took in what was probably my wide-eyed expression.

Pia smiled. "You're just like my sister, Tabitha. A bona fide history nut."

Doug broke into a grin at the mention of Pia's sister, the director of the historical society. "Tabitha has been immensely helpful planning Cordials and Cannonballs and bridging the gap between my general academic knowledge of the Revolutionary War and what happened during the battle in Port Quincy in particular."

His smile dimmed a degree. "I'm afraid your grandma wasn't too happy with me the other day, though." My stepfather turned positively sheepish. "Claudia tried to sell an impressive collection of authentic Revolutionary War weapons to Quincy College. Part of my growing duties at the school is to consult with the archives department. After a lot of consideration, the college archivist and I agreed not to purchase the items." He shook his head ruefully. "Claudia is persuasive, but we ultimately stood firm. But a lot of people in the department heard her pitch. It got a little heated." A small stain of blush graced Doug's face in remembrance of the altercation.

"Yup. Grandma Claudia is used to negotiating until she gets what she wants," Pia added.

"But it all ended well. Claudia and I ended up grabbing dinner and a beer after the whole incident and that was that. It was as if it never happened." Doug chuckled again. "We actually argued more about whether I was trying to defend her honor too much regarding Helene Pierce."

I frowned and leaned forward. "You never told us this, Doug."

My stepfather shrugged. "You know how that old biddy is. She doesn't want women on the reenactment field, as you heard firsthand," he said drily. "I intervened and tried to get Helene to reason."

Pia, Rachel, and I roared with laughter. "Your first mistake," I counseled my stepfather. "No one can reason with Helene Pierce."

"Yes, a mistake I'll never make again." Doug shook his head. "Pia, your grandmother was more ticked at me trying to fix her problem for her than Helene was that I tried to intervene. But all's ended well. There will be a few women on the battlefield tomorrow, and Helene can't do a darn thing about it."

"And I'll raise a glass to that." I held a delicate buttercup teacup aloft, and Rachel and Pia followed suit with their cups. We clinked with Doug's Gatorade bottle and shared smiles all around.

Doug bade us goodbye and set off toward the house he shared with my mom to change back into twenty-first-century garb. Pia and Rachel and I made plans for Pia to start work the next day. We were eager for her to help with Cordials and Cannonballs. Things were looking up.

But the universe had other plans.

The doorbell rang with an ominous tone.

"Are you expecting anyone else?" Rachel paused with the last slice of cranberry bread held aloft in front of her.

"Nope."

Before I could rise from the loveseat, we heard the wide front double doors swing open.

In minced Helene Pierce, her kitten heels striking the herringbone-patterned wooden floor with characteristic force. I was surprised the smell of fire and brimstone didn't follow in her wake. She seemed to have recovered from yesterday's come-uppance witnessed by all on Main Street. She was dressed head to toe in 1980s finery, a red power suit with nautical striped epaulettes and gold buttons giving her a comically commanding air. A sharp and expensive cloud of Caleche wafted around her.

"Hello, ladies. I thought I'd drop in to tidy up some last-minute details for Cordials and Cannon-balls."

I raised a brow in response and turned to my sister, ignoring our unwelcome interloper. "I suppose we left the front doors open for interviews."

"We'll need to be more careful next time," Rachel agreed with a practiced serene air.

I wasn't going to let Helene rattle me, not in my own house and place of business. Too bad my heart was secretly racing. Helene was technically trespassing. I didn't want her here a second longer than she needed to be. Still, I would keep my cool. I was proud that I was no longer afraid of Helene, just annoyed that I had to think of a way to get her out of my house. The biggest battle I'd ever had with Helene had been over this mansion. It hadn't been a Revolutionary War–size fight, but it had been big enough for me to want to avoid her for the next few decades. Helene's mother-in-law, Sylvia, had changed her will in her final week on earth and bequeathed the hulking mansion to me, effectively cutting out Helene and her son, Keith. It was an unexpected act that changed the course of all of our lives. I was eternally grateful for Sylvia and sent a smile over my shoulder at the picture of her I kept on my desk. I mustered up some of the sass and vigor Sylvia had retained even in her nineties and squared my shoulders. I was ready for whatever Helene was bringing today, probably about the veil.

"Hey!" I nearly ducked for cover when Helene reached into her snakeskin power briefcase and flung a manila folder in my face. "That was un-called for."

"Sorry. Poor aim." Helene sent me a smirk and included Pia in her disdain. "Not all of us were star softball players, like your mother, June."

Rachel sent Pia a steadying look, willing her not to take Helene's bait.

"I have some last-minute changes for Cordials and Cannonballs. See to it that my choices are enacted by sunrise the day of the event." Helene primly seated herself in a chintz wingback chair, despite not being formally offered a seat.

I breathed out a sigh of semi-relief. This I could deal with. "Helene, I already got these updates, in the documents the committee shared on the cloud."

I winced, knowing that Helene wasn't technologically astute enough to have added her tweaks to the event checklist herself, but had spent last night ruthlessly dictating her changes to the town council's assistant. But I would be professional and diplomatic, especially in front of our new hire.

"Some of your ideas are good, Helene, like spacing out the refreshment tables amongst the craft tables. But others can't be changed at this late hour." I hoped she'd be willing to take the single bone I offered, cut her losses, and get the heck out of here. But that would be expecting the impossible.

"I knew you wouldn't be able to pull this off, Mallory." She adjusted the heavy gold bangle bracelets threatening to escape her skinny wrists. "But time is of the essence. I guess I'll take what I can get."

*Huh?!*

Rachel and I exchanged confused looks. Helene never capitulated when there was a centimeter to haggle over.

"Now, to the real business at hand." Her lips curved up in a sinister smile.

This was more like it. Of course, Cordials and Cannonballs business was just a pretext.

"You will return my veil to me this instant, Mallory. I'm not playing games. I've given you a wide berth to do your little thing here in Port Quincy." She waved her hand around in the air, as if to dismiss the whole grounds of Thistle Park that served as my B and B and the anchor for the carefully and successfully built business I'd worked so hard to create. "But I'll have you know this. You will return the veil, a once-in-a-lifetime artifact, or your days in Port Quincy are numbered."

*Interesting choice of words.*

I couldn't stop my spine from tingling. I should have been worried about Helene's threat to smote me from my beloved hometown, but I was used to her hyperbole. A subtler bit of information she'd just shared was giving me real pause. Calling something an artifact was different. The now torn swath of lace was pretty and certainly an antique, but that didn't quite equal an *artifact*.

But there was no time to waste. I left my thoughts to actually address Helene's presence. I had to get this loon out of my house. Thankfully Rachel was already on it.

"Who cares, lady? I've seen that veil, and it's nice if that's your jam, but really, there are much better wedding headpieces out there. If you'll just be going we can all get back to having a pleasant afternoon." Rachel bore daggers into the glare she volleyed at Helene. But Helene just sat there, staring us down. Finally, she looked over our shoulders as if to guess where we'd hidden the veil.

I was secretly happy I'd stowed the fragile fabric in the safe concealed behind a portrait in this very office. I had to will my neck muscles and eyes to not inadvertently swivel toward the safe. Helene was intimately familiar with this house, as once upon a time she was due to inherit it. But the modern safe was new. Thankfully, she had no clue where it was. My gaze swept to take in my sister. I hoped Rachel was able to keep from giving away our hiding place.

Rachel trained her eyes upon the herringbone-patterned wooden floor and busy floral rugs scattered throughout our office.

*Phew.*

I closed my eyes and pictured the space over our little office fireplace, outfitted with a modern gas insert. The slim slit of a safe was fireproofed and secret and only accessible by pressing a certain piece of molding mounted to a spring on the original teak mantel. No one would look there. I opened my eyes to see Rachel's will finally broken. Her long-lashed eyes flicked toward the safe.

*No, no, no!*

But we were okay. Helene's steely eyes were trained inexplicably on Pia.

"Mother?"

*Oh great.*

Keith Pierce, my former fiancé and Helene's son, arrived on the scene. He swaggered into the office as if he owned the place. Indeed, Keith had grown up believing he would inherit the Gilded Age mansion. Too bad he'd cheated on me right before our wedding, and his grandmother had gifted the colossus of a building to me instead.

I craned my head to see if his wife, Becca, had accompanied him. Thankfully Keith seemed to be traveling alone.

"It's time to go, Mother. You have better things to do."

*Ouch.*

Despite having had a long engagement, I'd rarely witnessed Keith crossing his mother, no less putting her mother in her place.

"What gives?" Rachel mouthed sotto voce. I shrugged, as flummoxed as she was. Pia just sat in silence, her dagger gaze lasered in on Helene.

"Keith." Helene's voice was low and strained. "I am not leaving without my veil."

I'd had enough of this weird visit. "Do we need to call Truman?"

Keith had had enough, too. "This is not the same scrap of lace sewn by Betsy Ross, Mother."

*Mic drop.*

Keith seemed proud of his declaration and for standing up to Helene. Until a flicker of doubt skittered over the features I'd once upon a time found so handsome. His perpetually haughty and annoyed arrogance dimmed a fraction. His eyes swiveled to Helene's and seemed to read, *Oops.*

Keith had seemingly inadvertently revealed the veil in question could have been sewn by Betsy Ross. Make that a major oops.

I gasped at his admission once I realized the gravity of his claim.

Helene looked utterly crushed. She recovered and hissed at her son. "Don't tell these rubes! You just ruined everything!"

Keith sighed. His fleeting hesitation was gone. Keith thought he was impervious to mistakes. The usual swagger he wore like a cloak came rushing back. He dismissed Helene with a tilt of his head.

"That veil is long gone, Mother. There's no way it was stowed away at that antique shop. My father —" He stopped short and seemed to realize he'd said too much.

I couldn't conceal my shock. Keith was a skilled corporate trial attorney. It wasn't like him to make an admission like that. I nearly squinted as I considered him. He was adept at handling the stress of working at a big firm. But today was different. A drop of sweat rolled from his balding head and landed with a silent plop on his elegant cream-and-blue–striped tie. His complexion sported a gray cast instead of its usual hale and hearty pink. His eyes were even a bit red and rheumy. The man was not well.

I silently tsked at caring so much about him in the moment to closely observe those details, even though several years ago I'd been betrothed to him. In any event, he was stressed. Even revealing that the veil might have something to do with Betsy Ross was a gaffe of colossal proportions.

Helene looked fearful. And for once, she had nothing left to say. She swept from the room, her kitten heels nearly boring holes in the floor. The sharp scent of Caleche stirred and eddied with her exit. Keith gave me a steady look before he turned to trot after his mother. He seemed to want to apologize for her, but then thought better. His stressed look was overtaken by something even deeper and more melancholy. I couldn't remember a time he looked genuinely morose. He finally gave a weak half shrug and left the room.

Pia, Rachel, and I were quiet for a full ten seconds. My younger cat, Soda, chose that moment to skitter into the office and jump on Pia's lap.

"Your suit—" I moved to pick up my kitty.

"I don't mind." Pia petted the little orange Creamsicle-colored cat and let out a shaky laugh. "And I thought yesterday was intense."

The three of us burst into happy laughter. Rachel's eyes were shining. "Is it possible our veil was really crafted by *the* Betsy Ross?!"

I couldn't help but smirk at my sister's choice of words. Rachel had a secret hankering to live as large as a true celebrity. I could nearly see the dollar signs flashing in her eyes like a slot machine at the casino. If Bev and I had rightfully purchased a piece of Americana made by legendary Betsy Ross, it could be worth more than I could even fathom. But Rachel had just done that quick calculation herself.

The three of us chatted for a few minutes. "I'm so sad Doug just left," I moaned. "I was a history major in college, but he's the true expert. His specialty and PhD are on immigration in the colonial era. He'd love to be here right now."

"No wonder Helene was so hot and bothered to get it back," Rachel mused. "When all along it's just been sitting in that safe, fifteen feet away." Rachel blushed a second later, realizing she'd let slip where the veil was. I sent my sister a kind look.

I wasn't sure why, but I felt like I could trust Pia. Pia looked long and hard where Rachel had gestured. Was she a bit too interested? I shrugged away my concern. She'd need to know about the safe soon enough. We used the security device for about half of the weddings held at Thistle Park.

I crossed the room and pressed the specific knob on the panel, revealing the digitally locked safe. "Brides often drop off their rings and family jewelry the week of their wedding. It's nice, and crucial even, to have a safe place to put them."

Pia nodded, her interest seeming purely professional. It wasn't like I was giving away the code to the darn thing, anyway. And I would have to trust my newest hire.

The three of us chatted for a few more minutes about the veil. Pia wanted to tell her family about getting the assistant wedding-planner job and reluctantly placed a purring Soda on her chair. Rachel and I made a pact to only tell certain trusted persons about the possibility of the veil being crafted by Betsy Ross. My sister skipped off to text her boyfriend, Miles, one of the few to make the list. I sat next to my cat and absently petted her fluffy orange head. She purred in contentment.

But I was anything but content. The revelation about the veil I co-owned with Bev should have been cause for celebration. But certain fraught memories made me less than elated to possess the pretty swath of antique fabric. I closed my eyes and cuddled my cat, willing the nightmare visions away.

I opened my eyes and took a breath in the relative safety of the present. The portrait I'd placed in front of the safe was an oil painting of the original mistress of this house, Evelyn McGavitt. Her visage in the painting was chameleonlike. Most days her pretty face cast in oil-paint brushstrokes appeared to playfully smirk and twinkle. Today the enigmatic expression seemed to send me a message of caution. I turned my back on the portrait and the veil concealed behind it. The innocent lace seemed to be stirring up a whole heaping helping of trouble.

Bev and I had purchased the veil for a mere twenty dollars. Now the pretty scrap of lace didn't seem worth it if it meant this much trouble. It was turning out to be more than I bargained for.

# CHAPTER THREE

The next day arrived bright and early. I yawned and opened one eye to greet the sharp slice of sun sneaking through my blinds. Rachel and I occupied the third floor of the mansion, a space converted from storage and servants' quarters into an airy and lofty apartment decorated by our mother. The space was a definite contrast to the B and B portion of Thistle Park. My mother had decorated the third floor in cheery and whimsical Emerald Coast style. It was cozy and bright, but last night I hadn't been able to enjoy the space. My mind was laden with new worries fueled by the so-called Betsy Ross veil. After a fitful night of sleep, I'd finally dozed off. Which was a good thing since some solid hours of sleep seemed to have knocked some sense into me. In the clear, early morning light I now doubted the lace in my possession was really sewn by Betsy Ross.

But I decided to contact the Smithsonian, just

in case. I was only opening what could be a giant can of worms at Doug's suggestion. I had conferred with my stepdad via cell phone before I'd gone to sleep. He said that between Truman and the Port Quincy Police and the venerable Smithsonian Institution, it would all be sorted out soon. And hopefully without Helene's input.

I called the Smithsonian at the respectable hour of nine a.m., fueled by a giant mug of gourmet coffee. Doug had given me the name of an actual contact, passed along by the Quincy College archivist. I giggled as I dialed the number, thankful for the lead. I wondered what the Smithsonian would have said if I'd called their general operator line, yammering on about a possibly famed Betsy Ross veil.

But it didn't seem to matter that I had a real historical specialist's contact and extension. The woman I spoke to seemed keen to blow me off. She took down my information quickly, if not unkindly. She said she'd look into it and got off the phone in the span of two whole minutes. I knew she'd given me the short shrift, but the information was heartening. The veil must not be a Betsy Ross creation after all. And the Smithsonian must have all kinds of wackadoodles calling, claiming to have important pieces of Americana tucked away in attics and basements that they wanted verified as the real deal.

Imagine my surprise when my cell blared a half hour later with a D.C. area code. It was a different specialist at the Smithsonian who seemed keenly interested that the veil had been discovered in Port Quincy, Pennsylvania. The man on the phone peppered me with questions, most of which I couldn't answer. He bid me a curt goodbye, but he couldn't hide the excitement in his tone.

*Darn it. Maybe there is something to Helene's claim.*

But Helene also liked attention and people kowtowing to her. I wouldn't put it past her to aggrandize the veil's provenance and history for her own gain. Keith, too, for that matter. I already knew their games from solving an earlier mystery that Keith's biological grandfather was the Thistle Park gardener, not a prominent attorney as the family had claimed. Helene was obsessed with inheritance and one's place in this world being influenced by family connections and heirlooms. Claiming that the pretty swath of lace had been crafted by Betsy Ross would be right up her alley.

But it probably wasn't even a real Betsy Ross–crafted artifact. Until proven otherwise, I would consider it to be just a neat swath of lace. Keith was pretty firm in his convictions. But even if it turned out to be a nameless piece of fabric, I wasn't sure I wanted to wear it now. And certainly not for my wedding. The lace seemed cursed with bad juju from Helene. Now the pretty lace sundress from the Antique Emporium moved front and center in my mind. I relaxed as I focused on the future. Maybe my mom and Bev were right, and I should even move up my wedding.

I had a crazy thought as I refilled my mug of coffee. Maybe it was time to move. I could create a nice separation from the zany things happening at my B and B by creating a different space where Garrett, Summer, and I could cultivate a safe home. A place a small distance away. I thought about converting the greenhouse, carriage house, or even the giant shed on the property into a new abode.

I wondered with a start how my sister would feel. She was spending a lot of time with her new beau, Miles. She was barely home as it was. I wondered if she'd miss my presence in Thistle Park. Despite our busy days working together at our business and the equally busy moments off from work that we spent largely apart, Rachel and I usually ended each day with a chat before bed or a shared dinner with our parents. I wondered how moving out would change our sisterly dynamic.

And despite avoiding the conversation about whether we'd continue to grow the little family I was soon to form with Garrett and Summer, we had waded into the tetchy waters of where to live. I gave a little laugh about my fretting over leaving Thistle Park, when Garrett and I had already decided we weren't going to set up our new homestead on the third floor. It wouldn't be great for Summer to spend her high school years in a bustling wedding venue.

I made a promise to begin the discussion with Garrett as soon as possible. I might be channeling Goldilocks too much, but I vowed to find a space that would work for Garrett, Summer, and me to start our lives together as an official family unit.

I finally made it to my office and jiggled the handle with a start.

"Just a minute." My sister opened the door, but only a mere inch. "Yes?"

"What's up? I'd like to come in and document on my laptop the call I had with the Smithsonian."

Rachel shook her head and I heard another voice giggle from within the office.

"Pia and I are working on something top secret. Now shoo." Rachel summarily shut the door. I did a huffy about-face and began my work straightening up the B and B. A tiny stab of jealousy rippled through me as I imagined Pia and Rachel working on a project without me, Pia perhaps temporarily ensconced at my desk.

*Don't be ridiculous.*

I'd nearly fought a death match with my sister to get her to even consider Pia for an interview. And less than twenty-four hours later, the two of them were thick as thieves, working on something so that I could focus on other matters. It was ludicrous that I was feeling shut out, even though Rachel had literally shut me out of our shared office. I felt a tiny prick of hope. It was a good sign that my sister and Pia were getting on so well. My instincts in the Antique Emporium had been correct. So what if Pia and Rachel were already starting a new project? I'd take it as a sign that Pia was a great fit and would help us grow our business while also lightening the load for Rachel and myself. I shrugged at my earlier concern and returned to the work I could do outside of my office, hoping their surprise project was something good in store.

A few hours later, Rachel and Pia made good on their pledge to share their surprise. I answered the front door of the B and B to greet my gorgeous fiancé, who swooped down for a long and languorous kiss.

"Why hello to you, too." I smiled up at Garrett. He managed to look crisp and cool in a gray wool suit, even in the humidity of June.

"I came as soon as your sister texted me." A slight frown did nothing to mar his lovely features. His hazel eyes turned serious. "Is everything alright? She said to hurry."

I let out a laugh. "I hope you didn't drop something important. Rachel and our new hire, Pia Battles, have a surprise. They locked me out of the office earlier this morning, then forbade me from even coming down from the third floor."

A look of relief and mirth commingled in Garrett's expression. He relaxed and slung his arm around me, drawing me close. "You've piqued my interest. I wonder what they have in store?"

"It's the best gift I didn't even know I needed. You and I are here for our very own wedding planning meeting, where we'll attend as guests and clients, not the planners."

Garrett's smile grew bigger. "That's fantastic news. And now that the weight of planning our wedding has been taken off of your shoulders, maybe we could even move up the big day."

My eyes grew wide at his suggestion that I'd been pondering myself just a few hours ago. We really were in sync. I let out a breath of air I didn't know I'd been holding in. Suddenly the prospect of talking about what our family might look like someday seemed a bit less daunting. "It could be a possibility. We'll have to ask our wedding planners." I giggled at the reality that I really and truly wasn't going to plan my own wedding, no matter when it took place. But someone who should also weigh in on the decision was missing. "Where's Summer?" I glanced behind my beau, expecting to see Garrett's daughter.

"She's working on her booth for Cordials and Cannonballs." Garrett gave a fond smile. "She's turning into quite the history buff. She begged for an extra five minutes of time and told me she'd bike over." His warm expression dimmed by a degree. "Although I think the real draw of working on that booth is a certain older guy, not the task at hand."

I giggled and gave my fiancé's arm a squeeze. "Who's the lucky guy?" Then I felt a rush of motherly concern that was both surprising and natural. "And wait—how much older are we talking?"

Garrett sighed and ran a hand through his dark hair. "A year and a half. One whole high school grade." He paused and seemed to spit out the name. "Preston Mitchell."

"Bev's son?" I let out a sigh of relief. "He's a good

egg, Garrett. You have nothing to worry about."
Bev's lanky teenage son was a star baseball player
and constantly on the honor roll, as his mother
was happy to report. I couldn't think of a better
crush for Summer.

"You're probably right," Garrett gruffly agreed.
"I just wasn't ready for this new phase of her life
where she's seriously interested in boys. I feel like
she's growing up at lightning speed."

I reached up to brush a strand of hair back into
place, and he dipped down for another impetuous
kiss.

"Ew. Knock it off, you two." Summer breezed
through the door and hung her bike helmet on
the coat rack. "Just kidding. Hi, Mallory."

I gave my soon-to-be stepdaughter a hug, mar-
veling that at fourteen she was already half a foot
taller than I was. I peeked around her to silently
confer with Garrett. I knew we both wondered how
much of our conversation Summer had heard.

"What are we waiting for?" Summer eagerly
peered into the office door, opened barely an inch.

I shrugged and made a move to go in.

"Hold on a second, Mallory." Garrett gestured
toward the door. "We're technically the clients, for
once. We should wait to go in."

I giggled at the formality, and Garrett, Summer,
and I waited on a small divan outside of the office
until Pia and Rachel ushered us in minutes later
with great fanfare.

"Sit here, you two." Rachel guided us to the
aptly named loveseat where we placed each cou-

ple. It felt bizarre to view my office from the client seat. Summer sat next to us and eagerly awaited Rachel and Pia's plans. I gave an involuntary start when Pia took the rose-and-trellis patterned chair I usually sat in to conduct client meetings.

My mother and stepfather breezed into the room, and finally Lorraine, Garrett's mom, made her entrance. "I'm so thrilled you two are setting a date and making it official!" Lorraine dropped a kiss on my cheek and pulled back with an impossibly large grin, leaving a waft of snickerdoodles in her wake. She settled down next to her granddaughter and eagerly awaited the start of this meeting.

"A full house," I murmured to Garrett, suddenly nervous.

"Ahem." Rachel cleared her throat, revealing a frisson of nerves. She'd pitched wedding ideas before, and she'd never seemed tentative or flummoxed. Maybe it was being at the official helm of planning my big day, and presenting her ideas to our assembled families that heightened the stakes. "Thank you all for coming. I'd like to introduce you all to our new assistant, Pia Battles."

Pia sent everyone a smile and a wave from her perch on my chair. "Mallory, I hope you and Garrett like the suggestions we've put together for your wedding and reception."

And with that they were off to the races. Pia turned on her tablet and began a short presentation of ideas that showed up on the large flat-screen TV we kept concealed in an antique armoire, only brought out to show larger groups our proposed plans. Rachel and Pia took turns guiding us through a fall wonderland of rustic colors and textures.

"We chose a palette that will be more neutral and malleable. The main colors will be a cool sage green and cream with some yellow and silver accents." Pia displayed a trellis draped with light green fabric.

"We'll accent with pieces that celebrate the outdoors for a brief ceremony in the crisp weather." Rachel pointed out the wind chimes hanging from the trellis and back porch, as well as subtle fall pops of color achieved by spheres crafted from rust and pumpkin-orange mums hanging from the trellis and back porch ceiling. "We'll have a fire pit going for guests that want to continue hanging out in the cool air, with pumpkin s'mores and hot apple cider."

"And inside the mansion, we'll continue the sage-green palette with accents of orange and rust." Pia took in our approving nods and oohs and aahs. It was a gorgeous and unexpectedly simple yet chic display. I felt a weird mixture of pride, gratefulness, and a strange sprinkle of unease as I realized my sister and Pia had whipped up a beautiful and innovative plan in less than twenty-four hours.

Pia sent me a shy smile, snapping me out of my mental wallowing. "And these colors would work for other seasons, too, if you were considering moving the time frame."

"Yes, yes, yes!" My mother burst out her exuberant approval of that idea to the chorus of laughter from everyone else. "I mean, your wedding date is totally up to you two," she amended with a blush.

Garrett sent me a wink and squeezed my hand. I wasn't too sure how serious he'd been about moving up the wedding, but it seemed like everyone was game.

"We love it." I gestured toward the screen and brushed a tear from the corner of my left eye. "I didn't know I'd get so emotional. This is usually just business."

My sister crossed the room and gathered me up in a hug. "*Your* wedding would never be just business."

"Thanks, Rach, and thank you, Pia. I think I speak for all of us when I say you really blew us away."

I was pleased with the cozy and less formal affair they'd designed. The wedding could focus on Garrett and Summer and me, and the joining of our family with friends and loved ones. In a few short years of planning, I'd seen it all. Weddings with massive ice sculptures and choreographed first dances. My sister had toiled to bake and sturdily assemble seven-tiered cakes, and I'd tentatively superglued real rubies onto slippers the night before a ceremony. My wedding, in contrast, would be gorgeous, but a bit pared down.

"As a stager, I can see how you want your own shindig to be a bit more minimalist." My mom gave grudging approval of the work Rachel and Pia had done. I reached across the low coffee table and gave my mom's hand a squeeze. And I realized with a start that Rachel and Pia's lightning fast planning had swiftly and diplomatically cut my mother out of the loop, preventing her from making my nuptials a re-creation of her most beloved staging ideas.

*Good one, Rach.*

I didn't want my mom to have all the power, but she wasn't done just yet.

"And we'll have to find you a dress befitting this pretty and elegant design." My mother's eyes lit up at being able to helm that duty. "I think there are some stores we can visit in Pittsburgh or even Cleveland or Philadelphia that will have something just sophisticated enough to match Rachel and Pia's plans for your wedding."

*Anywhere but Bev's store right here in Port Quincy.*

"I was thinking of something simple and satin," I began, wondering how I'd maneuver my way through this potential quagmire. "And I want to make planning as stress-free as possible." There. I'd start by appealing to my mother's sense of empathy. "Pia is a fantastic addition to our team. A team we expanded because Rachel and I have been ludicrously busy with our growing business. I really would prefer to look for a dress here in town."

The vision of the pretty lace sundress from the Antique Emporium floated up unbidden from some recess in my brain. I batted away the thought and focused on Carole. She'd puckered her lips as if she'd taken a healthy bite of a lemon. We all watched her wrestle with her emotions. Summer giggled behind a throw pillow.

"Fine." My mother nearly spat out her consent. "We can take a little trip to Silver Bells to get some ideas. Though I bet you won't find anything there even half as lovely as what you need."

*Phew.*

My mom talked a big game, but I knew she'd be professional when the time came to select a dress. Everyone would win. Rachel and Pia would plan the big day with a bit of help from my mom, and Bev would work well in her own wheelhouse, providing me with a dress. My stepfather sent me a quick wink.

"At least you already have your veil." My mother was happy that Bev couldn't assist in selecting my entire look.

I shuddered at the thought. "I don't think I want to wear it anymore."

Summer nodded. "Now that Helene Pierce ripped it, you'd need an exorcism performed on that veil." The room collapsed into gales of laughter, all but Lorraine, who seemed a bit shocked by her granddaughter.

A timer went off in some distant part of the house, and Pia clapped her hands together with glee. "It's time to talk about the food!"

Rachel and Pia had outdone themselves. They returned to the office with carts full of mini plates laden with a sumptuous fall feast. There were tasting portions of pumpkin–sweet potato soup, roasted root veggies, tender slices of beef and lamb. My eyes grew wide at the sumptuous feast. We all murmured our appreciation and were about to tuck in. My sister and Pia must have kept the doors to the kitchen shut to keep the yummy smells from drifting out.

"Too bad there's so much meat." Summer muttered her critique in a small voice. "There are so many meatless options you could incorporate instead."

"Now, Summer—" Garrett began to respond when Rachel jumped up. "I forgot the last tray! I'll be right back." She returned with a last domed silver tray and whipped off the top with a flourish. She gave Summer's arm a warm squeeze. "I've got you covered, sweetie. Here's some harvest eggplant parmesan, but with vegan nut brie toasted and shaved instead of traditional cow's milk parmesan. And roasted root veggies with coconut oil instead of butter."

"Yes!" Summer pushed away her offensive meat-laden first plate and took a bite. She closed her eyes and sighed. "This is to die for. And it would be good for a summer wedding, too." She wiggled her eyebrows and grinned as we all laughed. "Seriously, though. What are we waiting for?"

Summer's use of *we* melted my heart. I felt Garrett's palm wrap around my hand and turned to peer into his lovely hazel eyes. "She's right. What exactly are we waiting for?"

My fiancé rewarded me with a kiss, to the cheers of our families. Somehow when Summer asked us to move up the wedding, it was a sweet nod to the family we'd be forming, not a nagging directive, as it was perceived when my mother made the same plea.

"This is totally doable." Rachel's fingers swiped her tablet's screen and she held up our summer calendar. "We have several open Friday nights or Sunday afternoons left in the summertime schedule."

"And all we need to do for our menu is to change some spices and starches to lighten up for summer." Pia sent us all a dazzling smile. "We can use the same meats, but grilled right here instead." She included Summer in her plans. "With some tempeh options as well, and the eggplant. We'll also do cool soups and chic salads. Maybe a couscous and kale side dish, with gazpacho to start. Some mint and lemon cocktails. White wine and Moscato. Pita and hummus and fruit for your guests between the ceremony and the start of the meal."

"We love it." Garrett and I gushed over the revamped plans. Pia and Rachel executed an exuberant high five. Those two were thick as thieves already, fast friends and efficient partners despite forming their collaboration a mere twenty-four hours ago. I was excited about Pia's addition to our team, but a bit wistful, too. I realized with a rush that being officially married would change both my personal and professional dynamic with my sister. No longer would we be able to chitchat into the wee hours in our third-floor apartment after I married and moved out. I was a bit sad and wistful to be leaving this part of my life behind.

Another wave of emotion hit me as I observed my mother holding aloft her flute of champagne and talking animatedly with Lorraine and Summer. This feeling I had about my sister and Pia forming such a great working relationship already, and my impending move, was probably akin to my mom's feelings about Bev. She must've just been worried about our special bond, and keeping it. I felt a rush of pathos for her, and vowed to include my mom in my plans.

"If we're really moving this shindig up, we need to decide where we're going to set up house." Garrett turned to me with an insistent but excited gleam in his hazel eyes. "Maybe this new plan to get married this summer is just the nudge we need."

My sister must have supersonic hearing, or a newfound ability to read lips. "Where are you guys going to live?" She gestured above her. "It'll be kind of crowded in the apartment."

"You're kicking me out?" I drew my sister's laughter with my mock outrage. She already knew Garrett and Summer wouldn't be moving in.

"Truman and I had an idea the other day," Lorraine tentatively put in. Her eyes sparkled as she set down her long-stemmed champagne flute. "I don't want to be too forward." Her visage dimmed for a bit. Lorraine had nothing to worry about. She was the least pushy person I knew. "What if you built a new structure on the land adjoining Thistle Park and our backyard?"

The room grew quiet as Garrett and I considered his mother's suggestion.

"A new house to join our families. Literally." Garrett slowly nodded. He turned to gauge my reaction. I wordlessly answered him with my second spate of emotional tears in one day. Garrett retrieved a tissue and gave me an embrace as I dried my eyes.

"I love it, Lorraine." I'd first met Summer the day Rachel and I moved into Thistle Park three years ago. She'd walked the length of the woods that began on my acreage and ended abutting her grandparents' backyard. She still often traversed the path leading through the woods to visit me at Thistle Park. A cottage or small cabin constructed deep in the woods, but adjoining the two pieces of land, would keep me close to work, and Summer close to the grandparents who had helped raise her, but give us all much-needed space to grow and thrive. We'd be joining our families in a symbolic and practical manner. It was a beautiful idea.

"But that might mess up a summer wedding." Dark clouds gathered in my mom's eyes. "I'm not sure you could build a new abode fast enough to be ready after the wedding!" Carole's voice rose to a frenzied pitch, and Doug placed a steadying hand on her arm, which she batted away.

*Thanks for the wet blanket, Mom.*

I sighed and moved to acquiesce to my mom.

"Oh, give it a break." Rachel was already on the case. "Jesse Flowers can do it. He's like a contractor superhero, and I'm sure he'd jump at the chance to help Mallory." Rachel suggested Bev's fiancé, a master restorer and builder, for the job. I had no doubt Jesse could do it, but I hesitated to ask.

"I'm sure Jesse would love this job," I mused. "But he is getting married in a few weeks, then off on his honeymoon with Bev and Preston." I didn't want to saddle him with a new project so close to his wedding to Bev.

Summer stared at her hands. She glanced up at me, a rich berry staining her cheeks. She must have been pretty smitten with Preston to break out in a blush at his mere mention.

"Yes, Jesse is just the person for the job!" My mom rubbed her hands together, dismissing my concern. I sent Rachel and Pia a snicker. "And I will design the interior of your new abode!" My mom prattled on with ideas for a structure that hadn't even been designed yet. She seemed to have forgotten all about her promise to help me find a dress at Bev's store. I felt my heart grow warm. My mom would be able to contribute in her own way, and not have to wrestle with Pia and Bev and Rachel taking over the wedding planning.

*Now I just have to get Jesse on board. And speed up my wedding, and move out of the third floor.*

"I'll call Jesse right away," I pledged. My earlier elation and gratefulness for Rachel and Pia planning my wedding was severely subdued. Moving forward with our plans was a bit like playing Whac-A-Mole. The wedding itself was in great hands, but if we stuck with the plan to move things up, I'd be inconveniencing Jesse and heading up a super-fast construction project. I stood and nervously grabbed a second flute of champagne from the sideboard. Perhaps I should have stuck with the sparkling punch Summer was consuming.

"We don't have to do this right now," Garrett murmured into my ear. My tall beau, a foot and two inches taller than me, leaned down to deliver his comforting message. "The house built between Thistle Park and my parents' backyard sounds perfect. But don't forget, we're in charge here."

I nodded, refreshed by his reminder.

"I think it should be at least four bedrooms," I heard my mother gush loudly from across the room.

"Why?" Summer wrinkled her nose and popped a piece of pine-nut-topped ciabatta into her mouth. She finished chewing and corrected my mom. "We'll only need two bedrooms, Carole."

My mother sent Summer a sly look. "You'll need the extra room for my grandbabies!"

*Mic drop.*

I coughed and sputtered as a bubbly trickle of sparkling red wine made its way to my lungs instead of my stomach. Garrett soothed me and sent Carole a well-earned death glare.

Summer clapped her hands. "I knew it, I knew it!"

I glanced at my midsection, wondering what had given all assembled the wrong idea, beyond my mom's wackadoodle announcement.

Summer grinned. "I wondered why you guys were actually okay with moving up the wedding, and now I know!" She nimbly plucked the flute from my grasp. "Should you be drinking that in your condition?!"

"Mallory, Garrett, why didn't you tell me?!" Lorraine hopped up from her seat and nearly danced a jig, the most animated I'd ever seen her.

"And how did you manage to keep this a secret from me?" Rachel shook her head, a warm smile lighting up her face.

I turned to Garrett. He looked like a deer caught in the headlights of a semitruck.

*Make that a deer flattened by a semitruck.*

I felt him take a deep breath as he dropped my hand.

"Whoa, whoa, whoa. There's been a mistake. We're not having a baby." Garrett's voice boomed across the office space. The force of his pronouncement nearly knocked the wind out of me.

I felt each pair of eyes swivel from my fiancé to me to gauge my reaction. I didn't have to guess that I must have appeared absolutely crushed. Garrett turned to take in my stricken expression and gently amended his statement. "Not anytime soon, that is."

*I guess I have my answer.*

I was stunned by the double whammy of my mom's crassness, and Garrett's forceful rejection of having another child. A child I wasn't even sure I'd wanted until yesterday when I'd cuddled little Miri.

"Mallory—" Garrett seemed to have realized the harshness of his statement. I gently placed my hand on his arm and shook my head.

"There's no bun in this oven." I gave a shaky laugh. My eyes must have taken on a desperate cast, because everyone resumed their chatter.

"Sweetheart." Garrett's voice grew tender as he turned to face me. "I guess we need to talk."

I gave him what felt like a weak smile. "It's three now. Aren't you meeting a client in half an hour?" My reminder wasn't entirely innocent. It reeked of dismissal, and we both knew it. But I didn't want to have this conversation here. In fact, I just wanted to sink into the polished wood floor.

My fiancé flinched and sent me a wounded look before he glanced at his watch and let out a sigh. "You're right." He brushed a kiss on my forehead. "Thank you, Rachel, and Pia, and Mom. I'm sorry, I have to run back to the office." He ducked out of the room after giving me one final, long, regretful gaze. I took in his retreat and breathed a sigh of relief.

*Uh-oh.*

I'd never been happy to see my beau go. But after airing our dirty-relationship laundry in front of our families, I was ready for a breather. I felt exhausted by my roller-coaster emotions. I'd been elated by the cottage idea, then stunned minutes later by Garrett's unexpected reaction to the topic of having kids in the near or far future. But what upset me even more was my inability to gauge my own reaction. In truth, I'd only given the idea the most fleeting of thoughts up until yesterday. Strange thoughts and emotions I needed to dissect were eddying and bubbling up from my subconscious.

Summer, at fourteen, was perfect and amazing. She was the kindest and most vivacious stepdaughter a woman could hope for. Before this week, my mom's annoying tick-tock comments had been a mere blip to dismiss.

"Garrett?" I ran into the hall, desperate to catch my fiancé before he left.

*Too late.*

I watched from the open front door as his Accord made its way down the long front drive. But then the vehicle stopped, executed a three-point turn, and drove up to the front of the mansion.

"I don't want to leave things like this." I cleared my throat and dragged my gaze to meet Garrett's. "First things first. I'm not sure what I think about expanding our family. But what I am sure about is that I'm unbelievably excited to get married. Let's focus on that."

The tense line running down the length of his broad shoulders relaxed. He gave me a thankful smile and found my hand. "I don't want to close that door. I just honestly hadn't given it too much thought." A painful wince marred his lovely features. He pinched his nose and let out a sigh.

*Uh-oh.*

I braced myself for what was to come.

"Your mother—"

I interrupted his declaration with a whoop of laughter. "My mother is ridiculous."

"Let's just say I wasn't ready to have a grand-baby-for-Carole-Shepard talk in front of a room of people." The corners of his mouth curved up in a rueful smile. "Though I believe her heart is in the right place."

I kissed my fiancé goodbye and he left once more. I returned to the house feeling much lighter and at ease. My worry over the possibly-crafted-by-Betsy-Ross veil seemed long gone. I had bigger fish to fry, but I had my family and Garrett to navigate the upcoming changes in my life.

When I returned to my office, the wedding planning session was winding to a close. Carole looked appropriately chagrined. I gave her an expansive smile and saw her relax. She'd been too nebby—that's Western Pennsylvania parlance for nosy—but Garrett was right, her heart was in the right place. A thirsty-for-itty-bitty-grandbabies place, but nonetheless, a well-meaning one.

Still, I couldn't help feeling a smidge sad at all of the plans coalescing at lightning speed. I wouldn't be living with my sister anymore. We'd grown so close these last two years, rooming just feet away. Rachel seemed to sense my sadness. She crossed the room and slung her arm around me.

"One of our vendors is calling us back!" Pia appeared as well and held up her cell. "This is the one that I wasn't sure could get us the lavender tablecloths in time for next week."

Rachel dropped her arm and went scurrying for her desk. "Hold on a sec before you answer, I'll get you the file."

*They make a great team.*

I reflexively started to wander over to my desk to help out. Cordials and Cannonballs was a mere day away, and I wanted to go over my checklist as the head planner for the event.

"Uh-uh. You deserve a day off, and to bask in the glow of our lovely plans for you." Rachel nearly frog-marched me out of the room.

"But Cordials and Cannonballs—"

"We can handle it, Mallory. You did all the heavy lifting, and Pia and I can tie up the last few loose strings." Rachel gave me a not unkind, sisterly push out into the hallway. When the door shut crisply behind me and the other guests, I realized the meeting was over and my role as bride for this planning session was, too. I bade my parents and Summer and Lorraine goodbye.

"*Meow.*"

My Creamsicle-orange fluff ball of a petite cat seemed to notice my confusion.

"That makes two of us, little one." I picked up the little gal and was treated to an outsized purr. Together we stared at the paneled door to my office. It may as well have been Fort Knox instead of the welcoming space where I spent most of the workweek. There was no use staying downstairs. Rachel and Pia had ushered me out, forcing a rest from work that I no longer wanted. My brain was buzzing with alarm about my personal life, and work would help me avoid untangling all of the knots I'd just discovered. But it was time to face the music, and my cat and I curled up on a fluffy window seat, lost in thought.

Several hours and cups of Lady Grey tea later and I felt a lot better. I'd passed the time going over Rachel and Pia's presentation, which they'd thoughtfully emailed to me, as if I were a real client.

*You are a real client.*

I smiled at my new status and made my way downstairs after I saw Pia's tiny red Nissan Versa proceed down the drive. It was past dinnertime. I assumed my sister and Pia had shared a meal in the office, a ritual Rachel and I partook in several days of the week.

I was about to help myself to some goodies from the tasting. But my heart skipped a beat when a shadow appeared over my shoulder.

"Greetings, Mallory." Truman offered me a smile, but his attempted cheeriness couldn't conceal a hint of worry. He must've wordlessly entered the kitchen from the back porch. I cursed my efficient decision to give the usually whiny hinges to the door a good dose of WD-40. Now I had no warning when someone came into the kitchen.

"Geez Louise!" I dropped a basket of the yummy varieties of olive, sun-dried tomato, and pine-nut focaccia my sister and Pia had whipped up. Thankfully the precious cargo within remained in the basket, secured by the fall-leaf-patterned napkin wrapped around the bread.

"Sorry to startle you. I'd be on high alert, too, after Helene busted in here."

"No worries." I willed my still-racing heart to slow down as I busied my hands pouring two quick glasses of iced tea with sprigs of mint. I grabbed little tureens and Tupperware containers, which held the last servings of food from the yummy tasting, from the fridge.

"I know you have to work, but you can still sample everything my sister and Pia made for our families at the tasting." I loaded the goodies, two sets of silverware, and several plates onto a wicker tray. Truman gallantly picked up the heavy feast and followed as I motioned for him to follow me to the back porch. I set our drinks on a low table overlooking the vast gardens of Thistle Park. Neon-green lightning bugs lit the air in an errant polka-dot pattern, warming up for the final setting of the sun.

"What's up?" I gestured to the porch swing and the chief eased into it with a grateful sigh. He took a swig of the iced tea and wiped a drop of sweat from his forehead.

"I hope it's cooler tomorrow for Cordials and Cannonballs." He gave up on his ministrations to his forehead with his hand and liberated an old-fashioned cloth handkerchief from his pocket to assist. "You all set for tomorrow?"

I winced as I recalled my office door shutting

me out a few hours ago. "Mm-hm. Rachel and I have a new assistant on board. She's been a tremendous help on only her second day on the job. We're all set."

*I hope.*

I suppressed a giggle as Truman shut his hazel eyes, so similar to Garrett's, and began swinging on the porch swing. He had to bend his knees and flare his legs out to avoid scraping them on the green-painted floor, a result of his six-feet-four stature. He looked for a moment like a little kid all dressed up in a policeman's uniform, rather than the esteemed chief he was. But suddenly his eyes flew open, and he stilled his swinging with his feet.

"I hear congratulations are in order. Lorraine told me you and Garrett are excited about the idea of building a new home for the two of you and Summer on the shared land between our two houses."

I nodded eagerly, embarrassed not to have already thanked Truman for his and Lorraine's generosity. But he cut me off at the pass.

"But that's not really why I'm here. I want to talk about that veil."

*Uh-oh.*

I'd pushed the filmy scrap of fabric out of my mind in order to deal with the other issues of the day. I'd barely thought of the thing while we all convened in my office, a mere few feet away from the safe. I bought myself some time by lighting a row of citronella candles on the porch. If I didn't hurry, the mosquitoes would arrive in the gloaming and make an even bigger feast out of yours truly than the dainty leftovers Truman and I were making short work of.

My appetite sated, I was ready for whatever news he had for me. "Did Betsy Ross make the veil, or not?"

Truman sputtered and set down his glass of tea. Beads of condensation rushed down the glass and stained the napkin beneath. "News does travel fast in this town."

I chuckled and filled him in on what was probably a big-time mess-up by Keith. Truman nodded, affirming the story and filling my head with wonder. I possibly held an extremely significant piece of Americana in my little safe just a hallway away.

Truman bolted upright and peered into the darkness in the garden. "What in the heck was that?"

As if taking a command, the back spotlights were triggered and lit up a patch of wildflowers that served as a delicacy for the local deer population. A pretty doe blinked impassively at us and continued to munch on a blue flower.

"Let's go inside."

I was alarmed by Truman's gruff order. I snuffed out each citronella candle and followed him in, startled more by his actions than by the movements from the deer, which I'd grown accustomed to in the summer evenings.

"What was that all about?" I waited until Truman had unloaded the tray to grill him.

"Someone could be listening." Truman's eyes darted to the now dark backyard, visible through the back-door window. I'd never seen him so spooked. It was deeply unsettling.

"It's not like we're harboring state secrets, Truman." I smirked and waited for him to assert that he wasn't. He answered me with silence, his mouth set in a grim line. "We're not, are we?"

Truman winced and gestured for me to sit down.

"Oh, no. If you're going to be so cagey, I'm putting you to work." I motioned to my two kitties dozing in the window seat. "It's cat beauty-parlor day." I tapped the calendar to punctuate my point. "And since Rachel is out with Miles, and frankly, you're freaking me out, you're going to help."

"Excuse me?" Truman finally broke from his deep-state demeanor.

"Time is tight and tonight we're trimming the cats' nails."

Truman seemed almost relieved to have a task to do that didn't involve returning to the topic of the veil.

"Allow me." Truman solemnly scooped up my usually sweet, but now predictably ornery calico, and gently held her against his uniform. She squirmed a bit and then was still. I saw a nice pattern of orange, white, and black cat hair on his uniform. I moved in and deftly snipped Whiskey's claws with my kitty nail scissors. Truman set the small cat on the ground, and she began to purr, twining around both my and Truman's ankles.

"She does this every time. Acts like it's the end of the world getting her kitty manicure, then when it's done, she gives you a little thank-you."

Truman motioned to my other cat, Whiskey's daughter, Soda, as if to finish our pet grooming task before getting down to brass tacks. Soda, usually the little spitfire just out of kitten-hood, always calmly acquiesced. She had been adopted so young that she always knew this ritual was just part of the routine. But her mother, Whiskey, had spent some time on her own. Whiskey viewed clipping her nails as the greatest affront known to cat-hood.

The task done, Truman laughed as I gave him a lint roller. I moved to make us post-dinner cups of coffee.

"Sorry about the cat hair. Now what were you saying about the veil?" It was time to return to business now that we were both more relaxed and not on high alert.

Truman didn't mince words. "The veil you purchased yesterday? There's a distinct possibility it is a famed piece created by Betsy Ross."

His admission hung in the air. I finished my coffee ministrations with shaky hands and carefully handed Truman a cup.

"Is the veil in a safe place?" Truman's eyes bored into me as his coffee sat ignored.

"Mm-hm. Currently locked up in the safe in my office. Not many people even know I have a safe in there."

A flicker of doubt briefly marred Truman's poker face. "How many people know of the safe's exact location?"

I bit my lip and pondered his question. "Lots of brides and families know I have a safe. But I don't literally show it to them. Only Rachel and I know the precise piece of molding on the fireplace you need to press to get it to open."

*Phew.*

"Oh! And Pia knows, too. We showed her yesterday during her first day of work. She'll need to know about it. But she doesn't know the actual code."

I wasn't rewarded with the look of relief I sought. Truman's frown deepened. "I wish you'd just kept it between you and Rachel."

Truman's disapproval made me uneasy. "It's okay. Pia's trustworthy. Plus, she really does need to know about the safe as our newest assistant."

I was rewarded with another impassive blink from Truman. He said nothing, waiting for me to prattle on. I squirmed in the silence and tried to ease the tension with a sip of coffee. Truman could make you feel like you were under the glare of his censure without a single word. I didn't appreciate his lack of agreement that Pia was trustworthy. And I realized with a horrible start that I didn't know much about her. She'd passed a background check as part of the hiring process, and she'd done nothing to give me pause. But my trust in Pia was based merely on pure gut feeling.

"No one from the Smithsonian has gotten back to me," I carefully offered. "If the veil right here at Thistle Park could really have been made by Betsy Ross, wouldn't they be all up in my business by now?"

After the first interested callback, the Smithsonian had left me alone.

Truman raised a bushy brow. "Well, my dear, they haven't gotten back to *you*." He let his statement hang in the air.

"Ah, but they have filled you in."

Truman gave a mirthless laugh. "I spent much of yesterday afternoon discussing the incident on Main involving you and Bev and Helene, with the Smithsonian."

Truman seemed to squint at me over his coffee cup. He must have made up his mind to include me, because he opened up the floodgates.

"I may as well tell you the whole sordid tale." His hazel eyes twinkled. "Since we both know you'll drag it out of me anyway. Once upon a time, Helene did own a veil crafted by Betsy Ross. Or rather, Betsy Claypoole."

I let out a low whistle and nodded. I'd looked up Betsy Ross after the claim about our veil. She'd married three times and had been widowed just as many times. She'd become Betsy Claypoole upon her third marriage. "That must have cost a pretty penny."

And it wouldn't have mattered to Helene. She'd come from a family with a sizeable fortune, and had married the heir to the glass factory that had kept the town of Port Quincy employed for three quarters of a century. The glass factory had closed in the 1960s, plunging Port Quincy into decay like so many other former manufacturing towns. But the Pierces had made out alright, maintaining their own wealth through their investments, art collections, real estate holdings, and the sale of the business. The town of Port Quincy hadn't been so lucky; that is, until the last five years. I was happy to be part of the mini renaissance sweeping through the town as people rediscovered its charm. Downtown was filled once again with useful and whimsical shops and service purveyors. But it was still hard to believe that a veil crafted by Betsy Ross once resided in Port Quincy, even if Helene had predictably been its owner. Her rant on Main Street made more sense.

"I suppose a veil like that would matter to Helene, since we all know she's obsessed with her claim of being a descendant of the town founder." I felt my mouth twist into a frown. Helene loved claiming she was the descendant of a Revolutionary War participant. She was active in the Port Quincy Daughters of the American Revolution, and had spearheaded the coup to try to keep women off tomorrow's battle reenactment.

Truman shrugged. "It doesn't make her any more American than anyone else, though, which is why her love of this period of history isn't as innocent as it could be."

I nodded, sharing his sentiment. A loose fact from the matter at hand was rattling around in my brain. "Wait. You said she did have a veil made by Betsy Ross. But she lost it?"

Truman nodded. "The veil Helene lost was indeed made by the famous creator of the first American flag. It was authenticated and everything, with a genuine receipt made by Betsy Ross, when she was known as Betsy Claypoole. It was last

seen in the back seat of Richard Pierce's car, over
two decades ago." Truman paused. He was well
aware of my former engagement to Keith, Helene
and Richard's son. "You know of course that
Richard was killed during a hit-and-run accident.
By the time the police and emergency responders
arrived at the scene, the veil was missing."

I sat in stunned silence, my coffee cup held aloft
in front of me. I finally set it down and found my
voice.

"Keith never told me," I sputtered to explain.
"He did tell me his dad was injured in a car accident, and didn't make it. But he made it sound
like an accident, pure and simple. Not what
sounds like something that may have been intentional, and motivated by a priceless veil."

My mind floated back three years prior, to when
I was engaged to Keith. Though my ex-fiancé had
omitted this intrigue by just mentioning how his
father had passed away in a car accident, I had
been privy to the emotional damage the event had
inflicted on a young Keith. The death of his father
at age thirteen had thrown his and Helene's life
into sudden upheaval. It would have been painful
enough for him to have to revisit losing his father
in a car accident, without divulging the additional
sinister details of the tragedy being a hit-and-run. I
didn't blame him for the omission. It was technically his business to keep it to himself. Still, despite
being long over Keith Pierce, I was a smidge upset
to know that he hadn't told me the whole story.

"You didn't know." Truman's gaze was kind. "I

suppose it's hard for Keith to talk about how we initially thought it was a run-of-the-mill accident, then realized it was probably a planned hit."

"But why?"

Truman shrugged. "Richard Pierce wasn't well liked. He ruled this town, just like Helene does now. Just not as overtly. That woman stomps and blusters to get her way. Richard was subtler, his influence hidden. He was a skilled attorney, and he was both feared and revered. That meant there were lots of disgruntled parties to investigate, many with motives to kill him, and some of whom would have recognized and realized the value of the veil on his back seat." Truman paused in thought. "The only person who could stand up to him was his mother, Sylvia. He had a lot of enemies, Mallory. And after he procured the veil for Helene from Sotheby's, there were a bunch of splashy stories about it. The Pierces should have lent the veil to a museum, or obtained better security for it. It certainly shouldn't have been taken out of the safe and thrown in the back of Richard's Cadillac. We could never prove why he'd taken it out for a spin. Helene was no help in that matter."

"And the veil Bev and I bought? Could that be the same piece stolen from the back seat of Richard's car?"

Truman winced and swallowed a gulp of coffee. His expression looked like it was as pleasant as a glug of battery acid. He gave a regretful and barely perceptible nod.

I had my answer. An immediate cascade of chills

ran down my spine. "What if Richard Pierce's hit was planned specifically to get the veil?" I heard my voice go up in a squeak.

"Maybe we should get it out of here, Mallory. The Smithsonian wants to examine it, and Sotheby's has offered their services as well. Until then, I could keep it at the station."

It was a tempting offer. But for some reason I wasn't willing to give up the swatch of lace. "I don't think too many people know it's here," I offered in a small voice.

Truman snorted. "Just half of Main Street." He amended his judgment. "Although it was a big deal twenty-five years ago, I'm not sure many could put two and two together. Fair enough. Keep the veil. But no one else is to know about the location of the safe, and do not share the passcode. And start locking your back door, for Pete's sake."

"Yoo-hoo!" As if to prove his point, in through the back door streamed Carole and Doug. "I've got building permit applications!" My mom shook a stack of forms under my nose. Doug looked both sheepish and excited.

Our talk of death and veils had come to an abrupt end. It was time to talk about happier things.

"I can't believe I forgot to thank you for the lovely gesture of donating land to build a new house for me and Garrett and Summer." I formally thanked Truman for the offer Lorraine had made and was rewarded with a hearty hug. I wanted to keep my interactions with Truman more like this, rather than returning to the past events of murder and mayhem in Port Quincy.

"Of course, Lorraine and I want to give you and Garrett the land."

"And you have one less worry." My mom beamed. "I spoke to Jesse this evening, and he's on board to quickly design you a new structure that honors the architecture of Thistle Park, on a much smaller scale, of course, and that will be a cozy home for you and Garrett and Summer." My mother wisely left off a quip about the new abode being a place for the passel of grandchildren she was demanding.

Still, I was a bit miffed at her steamrolling. "That's very sweet of you, Mom, to get the ball rolling. I wanted to talk to Jesse and Bev myself though, and make it clear that this project can wait so they can focus on their wedding in three weeks."

"Fiddle fuddle." My mother waved her hand in my face. "I'm not sure what Bev Mitchell has to do with Jesse taking on the project to construct your new home."

I shared an apprehensive glance with my stepfather. I knew my mother was long over Jesse, but didn't like how she seemed to be weaponizing her connections to the man in order to get to Bev.

"Now, let's toast to your house!" My mom retrieved a chilled bottle of Moscato from the fridge, left over from the tasting, and busied herself pouring four glasses.

"To Mallory and Garrett and Summer's new

house!" My mom raised her glass, and Truman, Doug, and I dutifully clinked with hers.

I murmured my goodnight and slipped off to my office to wrap up the last bit of details for Cordials and Cannonballs. I needed a minute to make sure Rachel and Pia had tied up the loose ends, and to digest the bombshell Truman had laid at my feet.

I needn't have worried. My sister and Pia had taken care of everything with aplomb. Cordials and Cannonballs would be a roaring success. Yet a smidge of doubt crept in as I thought of the veil, currently residing in its metallic tomb. My eyes darted toward the safe nestled behind the oil portrait. I had a tiny bit of Moscato left in the goblet in my hand. I turned my back firmly on the safe and veil nestled within and raised a silent toast to myself, to the future.

# CHAPTER FOUR

The next day dawned in a hazy glow, a thick fog coating the town of Port Quincy. I stared incredulously out my third-floor aerie window at a gray sky, thick as cotton batting, that reduced the newly risen sun to a hazy orb.

"This weather stinks." Rachel appeared at my side and squinched up her pretty face in disapproval.

"At least it isn't raining." I turned my back to the window and determined we'd have a wonderful inaugural Cordials and Cannonballs, despite the soupy mess outside.

Despite the surprise fog, I shrugged on the duds I'd selected the night before. I'd selected a summery yet professional khaki sundress with palm trees scattered all over the fabric, a rattan belt, and leather sandals. I'd planned on topping the whole thing off with a wide-brimmed sun hat, but the unusually cloudy sky and thick fog nixed any need for headgear. I decided a heavy coating of sunscreen would suffice.

Rachel in contrast had donned a daringly short, pink floral denim romper, her long legs showcased in wedge espadrilles with a healthy two inches of rattan wedge. I seldom saw my sister in anything but heels, and she could walk in all types of stilt-like shoes with aplomb. But the romper gave me pause.

"Are you sure you want to wear that?" I squinted at her outfit. "We only have porta-potties at the event. *Fancy* porta-potties, but you'll still have to contend with doing business in a romper."

Rachel laughed and flicked away my concerns, her sparkly metallic acrylics catching light from the kitchen light fixture. "Don't worry about me. I'm a romper pro."

We quickly assembled industrial-size carry cups of strong French roast, and fueled up on hearty breakfast fare. I filled bowls with fresh kibble and gave our two cats goodbye pats on their furry little heads.

Rachel held up her sequin-covered iPhone. The weather app showed a staggering number. "Ninety-nine percent humidity?!" Rachel swiped her screen closed. "Doesn't that just, like, automatically turn into rain?"

I shrugged, more preoccupied with the event checklist affixed to a clipboard. "Nothing we can do about it now. It's been ridiculously humid all week. I've nearly forgotten what normal weather feels like, anyway. I just hope this fog doesn't keep people home, and that cars are able to see well enough to arrive without any accidents." I recalled learning that Helene's husband wasn't felled by a mere car accident, but instead a calculated hit, and shrugged off a shiver. I only wanted to focus on positive thoughts as I ushered in the first Cordials and Cannonballs and tried to keep Truman's revelation out of my mind.

Rachel and I packed light messenger bags with our clipboards, coffee, and walkie-talkies for the day. My sister pushed away a tear as she regarded me locking the big double doors.

"What's up?"

Rachel sent me a sweet smile. "I'll miss this." She waved her hands around. "Getting ready and discussing the day's event, then setting off together."

I returned Rachel's smile. "Don't you worry. Even when I've technically moved out, I'll be over here and bustling around in the kitchen each day at the crack of dawn, Rach. You won't be getting rid of me." We shared a sisterly hug.

"Hi, you two!"

I jumped back as Pia emerged from the fog.

"I parked my car at the edge of the drive," she explained. "I didn't want to run into you guys, this fog is so thick."

The three of us set off for the event in my trusty 1970s station wagon, a useful artifact in itself, also left to me by Keith's grandmother Sylvia. I'd long ago christened the behemoth car the Butterscotch Monster, and thanked my stars that I'd kitted out the old vehicle with more modern shoulder belts and more responsive brakes.

We cautiously wended our way down the hill from Thistle Park's high perch, surrounded by Victorian and Georgian homes. I turned left toward the Monongahela, the yellow brick roads of Port Quincy making their usual pleasing thrum under the station wagon's tires.

"Whoa." Rachel let out an appreciative sigh as we crested a slalom-like hill to the pretty park where Cordials and Cannonballs would be held. Despite the thick cover of fog, we could see that the event was packed, even this early in the morning. I drove the Butterscotch Monster under a jaunty marquee sign. The custom-made banner proclaimed this as the Cordials and Cannonballs celebration and fundraiser to jointly benefit the Port Quincy Historical Society and Quincy Park. The festivities would be highlighted by the Revolutionary War reenactment battle; the original battle had taken place at noon sharp, according to the few first-hand accounts from the 1700s. We'd mused that it would be too hot to have reenactors on the field in the afternoon summer sunshine, but it looked like we were wrong about that, too.

Pia, Rachel, and I set up our command booth and got to work putting out small fires. Pia proved herself once again to be a patient, calm, and efficient planner. She soothed a few event-goers after respectfully listening to their complaints, and jumped on her cell phone to call in bottled water reinforcements. After two hours of triaging run-of-the-mill event issues, we were ready to take in some of the event as attendees.

Despite the unusual mist, I was proud to say this inaugural Cordials and Cannonballs had drawn an impressive crowd. There were more than forty booths for citizens to sample colonial-era food, drink, and artifacts. Despite the early hour, guests already sipped homemade whiskey and mead. People tried their hands at replica crafts such as weaving on looms and grinding up grains. Little kids had a blast chasing each other around in their tricorn hats. Their incongruous looks—with their sandals, light-up shoes, and cartoon-character T-shirts—made me giggle. And over everything loomed a thick, woolen fog. One that I hoped would soon dissipate with the breakthrough of the sun. But it was nowhere to be seen. Still, the large gathering and staged battlefield looked magnificent. The day so far was a roaring success.

"Ooh, there's Summer!" I hustled over to the teen's booth with Rachel and Pia not far behind, and I gave my soon-to-be stepdaughter a hug. She was wearing normal twenty-first-century clothing, a tank top and jeans, but had topped off her look with a pretty, historically appropriate bonnet. The front of her booth read "Vegan Versions: a vegetarian take on colonial food favorites."

"Hi, Preston." I waited until Bev's handsome son was finished with his transaction and had tucked away several dollars in the till. "You guys look busy."

Preston nodded, sending a shock of dark hair

tumbling into his eyes. He dug a Port Quincy High School ball cap from his jeans pocket and donned the accessory backward, seeming to use it more as a way to contain his locks than as a way to shield his eyes from the nonexistent sun. "We're doing gangbusters. We've run out of tempeh sandwiches and chickpea hash." He paused with a nearly in-candescent smile for Garrett's daughter. "Summer's idea for this booth was amazing."

Summer gulped a swig from her glass water bottle and appeared to nearly faint with glee. She didn't even answer Preston, just stared at him with moony adolescent ardor.

The two teens were adorable. But I found Garrett's alarm creeping into my observations. Summer's obsession with Preston, an undeniably good kid, was cute. But my almost-official stepmom hackles were raised.

Rachel leaned down for a whisper. "That girl is a goner."

We observed Summer, already a tall teen, look up at Preston and bestow him with a radiant, magenta-braces grin. He looked smitten, too. The new customers they were serving seemed amused at their apparent puppy love.

*She's growing up so fast.*

I split a lentil hoagie with Pia and my sister and we made our way toward the field. I was on the clock and couldn't imbibe, but I admired the cask-aged whiskey and eponymous cordials that many of the booths served. Not all were historically ac-curate, but instead were sweet and fun, jazzed up with lemonade, honey, and maraschino cherries. There were mimosas for this pre-noon hour, as well as home brews and ciders, too. I was grateful again that the weapons on the field were mere replicas, as I'd never want to mix alcohol and firearms.

"Mallory! Rachel! Hello, Pia." My stepfather waved us over to his station under a tree. He was putting the finishing touches on his colonial costume. "Mind giving me a hand with this getup?" He struggled to keep his pants rolled up, and I giggled as I procured an emergency safety pin from my dress pocket. Hidden in my bag and dress were all kinds of little tools to help me MacGyver through any event malfunction.

"Nice turnout, ladies." Doug gestured appreciatively toward the crowd.

"Thanks to your idea to have a reenactment," I reminded him. "I just hope the people watching will be able to see everything." We were fast approaching noon. The June sun that I'd hoped would burn off the haze hadn't been able to permeate the thick atmosphere. It was as humid as ever, and still some residual fog remained. The reenactment was to take place in a field somewhat resembling a bowl of earth. Regrettably, the low-altitude spot had the greatest concentration of impenetrable fog in all of Quincy Park.

"Maybe we should have moved the reenactment to higher ground in light of this weather," Rachel mused.

"No!" The force of Doug's answer caused us all

to blanch. "I mean, the original skirmish took place right in that little gully. It's so neat to recreate it down to the last detail. And get this—" Doug stopped to rub his hands together with glee. "Our few primary documents giving firsthand accounts of the battle indicate that there was an unusual cover of fog on that very day!"

"It's remarkable." My friend Tabitha, Pia's older sister, arrived to geek out on history with my stepfather. "Can you believe it? All the stars are aligning to create a picture-perfect reenactment."

"I certainly wouldn't say picture-perfect," my sister grumbled. "It'll be like fighting in pea soup."

"Historically accurate pea soup," Pia reminded us, earning a laugh from my sister. I wondered how my sister would navigate her residual and somewhat silly ire toward Tabitha, when she was becoming fast friends with her younger sister, Pia.

Tabitha, wearing her own late-1700s garb that she usually dressed in for historical events, carried on her impromptu history lesson with Doug. As noon drew near, the air was heady with their excitement, nearly as palpable as the fog. I felt my own trill of excitement wondering if Bev and I owned a real piece of Americana, a veil crafted by Betsy Ross. In light of the town's celebrations today, I could see why Helene was so covetous of it. All around us history was brought to life.

Doug gave us a salute and a tip of his tricorn hat before he made his way to the reenactment field. I drifted toward the sidelines to observe, along with several hundred denizens of Port Quincy. There were so many reenactors taking their places in the fog I could squint and believe we really were back in Revolutionary War times for the minor Battle of Port Quincy. The reenactors were taking their places in line, with others pretending to man giant cannons and antique howitzers. Then I caught a glimpse of a cell phone and people in their shorts and flip-flops taking selfies with their friends. My belief was no longer suspended, and the time-travel spell was broken.

"There's Grandma Claudia." Pia pointed out one of the few women on the field. She smiled contentedly. "Helene wasn't able to stop her."

"I'm not so sure anyone on this planet could stop Claudia. Your grandmother is a force of nature." The older woman looked particularly fierce as she gripped her rifle. "And I guess I can see where your sister gets her love of history from." I cocked my head and considered the Battles family business. "Your mom, too, with her antiques."

Pia nodded her assent, and we settled down on a swath of gingham picnic blanket to watch in earnest. I was pleased to see Truman and Faith checking each replica weapon on the field. Some of the bayonets and axes were clearly made from plastic. But others, like Doug's musket, were so carefully crafted that the weapons could be filled with ammunition and used. I squinted and took in Faith running a wand over participants' clothing, no doubt to ferret out concealed weapons.

Rachel followed my gaze and wrinkled her nose. "Is that necessary?"

I blinked and stifled a guffaw. "We don't have the best track record with our events, Rach." I stopped and knew she was thinking of the replica *Gone with the Wind* pistol that had been used to dangerous effect. Rachel's smirk fell, and she turned her attention back to Faith's examination of weapons.

*You can never be too careful.*

I turned to happier thoughts as my fiancé made his way to the picnic blanket. Ever the cool cucumber, he looked chill and calm in the blazing humidity in a pair of khaki shorts and a short sleeve button-down. "Your event is a roaring success. Congratulations." He graced me with a lovely kiss. Our concerns about more weighty subjects seemed far away. I felt myself relaxing, despite the ludicrous humidity.

My stepfather ambled over to our blanket in full regalia. "Take lots of pictures!" He gestured to the field.

"Will do, but I don't know if they'll come out." Rachel gestured to the other participants, half of them partially occluded by the rare fog.

"Hello, Mallory." Bev stooped down to give me a hug, and Elvis helped himself to a fourth of a ham sandwich from our cooler before his mistress could stop him. "Elvis! Where are your manners!"

"It's okay. There's plenty more where that came from." I scuffed the basset behind his floppy ears and took in his usual pungent scent of Cheez Doodles and Stilton cheese.

"It's your mother who could stand to take a few

lessons about manners," Bev muttered under her breath.

*Uh-oh.*

I winced at the same time Bev did. My friend the seamstress clapped a hand laden with costume rings over her mouth. "I'm sorry, Mallory. I just don't know how Carole convinced Jesse to take on a project designing you a whole home from scratch a mere few weeks from our wedding." She shook her head, the glass butterflies in her beehive threatening to take flight. "And don't worry." She held up her hand. "I know you didn't put her up to this."

But before I could address her concerns and mollify Bev any further, a bigger kerfuffle kindled a few feet away.

"This is an abomination, and I will stop it as promised! Our Founding Fathers would be rolling in their graves if they saw women on the battlefield." Helene delivered her message with a little stamp of her toeless peach pump and succeeded in getting the heel stuck in the grass. She shrugged off help and struggled to extricate her foot, nearly toppling backwards. A small segment of the crowd turned their attention from the reenactment field to witness her tantrum.

"Do you want to, or should I?" Rachel waved a sandwich and gestured toward my enemy. Pia looked ready, eager to spring into action.

"I'll do it. You two have tended to enough fires today." I stood to go when Garrett gently rested his hand on my arm.

"Just let Truman and Faith handle her, Mallory. You don't know what she's capable of." The look of tender concern in my fiancé's eyes was much appreciated. But I felt a teeny tiny spring of annoyance, too. This may have been what Claudia experienced when Doug gallantly offered to handle Helene for her.

"I've got this, sweetie. Be right back." I dropped a kiss on Garrett's cheek and rose to handle Helene.

"You're single-handedly ruining this event, Claudia Battles!" Helene was a sight to see as a protester. Her skinny hands were clad in white gloves, and her usual shoulder pads were present, raising the profile of her toile Lilly Pulitzer dress. I could see she'd paired her summer pumps with pantyhose, and she'd insisted on protecting her head with a wide-brimmed hat more appropriate for a little girl's Easter Sunday garb, or perhaps the Kentucky Derby. I couldn't suppress my giggle as I advanced. She looked like she was channeling Princess Diana during her courting Prince Charles phase, but with none of the charms or graces. Then, at the last second, a peculiar rush of pathos overtook me. I stood to watch my archnemesis directing her screeches at Claudia and the two other women on the field. Now I knew about Richard, and the extra sadness she'd suffered at knowing her husband was murdered in cold blood.

But I couldn't let her ruin the day. Not even the preternatural fog had managed to do just that, and I wasn't going to let Helene get away with it.

But she was skilled at intimidation, and upon my approach, took the first volley. Literally.

"This is all your fault, Mallory." Helene gave my collarbone a healthy shove.

"Time to go, Mrs. Pierce." Truman saved me the trouble and stood with all imposing six feet, four inches in front of Helene. "You have ten seconds to leave before we cuff you and book you for disorderly conduct. You also just committed assault on Mallory, but I'm sure she'll be willing to overlook it if you go now."

I rubbed my collarbone and placed a steadying arm on Garrett, who had materialized at my side.

Helene sized up the chief and the murmuring of the crowd around her. "Fine! I wouldn't want to witness this abomination of a reenactment anyway. This is completely beneath me!" She minced off as fast as she could, doing a strange walk on her tiptoes to avoid her heels sinking into the earth again. The crowd parted for her, tittering in her wake.

"I told you I should have handled her." Garrett ran a tender finger over my collarbone.

"I appreciate it." I smiled and gave his hand a squeeze. "But I can handle her."

The boom of a cannon made us both jump. I glanced at my watch. It was high noon, and the reenactment had begun. Garrett and I returned to our picnic blanket. I waved to June, who had spread her own quilt next to ours and was chatting animatedly with Pia over the loud noise of the occasional cannon shot. Baby Miri was enjoying some tummy time, her adorable little ears covered with noise-canceling headphones. June gave the baby a fond pat as she stood to make her way to the portable restrooms, her foster daughter tended by Pia in her brief absence.

I took in a deep breath when my mother joined us, her pug, Ramona, making a beeline for Bev's basset. The two women thankfully exchanged frosty smiles and ignored each other from their respective picnic blankets. All around me the denizens of Port Quincy slaked their thirst in the humid day with water, lemonade, mead, and whiskey cocktails. The reenactment had been going for a good fifteen minutes, but was truthfully hard to see through the fog. People made toasts and chatted, getting a little tipsy, no doubt accelerated by the heat dehydration.

An unmistakable shout of pain emanated through the mist.

"Man, they're really hamming this up." Rachel finished her sports drink and retrieved another from the cooler. "I think this is pretty neat, but the reenactors are taking it to a whole other level."

Another yelp of pain pierced the air. The chatter around us grew restless. War was painful, and the reenactors were making that aspect come to life.

A final scream echoed up the field, making the hair along my arms stand at attention. A few children in the crowd burst into tears when the loud pops of replica gunfire, somewhat akin to fireworks, hadn't phased them before.

"Yeah, they're taking it a bit too far," I murmured.

"Is that stage blood?" Pia got up on her knees and peered toward the field, careful to maneuver around baby Miri.

I stood to get a better look, accompanied by a dozen viewers.

Jesse, Bev's fiancé, a lumberjack of a man, staggered up the hill. The fake munition rounds were still going, but some reenactors were screaming for the show to halt. I witnessed a frightening tangle of legs and arms akimbo, as soldiers on the field struggled to run away, and only succeeded in running into each other in the fog.

"I don't think that's paint or ketchup." Rachel had joined me and pointed to Jesse with a trembling finger.

"Dear God." Garrett left my side to help Jesse. The big contractor was carrying a limp body, his homespun pants deluged with blood. I couldn't tell if it was his, or the unfortunate soul he held in his arms.

I made to join Garrett on the field when June stopped me. "Hold her, Mallory." Once more, she thrust a confused baby Miri into my arms.

"Stand back!" Truman's voice thundered over a megaphone, barely cutting through the cacophony of screams and chatter. But he succeeded in stopping Garrett, Pia, and countless others from rushing the field. "This is an active crime scene. Men are down. It isn't safe!"

Doug appeared out of the mist, grasping his

bleeding right arm. My mother ignored Truman to rush to support her husband. Jesse finally reached the top of the hill, the agony of his journey written all over his exhausted face. One arm barely gripped the person he'd been carrying, now slung over his shoulder. His other attempted to stanch the flow of blood coursing from his own abdomen. The sequoia of a man gave up his fight and crumpled to the ground.

Bev gave a primal scream and fainted dead away, Elvis keening and pacing around her.

And I finally recognized the limp person Jesse had carried up the hill. She lay beside him, not moving an inch.

*Claudia.*

The feisty woman was barely recognizable. I reflexively turned Miri around, although I was sure she was too young to comprehend. The event was in shambles. It was a melee as redcoats, and soldiers in brown homespun, were pushed back by Truman and Faith. June wailed, but Pia and Tabitha were surprisingly stoic as they worked together to tend to their grandmother's wounds. Bev was revived by her son, Preston; her renewed screams were only drowned out by the approaching wail of sirens. Two ambulances caused the apoplectic crowd to further scatter as the emergency vehicles made their ungainly way over grass, hill, and dale to reach the fallen reenactors. Emergency plans flashed before my eyes, which I'd hoped to never put into play. I felt a sickening stab of fear and regret as the

EMS workers loaded Claudia onto a gurney, her dull brown homespun outfit slick with cherry-red blood. Truman and Faith's careful examination of each person on the field had been all for naught. Someone had been hell-bent on recreating a massacre on this field, and had succeeded in spades.

# CHAPTER FIVE

I paced the gleaming linoleum floor of the McGavitt-Pierce Memorial Hospital. I'd spent way too many hours in the structure, part of a large medical complex named after Keith and Helene's family. The earlier success of Cordials and Cannonballs had evaporated in a haze of screams, blood, and mayhem. I wished I could have pulled down the unusual blanket of fog over the whole mess and carnage and done a redo of the day. Instead I spent the late afternoon waiting to hear news of my stepfather. The sun hovered like a giant orange orb from my western-facing view out the emergency room's sliding glass doors. The haze that had allowed some miscreants to wreak havoc at the reenactment had finally burned off of the horizon. It was a gorgeous sunset, the clouds tinged a lurid magma-like magenta. But what should have been a glorious view was a reminder of the red blood spilled on the field of what was supposed to be a pretend skirmish.

Doug had been carted away in the second ambulance. His arm was bleeding profusely, but the EMTs had deemed his wounds non-fatal. I would have preferred to have had my loved one healthy and whole, but compared to some who were not as fortunate on the battlefield, I'd take it. The eerie fog had ended up being premonitory. And from what I could tell, it didn't help the first responders who'd come screeching up to the field. I could tell from Truman's agitation before I left that it was a muddle of a crime scene. No one really knew what had happened. It was almost as if the perpetrator was in cahoots with the weather. The thought sent trickles of fear dancing across my shoulder blades, aided by the overzealous hospital air-conditioning.

I knew Rachel longed to be here, too, but she had remained to triage what must have been a messy and chaotic early end to Cordials and Cannonballs. My one relief had been to receive a text from Garrett assuring me that he and Summer were safe and sound.

I jumped each time a nurse exited the sealed security doors to the inner part of the emergency room. Doug had been in the back for quite some time. And though I worried about him, I couldn't help but glance up at the ceiling from my spot in the waiting room. I knew two floors up in surgery, there were two families whose concern and anguish were immeasurable. The first two ambulances

to arrive to the reenactment-turned-real battlefield had triaged Jesse and Claudia first. It hadn't
looked good. Neither one had moved as they were
loaded onto separate gurneys and carted away,
though Jesse had let out a stifled and burbling
groan. I sent a silent prayer for them skyward and
closed my eyes, willing my memory to shut off the
constant replay of the last five minutes before the
event had been irrevocably ruined. I sank onto a
green vinyl bench. The constant worry and constant pacing had finally overtaken the shock of
adrenaline and cortisol coursing through my veins.

At least I had a friendly, furry companion to
distract me. In the melee of first responders and
wailing attendees, Bev had handed off Elvis. The
dolorous pup seemed more sad than usual. The big
guy definitely knew something was up. He opened
one droopy eye and settled a paw on my lap before
letting out a high-pitched yawn and going back to
sleep. I petted the basset, his familiar loamy scent a
comfort. I absentmindedly scratched behind his
prodigious, floppy ears. He sighed in his sleep and
seemed to settle a bit.

The ER staff had allowed my mom to take in
Ramona the pug. Or more likely, my mom had
spirited her inside her big bag, and they were
choosing to ignore the little pup. But Elvis couldn't
be in the intensive care unit. I'd briefly peeked my
head into the ICU waiting room after my mom
texted that my stepfather was going to be okay. I
caught a glimpse of Pia and June huddled together, ignoring the National Geographic channel

blaring from the big-screen television mounted in the space, no doubt an attempt to distract the visitors waiting to hear word about their loved ones. I'd returned to the ER and gotten stuck in that strange time warp that was the peculiar purview of emergency rooms. A glance at my watch told me that three hours had gone by.

"Mallory."

The tall form of Truman blocked my own mindless TV viewing.

"Truman—"

"Claudia didn't make it."

My heart accelerated and promptly sank into the depths of my stomach. The feisty, dedicated, and loving mom and grandma was gone from this earth. Tears coursed down my face, and I dimly felt Elvis nestle closer. Truman wordlessly handed me a box of tissues he swiped from the intake desk.

"Oh, my goodness. I can't imagine what June and Pia and Tabitha are thinking." I failed to mop up the waterworks that I knew were just beginning.

Truman swallowed hard, too. His voice was gruff and laden with emotion. He was used to delivering bad news, but this time seemed especially egregious. "They're not taking it well, as you can imagine. June still has Miri with her, asleep in her baby carrier. She's holding it together the best of the three so as not to scare the baby. But Tabitha and Pia lost it. As is understandable."

Truman gave up his tough stance and crumpled

in the chair next to me. I noticed a bloodstain marring his handkerchief peeking out from his pocket and involuntarily winced.

A bubble of accusation percolated up, unbidden, and flew out of my mouth before I could stop it.

"That wretched woman."

"Who? Mallory?" Truman sat up, his attention definitely piqued.

"Helene Pierce!" I hurtled my suspicion with a screech loud enough to make the ER intake attendant jump. "Of course, it was her. The incident with the veil made that old bat unhinged. Her inability to stop women from taking to the battlefield pushed her over the edge."

Truman digested my theory for a mere thirty seconds before volleying back a question. "How did Helene manage to wound Doug, Jesse, and murder Claudia all in the span of about a minute and a half?"

I waved my hand around in frustration, taking in the happy fact that Jesse was still alive if Truman had designated him so. "She had reason to take out each person she wounded. She and Claudia argued over whether women could take part in the reenactment, everyone knew that." I held up one finger. "And Doug tried to intervene on Claudia's behalf and put Helene in her place."

"And Jesse? What beef did Helene have with him?"

I racked my brain as I stood again, carefully placing Elvis's paws on the vinyl bench. "That one's tougher. But Helene, of course, was furious about the veil. She couldn't take out Bev as a bystander in the crowd, so she went after her fiancé." I closed my eyes and stopped short. "Helene wears those silly little white gloves on occasion, but it's honestly a rare look even for her. Who did she think she was, Jackie O? No! She wore gloves to conceal her prints on the weapon."

This last idea got Truman's attention. I could tell because he rubbed his chin and seemed to consider the idea, rather than immediately shoot it down.

"Maybe you're on to something."

I took the miniscule bone he tossed and ran with it. "For sure, Truman! Helene is the only person who would have wanted to hurt those three particular people."

"But—" Truman's next question was cut short.

Bev shot into the room like a frantic cannon. She grabbed my hands in hers. "Jesse's alright! He's going to be okay!"

Elvis bounded down from his seat and wagged his stumpy tail. Bev knelt to hug the sweet basset, and he licked a trail of happy and relieved tears from her cheek. My friend appeared predictably exhausted from the crazy range of emotions she'd just gone through. She let out a somewhat frazzled laugh.

"And I feel like I owe your crazy mother a debt of gratitude."

*This should be interesting.*

Bev went on to explain. "I'm ever so glad she tasked him with building you and Garrett a cottage in the next month, even if it'll put a strain on our wedding prep. Did you know he was mumbling about blueprints and permits after he came out of anesthesia?" The seamstress chuckled. "I would like to think our impending marriage is the most enticing will to live for my Jesse. But he's vowing to complete your cottage in record time, even if it's by his bedside."

"I'm not sure that's such a hot idea." I'd been miffed at my mother, too, for whipping Jesse into a design and building frenzy when he should be finalizing wedding plans. But I was sure my house project should be tabled in lieu of Jesse focusing on his recovery. And I wondered about whether Jesse would be able to recuperate enough to get married in the next few weeks, much less design and build my cottage.

Bev seemed to follow my train of thought. "The surgeon thinks he will be okay to wed in two weeks." Her eyes twinkled. "My Jesse, good as new, just less dancing at the reception. The shot only nicked his spleen and part of one kidney. Barring complications, he'll be A-OK."

Bev would be able to give her strange thanks to my mom in person. Carole and Doug minced out of the inner vestibule of the ER. My stepdad was cradling his arm, but appeared no worse for wear. Unless you counted his bloodied and shredded homespun shirt the doctors and nurses must have cut to pieces in order to attend to his arm.

"Mallory." I shared a one-armed hug with Doug and promptly burst into tears anew. "It's okay, sweetie. Everything's going to be okay."

Truman waited a few minutes for me to chat with my stepfather. But then he got down to the business at hand. "I'm sorry to interrupt, and I know it's been a long day, Doug. But I do need to get some initial impressions from you while they're still fresh."

Doug nodded and sank into a vinyl chair. "I know I was jostled from behind—some redcoat taking things too damn seriously. But it seemed intentional, you know? Lots of us were tripping over each other and the rocks in the field because it was hard to see in the fog. But the shove that brought me down seemed to be on purpose." Doug winced at the memory. "I'm glad my bayonet wasn't real. Anyway, I dropped my musket when I fell, and I felt around for it, but several people stepped on my hands. I gave up, and almost immediately, people started screaming. I guess the real shooting began then."

Truman posed a few more pointed questions to Doug before taking in his exhaustion and hesitance to answer. "We can continue this questioning tomorrow after you've had a chance to rest, Doug." Truman's eyes turned kind.

"And Jesse, how is he doing?" My mother's query to Bev was friendly and neutral. But I don't think that's what Bev heard.

"Why are you so hot and bothered to know?"

Bev's eyes shot white-hot daggers in my mother's direction.

"Hot and what?! Pfft. As if." My mother stood like a pugilist in her little royal-blue mule loafers, appearing ready to spring into action.

"Mom, Bev. We've all had such a trying day." I awkwardly inserted myself between the two women. Elvis and Ramona hadn't picked up the tension and happily continued to sniff each other in doggie friendship. Too bad their mistresses never got the memo. In fact, Bev nimbly separated Elvis from his impromptu doggie playdate with Ramona, as if the little pug were his enemy by proxy.

*Ouch.*

"Let's go, Doug." Carole swept from the waiting room, Ramona dutifully if somewhat reluctantly trotting behind her. My mom stopped and hustled back to steady Doug, a blush staining her cheeks at her apparent prioritization of making a quick get-away over helping her wounded spouse.

I gave Bev a weak wave and followed my family out. At the last second, I glimpsed Truman. He stood in the corner, observing it all. Of course, he had to know the bad blood between my mother and Bev was just a silly misunderstanding, not anything to do with the carnage of today. The little squabble the chief had just witnessed must be small potatoes in light of Claudia's death and the other unsolved mysteries of the day. But Truman had his game face on, and seemed to be exploring all of his options.

*Uh-oh.*

\* \* \*

I awoke Sunday morning hoping the prior day had merely been a nightmare. But a quick perusal of the digital version of the Port Quincy *Eagle Herald* newspaper showed the ruined aftermath of Cordials and Cannonballs in lurid, blood-red detail. I swiped my phone's screen closed and went about my duties straightening up at my B and B with wooden inattentiveness. I was happy to chat with my mother and Doug and get a good update on his continued progress.

And though my appetite seemed to be gone for good, I decided to keep a long-standing lunch date I'd scheduled with my best friend, Olivia. She was due to have her first child in two weeks, and I was planning her rather last-minute baby shower. I was grateful to have a chance to turn my thoughts to properly celebrating the new addition to Olivia's family, rather than replaying the grisly events of yesterday in a loop in my head.

A few minutes before noon I dragged my sorry self across the threshold of the Greasy Spoon, a usually cheery and kitschy diner decorated with yards of black and gold vinyl and smooth, polished chrome. Today the place was alive with what was no doubt gossip about the ruined and deadly events of yesterday. The initial quieting of the buzzing chitchat when I entered the restaurant affirmed my suspicions, but soon the chatter picked up, with some diners glancing at me and lowering their voices.

"I'm so sorry about your event yesterday, love."

Olivia jumped up from her booth in the back corner and attempted to give me a hug. Her giant, late pregnancy belly prevented her from delivering one full-force. But that didn't stop her from trying. She appeared chic and collected, even at nearly nine months. She wore a ruffled denim jacket over a black tank and leggings, the cream enamel earrings swinging against her shiny black hair a gift I'd given her several years ago.

"Thanks, Liv. I needed that." I sank gratefully down in my side of the booth. When the server took my order, I barked out a request for chicken noodle soup and cornbread. The meal wasn't very fitting for an unusually hot June, but if anyone needed to try to choke down some comfort food, it was me.

"Doug was lucky. He lost a lot of blood. But whatever ammunition nicked his arm was basically a surface wound. Beyond lots of stitches, he'll be okay." I gave my peremptory report to stave off further questions. Olivia seemed to catch my drift. Especially when I brought out my tablet and the manila file I'd assembled for her shower.

"Yes, let's get this done." Olivia turned her efficient and analytical attorney's mind to the task of winnowing down choices for the shower. She'd begun her second litigation career in January, teaming up with Garrett, and had fully transitioned into her work as a plaintiff's attorney in small-town Port Quincy. "I think we're the last couple on earth who isn't interested in finding out the sex of the baby." She gave her belly a little pat.

"Too bad all of the gender-neutral stuff is gray. Not that I don't like gray, but I'd welcome a pop of color. Your yellow and orange shower will be a welcome break from all those neutrals."

I nodded and swiped through the Pinterest board I'd created for Olivia's approval. The shower would be citrus themed, with little giraffe and elephant accents in orange and yellow. Planning the event should have been a joy, but was understandably muted from the events of the day prior.

"Garrett has been wonderful, too," Olivia gushed about my fiancé. "If I'd stayed at the big firm, my maternity leave would have been nearly nonexistent. Here, I'll be able to ease back in at a family-friendly pace. Maybe raising Summer as a single dad gave Garrett an unusual and much appreciated understanding of the need for real parental leave." Olivia cocked her head and considered me for a moment. She seemed to hesitate, but took the plunge. "Have you and Garrett thought about having kids?"

I felt a hot jet of delicious broth from my chicken soup skitter down the wrong pipe. Several diners looked over in alarm as I gave a choking cough, only saved when Olivia thrust my cold glass of iced tea in my hands.

*Great. First Mom, now Olivia.*

"Um, I haven't asked."

Thankfully, Olivia didn't shriek in alarm, or offer immediate chastisement. What she did was worse. She put on her litigator game face, tented her hands under her chin, and regarded me carefully.

"What?!" I took another swig of tea to avoid her piercing gaze.

"*What* is indeed the question at hand, Mallory." Olivia leaned back, her pregnancy glow nearly casting a halo around her pretty face. "What do you want?"

"I don't know." My voice came out confused and low. "If I did have a clearer idea of what I wanted our family to ultimately look like, maybe I'd be justified in grilling Garrett."

The few times when the subject of having kids had obliquely crossed our radar, Garrett had been maddeningly unspecific. And to be fair, before this week, despite my mom's goading, I'd found myself ambivalent, too. Until I'd held little Miri in my arms in June's shop, and decided maybe I could entertain the thought of having a child someday.

"How would Summer feel?" I blurted out. "Honestly, her opinion matters just as much as mine and Garrett's." I loved my fiancé's daughter like my own. I would never try to usurp her mother Adrienne's place, but I couldn't wait to make our relationship official.

"You'll be a wonderful stepmother, Mallory. And if you and Garrett so choose, I know you'd be fantastic parents to another little one as well." Olivia graced me with a kind smile as she dug into her bag and returned triumphant with a giant bottle of Tums. "I'm starving these days, but there's no room in here." She gestured toward her unbelievably round stomach. "The heartburn is unreal."

We sat in content silence for a few minutes while we finished our meals. I couldn't believe the whether-to-have-kids conundrum was a welcome change of focus. But compared to yesterday, I'd take it. And Olivia wasn't quite done.

"Maybe," she began tentatively, "when you settle some of these big issues, like where to live and when you and Garrett are getting married, the even bigger questions will fall into place."

I filled in my friend on the exciting plan to build a new abode on the land adjoining my property and Garrett's parents'. "Although we were going to break ground soon, and with Jesse recuperating, I'm sure that will be on hold. As it should be. I think my mom got carried away."

"And Garrett mentioned on Friday that you two are considering scheduling your wedding for the summer instead of fall?" Olivia asked her question innocently, her long black lashes blinking in anticipation.

"That seems too rushed, too, in light of yesterday," I miserably put in.

Olivia reached across the table and grabbed my hands. "Close your eyes, Mallory."

"Huh?" I glanced around at the other diners, who had finally stopped staring at me like I was a zoo animal, and had returned to their food and conversations. "Come again?"

"Just try it." There was mirth and laughter dancing in Olivia's eyes, and I grabbed on to her happiness like a life preserver. "Now. How do you picture getting married?"

I tried not to think about how I was doing a vision quest in a booth in the Greasy Spoon and attempted to play long. "Okay. Um. Well, I see a dress." I gulped. "A dress at the Antique Emporium, to be exact. And I don't even think the season matters. I see my friends and my family, and we're having fun. It's casual, and meaningful, and intimate." I opened my eyes. "I guess I get it now. It doesn't matter when I get hitched, just that I want to do it. Thanks, Liv."

Olivia's brown eyes sparkled. "I do know that dress you mentioned is the key to it all, though. Why don't you go get it, and when everyone is all healed up and ready to go, just do it?"

I nodded at her enthusiasm. Then I clapped a hand to my forehead. "Shoot. I promised *Wedding Divas* magazine they could do a story on our wedding. It's a feature about how wedding planners approach their own weddings." I frowned. "It seemed like a fun idea, but it might not work for a smaller, more casual wedding."

Olivia's expression turned mischievous. "Then don't do it. From now on, do exactly what you want. *Oof.*" Her power talk trailed off as she grabbed her belly. "That was a strong one."

I glanced down at her stomach in alarm. "You're not going to have the baby right now, are you?"

Olivia let out a pretty peal of laughter. "Nope. The due date is still two-and-a-half weeks away. I bet that was just a practice contraction." Olivia's eyes sparkled.

My phone let out an insistent buzz, and I murmured an apology as I eagerly checked it. I was worried I'd miss an update from my mom or Bev.

"It's an email from the Smithsonian," I said with wonder. "They want to meet to discuss the veil."

I gulped down the rest of my iced tea and bid my best friend goodbye. I had a feeling that things were going to get even more complicated, if that was even possible.

Monday morning arrived with a periwinkle sky barely brushed with feathery cirrus clouds. There was no fog or humidity. Just calm, atmospheric clarity.

"If only we'd had this weather for Cordials and Cannonballs," I grumbled to myself as I glanced out my bedroom window. I'd tried to keep my mind busy after my lunch with Olivia. When things got too quiet, my brain tried to make sense of senseless things: the ruined event, Jesse's injury, the idea that anyone wanted to hurt my dear stepfather, and the unfair and cruel death of Claudia. And hanging over it all in the present was Bev's nonsensical anger directed at my mother. I had texted my friend a few times, and her cagey answers were crystalizing into a bizarre theory that perhaps Doug had been to blame for Jesse's injuries. I decided to chalk up Bev's claim on her need to make sense of what had happened to Jesse.

And despite Bev's nonsensical accusations, I was grateful for Doug's increasingly speedy recovery.

Doug revealed that the ER had initially been puzzled at how to handle a suspected musket shot, but had eventually just sewed and cleaned up the jagged flesh like any other wound. My stepfather felt better on a massive dose of ibuprofen. He also seemed to be enjoying my mom taking off work to flutter around him. Neither she, Rachel, or I had the heart to tell Doug that Bev somehow suspected him of shooting Jesse. The men were friends, and Doug was secure in his marriage to Mom.

I was almost happy to be entertaining the specialist due to arrive from the Smithsonian. It was possible I could offload the veil and maybe in the process earn enough good karma points to get this month of June back on track. I put the mess of Cordials and Cannonballs and its aftermath on the back burner, if only for a bit.

"Are you ready?" Rachel entered the library with a tray set for tea. A delicate curl of steam twisted up from the spout, ringing the plate of cranberry and white chocolate biscotti. Together with my sister I had selected a pretty purple violet and forget-me-not pattern from our eclectic collection of antique tea sets. A few summers ago, we'd done an inventory and kept all of the ones that were not made with lead glaze. We enjoyed bringing them out for events and to host. I thought the archivist might appreciate this set, made and commissioned right here in Port Quincy in the 1920s.

"I'm as ready as I'll ever be." My eyes strayed to the silver tray where I'd eventually place the veil for the Smithsonian representative to examine.

Call me crazy, but I hadn't even gotten it out yet. It could have been the stress from Saturday's reenactment turned shoot-out, but I imagined Helene wafting through the library window on a broom and absconding with the lace before I could stop her. Stranger things seemed to have happened, and I was taking no chances.

"They must really think this is the real deal if they sent someone from D.C." Rachel absentmindedly fluffed a throw pillow, her green eyes alive with schemes and calculations. I knew my acquisitive little sister was seeing little sugarplum dollarsigns dancing in her head at the prospect of me owning a real artifact created by Betsy Ross.

"They sat up and listened when I told them we'd found the veil in Port Quincy." I recalled the sharp intake of breath on the other end of the line when I'd mentioned the provenance of the found veil. "And then they really got interested when Truman collaborated with them."

I finished straightening the room and stood to face my sister. "But you remember what happened with the paintings."

Rachel blinked her ultra-long lashes. "What on earth do you mean, Mallory?"

I lobbed a pillow at my sister, nearly knocking her sky-high genie ponytail askew.

"Hey!" Rachel grabbed the pillow with her cat-like reflexes and set it down on a fainting couch with a pat. "That was uncalled for. Fine. It doesn't pay to stash precious artifacts in one's house. Especially this one." A brief cloud swept over her pretty looks. I know we are both thinking of what had happened when certain unsavory characters knew of some rumored valuable paintings in the house.

"Collecting rare pieces is great, but we're a B and B. Not a museum." I had texted Bev last night, and the two of us were moving in the direction of donating the piece if it truly had been sewn by Betsy Ross. Although I anticipated a vicious fight from Helene, and hadn't started going down the legal rabbit hole of ownership when one party fairly purchased an item that had long ago been stolen from another.

"Ugh. You're such a killjoy!" Rachel nearly stamped her foot as she saw profits from the veil slip from her sparkly, acrylic-nailed fingers.

But I stood firm. I no longer saw the veil as a whimsical find to share with Bev on our respective wedding days. The veil wasn't a boon, but a coveted chess piece that could bring me, my sister, and now Pia, and Bev as a co-owner of the veil, to real danger.

"At this point, Rach, I kind of want to jettison the whole darn thing. Or cede it to Helene."

Rachel's green eyes grew to saucer proportions. "No! Don't let that old meanie win."

"I shrugged. It might not be our choice." I suppressed a shiver. "What if it's already starting?" My question began as a whisper, and rose to a shrill pitch.

Rachel scrunched up her nose in thought. "Wait, like what went down at Cordials and Cannonballs was somehow tied to the veil?" A real look of panic flicked over her features.

"Precisely." I held up my fingers one by one. "Richard Pierce was ostensibly murdered because of this veil, albeit a quarter of a century ago. And it was controversial enough that my own ex-fiancé never told me." I took note of the look of shock on Rachel's face at this admission. "The hit-and-run that killed Helene's husband sounds much more like a straight-up hit. Two. Helene got all riled up when she found out we'd bought this veil. She was ticked at Claudia, whose family store sold Bev and me the veil. Now"—I gulped—"Claudia is gone. Which points to Helene."

Rachel nodded her assent. "I can't picture Helene pulling the trigger. But I can see that crazy lady calling in a hit on Claudia. She specializes in getting others to do her dirty work. But what about Jesse?"

"Ahem."

Rachel and I jumped when Bev appeared in the library. "Believe me, girls, I've been trying to figure out the same thing."

Rachel and I spent a few testy minutes arguing over who had left the front door unlocked. "We can't be too careful with the veil in here." I didn't want to leave the house open to attack. I felt a knot forming in my stomach when I realized my mind automatically jumped to macabre possibilities.

"It's okay, Mallory." Bev attempted to soothe me. "I locked the doors after I came in."

I was distracted more by my friend's unusual getup than calmed by her words. Bev was wearing the most somber outfit I'd ever seen on her plump figure. She'd dressed head to toe in dark colors, with nary a glittery accent. I knew she wore prescription glasses, but she still had over two dozen pairs. These ones were black tortoiseshell to match her black cap-sleeved top and dark wash jeans. Ah. If I squinted, I could see the resin frames were infused with the barest hint of microscopic glitter. Her sky-high beehive was still bedazzled with its usual butterflies, but these ones were styled in an unusual somber gray. The decorations almost looked like moonlit moths, but velvety, subdued ones.

"And I'm sure Truman will have this all wrapped up in no time." Bev raised one blond brow. She let her eyes stray toward a 1990s portrait of Mom, Doug, Rachel, and I. I didn't suppress my eye roll at her insinuation that my parents had had one iota to do with Jesse's attack.

I could count on Rachel to be even less subtle. "Oh, c'mon, Bev! You can't possibly think that Doug or Mom would want to hurt Jesse. What did Doug do, shoot your fiancé, then somehow wound himself?"

Bev gave Rachel a narrow-eyed look. "I just know that Truman is looking at all of the possibilities."

The front hall bell rang. The three of us jumped.

"Saved by the bell." Rachel gave Bev a somewhat unkind smirk. "And into the fray."

The man we greeted on the front porch and ushered into the mansion seemed overwhelmed to meet three women who claimed to have a stake in the veil.

"Hello, Ms. Shepard, I presume? I'm Horace Overright." The man before me was only a few inches taller than my five feet even. He was wearing an interesting mix of professional and casual. His top was all business, with a windowpane patterned shirt, polka-dot tie, and dapper suspenders. He completed his look with decidedly casual olive twill shorts and a pair of Vans slip-ons that had seen better days. He caught me visually critiquing his look and gave me a shrug. "It's as humid up here as it is in D.C. Not what I remembered."

I found myself laughing with the pleasant middle-aged man and ushered him into our cool, air-conditioned mansion. He nodded appreciatively. "And you upgraded Thistle Park, I see."

"Excuse me?" I waited until he'd made his introductions to Rachel and Bev to question him. "You've been here before?"

He nodded as he eagerly looked around. "I was a junior varsity point man in authenticating and examining the veil when Helene Pierce originally owned it. I had tea with her mother-in-law, Sylvia, when I was last in Port Quincy. It only makes sense that they sent me up today."

Horace appreciated the tea set Rachel and I selected for his visit, but he didn't dillydally. He made it clear this wasn't a social visit. After neatly consuming exactly one slice of biscotti, and one cup of tea, he clapped his hands together. His jewelry mirrored his clothes. On one hand was an ancient and pricey-looking gold signet ring. On the other was a simple silicone band. "Where is it?"

I felt a wave of panic wash over me at his request to see the veil. I'd taken to heart Truman's admonition not to let anyone know of the safe's location. That's why our little meeting was taking place in the library rather than the office.

"I'll get it." Rachel and I laughed as we both rose and declared we'd get the veil.

"I'll go with you." Horace stood and brushed off a crumb of biscotti.

"That's not necessary." It was Bev who batted down his request and dared him with dagger eyes to take a step out of the library.

"I always like to see where people keep their precious collection items." Horace refused to take no for an answer, and nimbly trotted down the hall in my and Rachel's wake, his Vans silent on the hardwood and antique runner.

*Darn it.*

Rachel and I exchanged rueful looks as we made our way to the safe.

"Whoa. That's awesome!" Horace's eyes nearly bugged out of his head when I pressed the little dragonfly carved into the teak mantel. "I've never seen anything like it."

"It was designed by my fiancé, Jesse Flowers, a master craftsman and historical restoration specialist," Bev gushed.

I realized with a start that Bev knew of the location of the safe, too, since Jesse had indeed designed and built the complicated hidey-hole. Truman would be disappointed when I furnished him with an even longer list of people privy to the safe's location.

I didn't feel as much trepidation from Horace knowing where we kept the veil. He was a professional, after all. But I still reflexively covered the digital keypad with my other palm as my fingers flew over the numbers. If I had to do it at the grocery store with my debit card PIN, I wasn't going to not do so here. I'd suffered enough weird occurrences over the years to justify my paranoia.

We held our collective breath as I slipped the tissue-paper wrapped bundle from the cool, metal confines of the safe.

"Ladies and gentleman, here it is." I peeled back the tissue and delicately plucked the veil from its folded pile, holding the exquisite and aged lace up to the light.

"Whoa." Horace seemed to make it across my office in a flash. "Mm-hmm. I'm willing to bet this is it." He tried to suppress a wince and gestured toward my hands. "Although, dear, you really ought to be wearing gloves."

I dropped the fabric like a hot coal and felt mildly chastened. I realized Horace had procured gloves for himself from his shorts pockets. "They're pretty clean," I murmured. "Except for that piece of biscotti." I felt a slow blush.

Horace chuckled and donned a pair of wire-framed reading glasses for a closer look. "No worries. People have residual oils on their hands that can damage the fabric."

Rachel lost her patience at his chastisement. "For Pete's sake, it was stuffed at the bottom of a hatbox!"

Horace gave her a gentle smile. "Yes, Truman did tell me that. Fair enough." But he drew in a sharp breath when his examination revealed the veil to be in two pieces. He gave a low and dolorous whistle. "And Truman told me about the melee on Main Street, too. But that didn't prepare me, in all honesty, for this." He held up the two jagged ends, viciously rent by Helene.

"*Meow.*" My sweet little orange kitten must have awoken from her nap in the parlor. She turned her pretty lemon-yellow eyes to the veil Horace held aloft, and the temptation was too much. Before I could stop her, Soda alighted on the desk and reached out a clawed, although recently trimmed, paw. She took a playful swipe at the delicate artifact and jumped when Horace let out a primal yelp.

"Oh, my goodness, Soda!" I scooped up the Creamsicle-colored fluff ball and gave her some comforting pats before I gently placed her outside the office and shut the door firmly behind me. Bev was fanning a nearly faint Horace, who had taken the liberty to sink into my office chair. Rachel was nearly purple as she attempted to keep from bursting into gales of laughter.

"I'm so sorry." My worry over the revelation of my safe's location seemed like a minor issue in comparison to my cat nearly doing a Freddie Krueger on the priceless veil.

Horace let out a strange wheeze. I wondered if I'd need to revive him with some modern-day smelling salts. But his wheeze grew and erupted into a hearty spate of laughter. "This town hasn't gotten any less crazy in the twenty-five years since I last visited."

We all joined in his mirth, relieved that the veil wasn't going to suffer any more tears. We grew quiet as Horace brought out a pricey-looking small digital camera, and took numerous close-up shots of the lace's patterns.

"Now, I just eyeballed this fabric." Horace neatly and lovingly folded up the veil and wrapped it up in the tissue paper. "I have our original authentication papers that we collaborated with Sotheby's to produce, around the time of the original sale of the veil. I'll need to compare the photographs, of course. But for now, I am going to make the official call and tentatively authenticate the veil as a piece of lace crafted by Betsy Ross."

Rachel cheered in response, as if heralding a Steelers' touchdown.

"But," Horace warned us, "we'll need to do a scientific analysis of the fabric back in D.C."

"Absolutely." I nodded my assent.

"Yes, that sounds right." Bev agreed and let out a whoosh of air and tension.

"No way!" Rachel furrowed her perfectly plucked brow. "The veil should stay here for now."

Horace nodded to my sister. "Of course, for today. I'm not taking that back to the hotel. The veil should be safe and sound in that ingenious little contraption you've got there." He gestured toward the mantel. "I do, however, need to ask." He took a deep breath and his kind face settled into a hopeful smile. "I bet you'll need to sort out some rather big chain-of-possession issues with the lace."

*He means Hurricane Helene.*

"But," he continued, "if you ladies get to keep it, I think you should consider donating the artifact to the Smithsonian." He tactfully ignored Rachel's rude snort. "Or even just lending it to us," he amended.

"But it's a liquid asset," Rachel muttered. "You've got some big—" Rachel stopped herself from saying any more.

*Say what?!*

My sister continued with an outright sour expression. "Think of how much it's worth! You can't give that up." She turned pleading eyes on Bev and me.

I didn't deign to respond, but didn't suppress my eye roll, either. After nearly dying, my sister had been quite happy to rid our house of a very expensive John Singer Sargent painting. I guess a few years' time had mellowed her memory.

Bev was more wistful than anything. "I really am sad. I so wanted to wear the veil on my big day."

Horace gave Bev a sympathetic look, but handed her a sheaf of papers in lieu of verbal comfort. "It's a bit premature, but these documents detail the process should you gracious ladies consider donating, or, ahem, lending the veil to the Smithsonian Institution."

"I guess we could have replicas of the veil created." I brightened at the idea that popped into my head. "Like Kelly Clarkson's Jane Austen ring when the British government didn't let her remove the original from the country."

"Oh, that's a lovely idea!" Bev's eyes sparkled anew behind her subdued spectacles.

Rachel looked like she wanted to sink into the floor.

"That is totally doable," Horace promised with a smile. "We could facilitate the creation of an exact replica." He winced. "Sans the giant rip down the middle, of course."

We bade him a good afternoon and walked him out, after bestowing the veil back into the safe, that is.

"I can't believe you're basically giving it away!" Rachel's protestations were loud enough to echo through Port Quincy. I was glad Horace had already advanced down the drive in his rental car.

"Don't worry, Rach." I wearily recalled Horace's warning, and my former training as an attorney. "It might be years until this dust has settled."

"Huh?" Rachel perked up at the prospect.

"Not necessarily in a good way. If this is indeed the original veil, Helene may have just as much of a claim to it, since it was hers, and stolen." I pinched the bridge of my nose to stave off a headache. "I can't even remember where my property case law text is. And it feels like a million years since I took the bar and practiced. I need to brush up on possession and the current stance on this."

But it looked like I wouldn't need to wait. A sharp rap on the front door announced another visitor. A person who next took the liberty to try the front door, which we hadn't yet locked since Horace had just left.

"Greetings, ladies." Helene let herself in, a whoosh of hot, fragrant air trailing behind her. She stepped aside to usher in a constable, who looked regretful to be taking orders from her.

"Stop directing him." A booming voice barked out behind Helene, and I was relieved to see Truman's large frame block the light from the outside as he brought up the rear.

"I just accompanied him to make sure that justice is served," Helene hissed. "And to see Mallory and Bev here be served their slices of revenge." Helene gave a sinister little chuckle. "They say it's a dish best served cold, but I don't know about you. I think it's just as lovely to witness in the heat of summer."

"Just get on with your charade." Rachel gave her large, rose gold Michael Kors watch an exaggerated glance. "We only have so many minutes a week to dedicate to your shenanigans, Helene."

I stifled a giggle, my sister's assertions making me feel better in an instant.

"Well?" Helene gave the young constable a little shove.

"Ouch! Okay. I have a temporary restraining order issued for Mallory Ann Shepard and Beverly Lynn Mitchell." The constable somewhat reluctantly handed two sealed documents over.

I snorted as I ripped open the envelope and skimmed the contents within.

*Utterly predictable.*

This wasn't the first time Helene had used the law to temporarily get what she wanted. It was one of her dearest tactics. A judge had signed a temporary restraining order prohibiting the removal of the veil from Port Quincy.

*There goes Horace's wish for a speedy donation to the Smithsonian.*

"What are you waiting for?" Helene turned her imperious gaze on Truman. She wafted a queenly hand in his face. "Tut tut, go get my veil!"

Truman answered her with a barely restrained smirk. "I got my own copy of the TRO, Helene. Your request for the veil to remain in Port Quincy was granted. However, given the complicated history of the matter, the judge decided the current chain of possession should be maintained. The veil will remain at Thistle Park."

Helene could charge to give toddler tantrum lessons. Her reaction to the judge not taking up her gambit in precisely the way she'd decreed sent her into an emotional tailspin. She gave the hallway an actual staccato line of stomps, and clenched her teeth so hard I feared she'd snap off her fillings.

"Just you wait. I'll see to it that my veil is returned!" She swiveled her murderous glare from person to person.

The young constable could take it no longer. His eyes watered, and finally he gave way to a spate of hysterical laughter. "I was warned about the serving process, and how some people have strong and irrational reactions." His laughter trailed off into a giggle. "But you, lady, take the cake."

"Excuse me, but I forgot my fountain pen." Horace reappeared in the doorway, his eyes going wide as he took in Helene. "Why, hello, Mrs. Pierce. You haven't aged a day!"

*You're laying it on pretty thick, buddy.*

It was a totally inopportune time for the archivist to come back. But his placating tones seemed to mollify Helene.

"Horace Overright. What a pleasant surprise." Helene held out her hand, and Horace awkwardly gave it a peck. I felt as if I'd tumbled into some alternate universe. Horace straightened up, and as Helene turned her glare to Truman, Horace gave me a sheepish shrug.

"Truman, I will get the judge to amend this order. There's no way Mallory's place is safe enough for the veil to reside."

Horace's eyes nearly bugged out of his skull. "Are you kidding me? Mallory and Rachel have one of the most ingenious safes I've ever seen, tucked away right over there in the office, above the fireplace."

*Oh. My. God.*

It was my turn for my eyes to grow wide and nearly bug out of my head.

"Good one, you fool. She's the enemy, don't you know?" Rachel had had enough, and chastised Horace with a withering glance. It didn't help that she towered over him.

The little man clapped a hand over his mouth. "I'm sorry, ladies. I don't know what came over me."

Helene's powder-blue eyes glittered in triumph. My safe was supposedly impenetrable. I trusted the contractor Jesse had hired to provide the actual metal structure and the digital entry system. And many a bride had stored pricey jewelry there on the eve of her big day, and at receptions to safely sequester money and small gifts. But that didn't mean someone couldn't try to *compel* me, my sister, or Pia to open it. With a threat of danger or even death.

*Gulp.*

A cold bath of unease trickled down my back as I considered the ramifications beyond just holding the veil for safekeeping in my safe. I thought of how Keith was adamant that the veil wasn't the famed one in question, yet Truman had revealed the veil as a possible motive in the death of Keith's father, Richard. And now the gorgeous yet tattered lace was residing in my safe for the foreseeable future. A decision canonized by a judge's pen stroke. A location now revealed to Bev, Horace, Jesse, Helene, Truman, and Pia. There were far too many cooks in this pressure-cooker kitchen.

"I'm sorry you have to deal with this." Truman offered his condolences as Horace apologized again and let himself out, his fountain pen found.

"It's okay." I shivered as I watched Helene peel out of my drive, pinging up gravel, her Cadillac engulfed in a cloud of dust. I felt as if a lurid red bull's-eye had just been painted on my back.

# CHAPTER SIX

I took a few hours to cool my jets after the tense showdown with Helene. I knew Pia and Tabitha must be hurting from the loss of their grandmother, Claudia. Both women had murmured appreciative words when I'd made brief calls of condolence on Sunday, and both thanked me for the flowers Rachel and I sent to them and their mother, June. We'd given Pia the week off to help make the necessary arrangements for Claudia's funeral and burial, and to grieve.

Imagine my surprise when I got a text from Tabitha to meet for lunch. I offered to pick up a mini feast for us to eat in her office, but Tabitha insisted on getting out and clearing her head. I selected a Port Quincy institution, Pellegrino's. While many of the movers and shakers dined there daily, it also afforded customers high-backed, recessed booths and little tables tucked into corners for a bit of privacy.

Tabitha beat me there, and I slid into the rich leather booth across from her. The business's air-conditioning was blasting full force. I tucked my denim jacket more closely over my sunflower-patterned dress and firmly adjusted my yellow scarf against the manufactured arctic air. I gave my friend's hand a silent squeeze over the table. Her pretty if sharp features faltered on the way to an expression I couldn't quite call a smile. Her gimlet-green eyes were ringed a rheumy red that nearly matched the dyed Ariel-the-mermaid jewel-tone shade she always selected for her hair.

I ordered a dinner reminiscent of a gourmet Thanksgiving, with free-range chicken baked with sage, tarragon, and rosemary; andouille sausage stuffing; and green onion and crème fraiche green beans. The chef must have tailored this hearty, hot winter meal to combat the chill created by the summer air-conditioning. My mouth formed a little O when Tabitha ordered only a simple bowl of bison chili with jalapeño cornbread on the side.

"It's hard to eat these days." My friend offered me an apologetic shrug. I could barely hear her voice, though Pellegrino's was playing a soft suite of cello music. The restaurant had a pleasant ambiance, and we were blessedly tucked into a booth that would afford us some measure of privacy. Yet all around us, people craned their necks and peered around potted plants to send Tabitha sympathetic glances, then bent low, no doubt to gossip about the mysterious circumstances surrounding Claudia's death. When our food arrived, Tabitha set down her spoon nearly as soon as she attempted to eat. I wanted to encourage her to get some sustenance, but didn't want to be pushy.

"I usually love this dish." Tabitha gave a rueful and mirthless laugh. "Actually, I make this bowl the first part of a three-course meal I have at Pellegrino's, not the main event. But all food tastes like sawdust in my mouth." My wounded friend took an obligatory three bites of the rich food. She burst into tears, her usual stoicism long gone. I thrust her cloth napkin into her hand, and Tabitha delicately dabbed at her eyes.

"I wish I could get my mind off of the reenactment for just a few minutes." She took a restorative swig of ice water. "Not to dampen Claudia's memory, but really so I can stop the gruesome mental replay of what went down on that reenactment field."

I closed my eyes and willed away the vision myself. "I guess I've had some crazy things happening to pull my attention away from the disaster that was Cordials and Cannonballs."

Tabitha nodded. "There've been rumblings about the Betsy Ross veil."

"You know about it?" I gave my friend an incredulous look, then realized the obvious. "Oh, duh. You're the town historian. And Bev, the biggest gossip in the western hemisphere, is the other owner. Who am I kidding?"

My outburst earned a small, tentative smile from Tabitha through her residual tears.

"Yes, I imagine you'll have your hands quite full with the fallout from that."

I didn't like Tabitha's choice of words to describe veil-gate. Yet a nuclear fallout was an appropriate analogy for the incident so far.

"It's okay. You can ask me anything you want to. I'm glad I picked this booth. I can see people watching me, but it would be hard for anyone to really eavesdrop."

I shivered at Tabitha's insistence on secrecy. But her booth choice was a good move. I was used to protecting my gossip in this small town. Especially since this veil seemed to be worth killing for, at least for some.

"What do you want to know about the veil?" Tabitha held out her hands in an expansive motion. She slipped back into her role of director of the historical society and seemed to revel in the familiarity. And I was happy to oblige if it eased her mourning for the duration of our lunch.

"Well, for starters, how did Helene get it? And was it really made by *the* Betsy Ross?"

Tabitha nodded, a faraway look in her pretty green eyes.

"You and Pia reminded me so much of Rachel and me." I blurted out a non sequitur and interrupted her thoughts. "You two look so alike, yet so different."

Tabitha gave a weak laugh. "We're half sisters, Mallory. A lot of people don't know that."

While I digested that probably unremarkable

fact, Tabitha was just getting warmed up. "Let's
see." She cocked her head and seemed to be consulting some kind of mental Rolodex. "It's pretty
darn irrefutable that the veil in question, if it indeed is the same one, was made by Betsy."

I filled Tabitha in on Horace's visit, and she
nodded along. "Well, then, Mallory, Rachel is right.
You have a nearly priceless artifact on your hands."

*And blood on them, too.*

Focusing on the veil may have directed Tabitha's attention from the carnage at Cordials and
Cannonballs, but sitting across from Claudia's granddaughter made it all too real again. I ran scenarios
over in my head again, thinking of how I could have
prevented the shootings.

"Earth to Mallory."

"Sorry, Tabitha. So how do you know the veil is
the real deal? Anyone could have made it."

"Ah, but there's a bona fide paper trail." Tabitha's pronouncement brought out her first real
smile of the day. She even set down the spoon she'd
been trailing around in the chili bowl and rubbed
her hands in anticipation. "A receipt!" She nearly
crowed.

"A receipt? I dumbly repeated her phrase, pic-
turing the important slip of paper that had helped
to prove to Truman that Bev and I had purchased
the veil from the Antique Emporium.

"A receipt written out by Betsy herself!" Tabitha
eagerly dug her phone out of her purse and typed
and slid her fingers over the screen. She held up a
link to the historical society's website, a closeup of

a frayed and yellowed slip of paper with spidery, slanting brown ink scrawled across. "It's hard to see, but this is a receipt made by Betsy. Betsy Clay-poole, as she was known at the time. For the cost of the veil, for one Anne Gray. The receipt was kept with the Gray family, who passed the veil down through their family line. When the patriarch had no one to pass the veil on to, he sold it at Sotheby's. In 1950, to Keith's grandfather."

I let out a low whistle and squinted at the screen anew. "And I suppose the Gray family had the veil before the legend of Betsy Ross was revived."

Tabitha nodded, and in her new spate of enthusiasm for the subject, she even managed a bite. "I guess you know a bit about Betsy. How her descendants, a century even after her death, popularized the idea that she had sewn the very first flag. That is a tidbit historians have never been able to definitively prove, but this veil was crafted with Betsy's very own hands."

"I know just a bit about her in passing." I recalled Horace's warning not to handle the veil too much with my bare hands. I admit I'd felt a frisson of connection when I lovingly if nervously wrapped up the veil and placed it back in the safe. It was a unique touchstone back to the days of the Revolutionary War, and I could scarcely believe the veil was still in my possession.

"Betsy is a beloved figure for a reason," Tabitha continued. "She went to work as a seamstress when she was just a young teenager."

"I can't imagine. Summer works so hard in school,

but I wouldn't want her to be working for wages at her age."

Tabitha nodded. "Betsy grew up quickly, but then most of the women of the time did, too. She eloped with John Ross, who was not a Quaker. She had to leave her church over it, and she lost him so early in their marriage. She married twice more. The receipt is labeled with the surname from her third marriage. She was widowed each time. She led a really interesting life."

"I can see why Helene is desperate to get the veil back." A rock sank into the pit of my stomach.

*Darn it.*

I would have to return the veil. In light of Tabitha's revelations, it truly did belong to Helene. I really couldn't keep the veil. A slow bit of wistfulness coursed through me. It had once belonged to her husband's family, and now it rightfully should be reunited with her. The woman's actions were often reprehensible. But, she didn't ask for her husband to be murdered or the precious family heirloom to be stolen from the back seat of his car. And though I had fallen out of love with the now-odious Keith Pierce ages ago, my heart still went out to what must have been a very scared adolescent who had to deal with the sudden death of his father at an age younger than Summer is now. I would return the veil ASAP.

*That is, if Bev agrees.*

I wasn't sure how my friend and co-owner of the veil would feel about handing it over to Helene, no questions asked. But I'd deal with that conundrum after lunch.

Tabitha wrinkled her nose. "Helene does celebrate colonial-era history, and I guess she does deserve to have her family's veil back." Tabitha must have read my mind. "But I'm afraid she celebrates it for all of the wrong reasons." She let out a withering sigh. "Not to go all soapbox, but Helene likes to collect artifacts to bolster her claim of being more American than others, whatever the heck that means. When the spirit of Betsy is about inclusion. She understood being shunned when she had to leave her church and not visit her family, for marrying outside of the Quaker faith. She was a working woman, and supported her family. All things that Helene wouldn't celebrate. It stinks that it really is her veil."

"Helene has dangerous and antiquated views, to be sure." I thought back to the delicate lace. "But be that as it may, I'll do my best to convince Bev to return the veil. Though it is interesting."

"What?" Tabitha went back to playing with the remains of her now half-eaten chili.

"I knew Keith's dad died in a car crash when he was thirteen. He told me all about it." I jumped as Tabitha's spoon clattered to the hardwood floor with a crash.

"Excuse me." She dove under the table and retrieved her cutlery, a warm-looking blush staining her cheeks. "Go on."

But she looked like she wanted to be anywhere but here.

"But what he didn't tell me was that it was most likely a hit-and-run. And that the veil was taken from the back seat of his father's car."

Tabitha looked at me as if she were staring down the barrel of a gun. "Who told you that?" Her voice was a mere whisper, hoarse and frightened and disbelieving all at once.

*Whoa.*

"Um, Truman?" I clapped a hand over my mouth. Maybe this wasn't my tidbit to reveal. "Oh. My. Gosh." I realized with a start that perhaps Keith had never told me the sordid details of his father's demise because he honestly didn't know all the lurid details. He was thirteen, and there was a possibility that Helene told him it was a car crash, not a probable murder for hire.

But the unnatural fear riveting Tabitha's face bothered me more. "Tabitha, are you okay?"

"That's not a widely known detail." Tabitha seemed to come to her senses and glugged down half a glass of iced tea. She looked around for a moment, then made the paranoid move to kneel on her leather booth seat and peer over the edge into the next little carved-out vestibule. "I'm not sure even Keith knows."

*Bingo.*

"I'll admit I was hurt when Truman told me. I thought Keith had kept an extremely important detail about his life from me. But now I suppose it is possible he just thought his dad was in an accident." I glanced at the pretty antique ring that had come from Tabitha's family's store. It really didn't matter what Keith had told me. I was with Garrett now, the love of my life, and couldn't worry about that part of my past.

"Okay, you got me to tell you how I knew. But what about you?" I tried to keep my voice accusation-free as I posed my question to my friend.

"Mallory." Tabitha's voice was low and rough and halting. My heart rate accelerated. She looked like she was about to pass out. "No one other than Truman and some men on the force who have since retired or passed away knew that tidbit about Richard getting struck on purpose. I only know because I saw it." Tabitha slunk back in the booth, a course of solemn tears running down her face.

"You what?!" My voice boomed across Pellegrino's dining room. "Sorry." I modulated my voice to a whisper.

*Too late.*

Our server appeared with a concerned look on her face. "You two ladies alright? Can I get you anything?"

I dashed off two orders of razzleberry pie and coffee just to get her to go.

"How did it happen that you saw Richard get killed?" I tried to keep my voice gentle, and not trip over the last word.

Tabitha finished dabbing her eyes with her cloth napkin and set it down on the smooth lacquered table with a sigh. "I know even more." She fiddled with the purple beaded necklace hanging from her neck and twisted the strand until it was nearly a tourniquet. "I knew Richard Pierce was having an affair. And Helene seemingly never knew. I was a nebby thirteen-year-old, and I was poking around in people's business when I shouldn't have."

"How can you be sure?" This was all over two decades ago.

Tabitha was a bit shrill. "I knew! Okay?" More of the lunch crowd turned to stare. "I volunteered at the library. I saw them kissing in the stacks. But never could figure it out. It was Keith's dad, alright. And he was with a dark-haired woman."

I nodded. I knew from old pictures that Helene had been a bottle frosty blonde during that era.

"The day it happened?" Tabitha seemed to muster the courage to go on. "I saw him kiss what looked like the same woman, but I couldn't really be sure. She was wearing the veil-like shawl. She got in the car with him, and they had a fight. The woman left. Ten minutes later, Richard Pierce got out of the car to smoke a cigar." She took a steadying breath. "He looked up, met my eyes, and I froze. I didn't see the other car barreling down the street toward him. It was some kind of nondescript sedan. Someone in a hat crunched right into him. He crumpled to the ground, the car screeched away, and I was beside myself."

Tabitha seemed far away, as if she were reliving the horrid event. I reached across the smooth, glass-like expanse of the table and gave her hands a squeeze. They were ice-cold.

"I never told the police I found Richard outside of the car." She shuddered. "But I had his blood on my hands. Literally. I went to help him up, and touched his front. I jumped back when I realized my hands were covered in the stuff. And I think it was too late anyway. I don't know, thirteen-year-old me didn't think he was breathing. Then I realized I'd wiped all his blood on my jean skirt. I wrapped my hoodie around my skirt, hurried home, and burned it like some vigilante criminal." Tabitha let out a strange incongruous laugh.

I watched her with a peculiar and unsettling mix of horror and awe. A thirteen-year-old had the wherewithal to try to help, then realized she should burn the evidence.

"The police never questioned you?"

"Obviously some psychopath just did this— should I have waited around to be found?" Tabitha's voice grew shrill in the face of my subtle accusations. "I know you were once engaged to Keith. Whose side are you on, Mallory?"

"I wasn't aware there were any sides to take," I said evenly, willing my breathing to slow down.

Tabitha gave a nervous chuckle. "Do you know strange stuff is happening now? Ever since the spring, items keep disappearing at the historical society. Expensive stuff. Valuable, irreplaceable items. I reported it, and Truman ended up giving me the third degree. I know that's his job," she conceded. "But every time he came back to my office to try to puzzle out where our artifacts are going, I thought he would spring Richard Pierce's twenty-five-year-old murder on me."

The true weight of her experience hit me like a full bag of laundry. "You've carried it all this time?"

"Yes. I'm the only witness." Tabitha was utterly miserable. This was a far different kind of emotion than the sadness over her grandmother Claudia's death.

Tabitha picked at her newly arrived razzleberry pie. The server had placed the pies on the table with a warmed dollop of French vanilla ice cream running in rivulets through the red-and-blue baked fruit. It looked like blood on snow. Tabitha pushed her plate away.

"Mallory." Her voice grew even more serious. "I love history. I love material culture. But I saw a man die over it. That veil is trouble. I want you to get it out of your possession."

"I couldn't agree more." The veil was seeming more like a curse at this point than a boon. I thought of the psychological damage keeping such a secret had wrought on my friend. I recalled how the Pierces' machinations and power had ruined good people's lives. I didn't want to get messed up in that. I gave my friend's hand another squeeze.

Tabitha took in a restorative, if shaky breath, and tried to drink some coffee, but only succeeded in spilling several sloshes on the table. "What I can't figure out now was how the veil, missing these twenty-five years, got in our shop."

"Your mom's store is the perfect hiding spot," I mused. "Or someone could be trying to frame you guys. But it looked like that hatbox had been in the basement of the Antique Emporium for a long time." I stared into space, feeling good enough to eat most of my pie. "What I can't get is whether what happened at Cordials and Cannonballs had something to do with this."

"Dear God, I hope not." Tabitha was even more subdued. "I don't envy Truman and Faith." The wry beginnings of a smile ticked up the corners of Tabitha's lips for a millimeter. "Just promise you won't go all Nancy Drew and try to solve this, Mallory." She held out her pinky and made me swear not to intervene. I joined in her laughter. No way would I touch this. Tabitha's mirth lasted a few seconds before the present circumstances dragged her expression back into an understandable frown.

I paid the check and we walked out into the sunshine. I gave my friend a bone-crushing hug. "Let me know if you need anything, Tabitha."

My friend blinked in the sunlight. "Just take care of yourself." Her blinking turned into a genuine wince. "And my little sister, too, now that she's working with you. And that reminds me. Are you thinking of moving up your wedding? We need something fun and positive to turn this summer around."

I gave my friend a genuine smile. "I think maybe we will. And when we do, will you be a bridesmaid?" In all the doom and gloom, my ideas were beginning to take shape. Or course I wanted Tabitha, my first friend in Port Quincy, to be part of the wedding.

Tabitha smiled and nodded her assent. "I'd love to."

We parted on the sidewalk in the clear light of day. I wished the sunshine could cleanse the icky feeling still clinging to me from Tabitha's revelations. The sunny day was incongruous with the gruesome and weighty tale Tabitha had just burdened me with. I wondered why she kept that secret for all those years. Who was she protecting? Or was she just an adolescent crushed under the weight of that burden, running scared? I thought of sweet Summer. I wouldn't wish the weight of what Tabitha had witnessed, and buried in her memories for decades, on anyone, especially not someone so young.

And Tabitha's admissions complicated the matter. I had a new suspect in the murder of Richard Pierce. Helene could have found out about his affair, called in the hit, and absconded with the veil herself.

*Don't go there.*

Tabitha's warning not to sleuth rang in my head. Okay, I wouldn't dig around. I'd let Truman figure it out. But Tabitha had to tell him what she knew, and the sooner the better.


Tabitha's revelations weighed heavily on me. I marveled at the gruesome turn the week had taken. What had started out as a time meant for celebration and reflection had turned into a deadly disaster. And I almost felt guilty, realizing that handling such issues in my early thirties was probably easier than trying to make sense of these happenings as a mere thirteen-year-old.

I drove home on autopilot. I didn't want to think of cars as weapons and the strange murder my friend had witnessed. I almost cried tears of joy when I spotted my mother's Prius in the drive. If she felt like she could leave Doug to pay me a visit, then my stepfather must be truly on the mend. Better yet, perhaps he was here with her.

But only the sounds of my mother's humming emanated from Thistle Park's kitchen.

"Hello, dear." Carole leaned over from her ministrations on the counter to give me a quick kiss on the cheek. "I made my famous savory biscotti and maple bacon biscuits and thought I'd pair it with a nice jasmine tea." Her eyes twinkled. "Doug sent me out for a little bit of fun tonight. The dear man thought I'd been spending too much time tending to him with his broken wing."

I giggled at Doug's characterization of his wounded arm and took a bite of the slightly spicy jalapeño and bacon biscotti. "Yum." I smiled as my mom's pug, Ramona, danced on her hind legs. The sweet little doggie wore a jaunty navy gingham scarf. The better to match my mother's own pretty gingham shirt and navy skirt. The outfit looked cute, and somehow Carole avoided looking like a tablecloth. I knew she liked to bring both Doug and Ramona into her clothing coordination mania. Neither the pup nor my stepfather ever seemed to mind. I bet Doug was recuperating at home in navy pants, a navy polo, and slides. I didn't even try to suppress my smile at the thought. I retrieved the special stash of doggie biscuits I kept in the pantry and rewarded Ramona with her own treat.

"Now, down to business." My mother set down the carafe of jasmine tea. "If you truly are going to get married this summer, you need to get busy, honey."

I poured a steaming cup and cocked my head. "This summer has been so dreadful so far. I saw Tabitha today, and she thinks getting married soon would be a good way to focus on something positive."

My mother nodded vigorously. "And if you can even pull this off, we'll need to get you your dress."

Like a muse that wouldn't quit, my mind strayed again to the pretty sundress in the Antique Emporium. I could briefly close my eyes and picture the floating and whimsical number. But there was no way I would bother any of the Battles women this week and try to see if I could purchase the dress. I'd let them bury dear Claudia in peace.

"Just promise me one thing." My mother's grumbling broke my dress reverie and brought me back to the present. "We will not be going to that woman's dress store!" She huffed and didn't let me interject. "I thought Bev was a pill when she was merely trying to usurp my role as your wedding planner." She stopped for a sigh and a sip of the fragrant jasmine tea. "Since you've ceded that task to Rachel and Pia, I will be in charge of the dress. But there's no way we're going to Silver Bells now that that loon is basically accusing Doug of trying to murder Jesse!"

I frowned. A few years ago, my mom and Doug had hit a bit of a rough patch. I firmly believed my parents' marriage was currently strong and healthy, and would continue to be so. But Mom had considered, for the most fleeting of moments in her confusion, her old relationship with Jesse. Bev didn't even really know that my mother had given it any thought. She just knew that Mom and Jesse had legitimately dated decades ago.

Before I could open my mouth to carefully wade into the fray, there was a sharp tap on the back door.

"It's Truman." I would normally have been happy to see him, but now all I could think of was Tabitha's confession of sorts. I wondered if Truman would be able to see the strange look that I felt must be written large on my face. But I always did have a decent poker face, and it seemed as if he had made this call for other business at hand.

"Would you like a cup of tea?" My mom beamed up at the chief.

"Don't mind if I do." Truman drained the delicate serving in nearly one gulp. He must have had an esophagus of steel to not get burned. My throat felt pain in sympathy.

Truman sighed and plunked his cup back on the kitchen table. "I'm afraid this isn't quite a social call."

*Uh-oh.*

"Processing that scene on the reenactment field was a real doozy," he began.

"Nearly every reenactor had a gun of some kind. Thankfully, most of them truly were inoperable replicas."

I felt a swig of now-tepid tea go down the wrong way. "Most?" I choked out. I didn't like where this was going. I happened to know a certain person who had explained to Rachel, Pia, and me that his gun was technically usable, though a replica.

"We found a musket." Truman let the statement hang in the air. Ramona gave a little doggie whine, walked around the window seat three times, and nestled down for a nap.

I saw my mother gulp. "You're basically family now, Truman. But I don't like where this is going, mister." My mother stood to add more hot water to the teakettle. She could outsass anyone, but right now her hands were shaking.

"I'm afraid you're going in the right direction, Carole." Truman did appear apologetic. "Doug's musket had real shot inside, ladies. And the ammo matched the musket balls found in Claudia and Jesse."

"That's preposterous!" Carole stood again, pacing anew. "I double-checked that horrid thing before he even put it in the car. I'm not a fan of guns."

"And didn't you check the darn thing on the field?!" My mind trailed back to the event, and Truman and Faith's work not only examining each replica weapon, but running metal detection wands over each person.

Truman nodded, as glum and stricken as I'd ever seen him. "But don't worry, Carole." I knew he was obliquely referring to the terrible week right before Christmas when my mother had languished in jail for a crime she hadn't committed. "I believe Doug. He said he dropped the weapon in the foggy melee. And you're correct, I checked the darn thing myself. There wasn't a speck of shot nor gunpowder in it."

"So, someone else puts ammo in," I mused. "Someone who wanted to frame him for shooting Claudia and Jesse. But why?"

Truman shook his head. "You're not going to like it, but there are a few reasons why it could be believable." He looked up as my mother delivered an angry guffaw. "I didn't say I believe it," he clarified. "Both Claudia and Doug were shot at close range," he continued. I believe other witnesses who said Doug was knocked down for most of the reenactment."

I set down my cup with shaking hands. "Close range? Doug told me a musket doesn't have good accuracy. It was like the killer was trying to execute them?" I took in Truman's wince.

"I believe so, Mallory. The working theory is that the killer took advantage of the fog to make it look like Doug did it, but he was actually just in the wrong place. Why, the darn killer even managed to graze Doug himself. My working theory is that was a mistake."

My mother's shoulders relaxed a mere centimeter at Truman's declaration that he knew Doug didn't really do it. "Fine. I'll take it. But back to the motive. There isn't a single reason why Dougie would want to hurt Claudia or Jesse!"

Truman stared impassively at my mother. "Doug argued with Claudia about whether she would allow him to help her stand up to Helene. It was an act of chivalry, but people heard them arguing nonetheless." He bit his lip and continued. "And, well, you had just announced your intention to work with Jesse to design a new house for Mallory and Garrett." Truman held up a hand to stop my mother's protestations that had already begun to loudly roll from her lips. "I know that is ancient history, but someone could make the case that Doug felt threatened at the prospect of you working with an old beau."

It was the working theory Bev was clinging to, and I nearly saw steam emanate from Carole's ears.

"What about Helene?!" My mother spat out a suspect loudly enough to wake Ramona in her window seat. "The silly, spiteful lady had it in for Claudia, and she was wearing gloves for goodness' sake! All the better to maraud around and shoot people without leaving a trace."

Truman cocked his head and seemed to appraise my mother. "An intriguing clue we all took note of. The musket did not have any prints on it, save for my own and Doug's."

Ramona danced in a slow circle at my mother's

feet and pranced over to the back door. Carole, long over this conversation, took her chance. "I've never been so happy to attend to Ramona's potty business than in this very moment."

She flounced out the door, leaving me with my soon-to-be father-in-law.

Truman rubbed the bridge of his nose in seeming irritation. "I'm not even done yet, Mallory."

*Oh, great.*

This little teatime with my mother was irrevocably ruined. Doug had sent her over for a chat and a snack, and she'd been ambushed instead. What more did Truman have in store?

He didn't mince words, having already semi–worn out his welcome. "Be careful around Tabitha," he cautioned.

"Beg your pardon?" I hoped he couldn't hear my heart beating with alarming alacrity in my ribcage. Had he somehow overheard her declaration of witnessing Richard Peirce's murder while we'd been at Pellegrino's?

Truman seemed to consider how to say his next statement. "Hinky stuff is going on with historical society holdings. Tabitha is cooperating, but I feel like she's not telling me something. Something big."

I felt a flare of irritation mixed with relief. "That's nothing. I mean, it's something, and I hope you catch who's doing it. But Tabitha told me about that today. Why would she if she had anything to hide?"

Truman tried to wipe away the shocked look on

his face before I noticed. "One never knows one's motives, Mallory. Just make me one promise this month. Leave the professional sleuthing to me."

I grumbled my assent, then stuck my tongue out at Truman's retreating form as he left Thistle Park. I wouldn't be jumping into the amateur detective fray this time, when bodies and stolen artifacts alike were piling up in Port Quincy. But I was irritated to be reminded twice in one day.

I had one more trick up my sleeve after dinner, compliments of Summer. I was eager to get out of the house. After Truman's visit, my mother had retired to the library for a nap. She'd kept her phone on in case Doug called, but soon dropped into a deep sleep. While she dozed, I received a text from Summer asking me to meet her at the Silver Bells dress shop around seven p.m. to pick out a dress for the Founder's Day dance. My heart melted at the request. I just wondered if I could convince my mother to accompany me to Bev's store if we weren't there to find me a wedding dress, but rather shopping for a semi-formal gown for my fiancé's daughter.

"Oh, alright." My mother sat up and rubbed her face, the seam of a pillow embossed on her cheek. "I guess I needed that nap. I'm still ticked at Truman, and Bev, and well, basically half of Port Quincy. But I'll go to that darn dress shop run by that darn woman. But make no mistake, missy.

This is only for dear Summer, and not to find you a wedding dress."

I giggled at my mother's decree and we headed out to Silver Bells shortly after a light dinner of sandwiches added to the tea goodies my mother had initially brought over. We stopped on our way to check on my stepdad, then headed on to downtown Port Quincy.

"I texted Rachel, but she's not answering," I murmured as I parked the giant station wagon in front of Bev's store.

"Oh, she's probably off with Miles, or Pia, even." My mother airily waved her hand. "I know she's been spending quite a bit of time with that lovely girl, trying to help her make sense of her grandmother's death."

I felt a strange mixture of feelings eddy up in me as I rolled up my window. And since the car was an artifact itself, I literally did have to crank the window closed.

On one hand I was happy that my sister could be there for Pia, as I had been for Tabitha. But an ugly green flare of jealousy also ignited inside me, and I didn't like it. I wondered how my relationship with my sister would change when I was no longer living at Thistle Park and the two of us spent most of our work-week hours with her seemingly new best friend, Pia. I pushed down the strange feeling as I simultaneously pushed open the door to Bev's pretty shop, the silver bells echoing the name of the store.

"Mallory!" Summer nearly bounded over in excitement. She gave a practice spin, already clad in a contender dress for the dance. "Do you like it?"

I blinked as I took in a dress that could have been at home in the late 1980s or early 1990s. Nearly every dress-up occasion in Port Quincy these days seemed to involve some kind of style time-machine. This dress was a daring magenta, the shade a precise match for the bands around Summer's braces. It featured a bubble satin skirt topped with a strappy sequin bodice.

"I love it. And you look amazing!" It was my second bout of strange feelings. Summer was lovely in the dress. With her lanky legs and tall stature, she looked much older than her fourteen years. I wanted to grumble about her growing up too fast, as Garrett was fond of doing these days, yet my heart simultaneously swelled with pride.

I sat on a pretty polka-dotted loveseat while I waited for Summer to change into another dress. My mother sat next to me, her arms huffily crossed over her chest, as if not wanting to cede an inch of goodwill in Bev's store. She needn't have worried. Bev's assistant manned the little shop, and I guessed Bev was still taking care of Jesse.

*Wrong again.*

The bell tinkled again, and in breezed Bev. "Hello, my dear. Jesse finally fell asleep over at McGavitt-Pierce Memorial." She referenced the hospital where Jesse was making slow but steady progress. "The poor man can barely get a wink with all of the vitals checks the nurses insist on doing." She leaned down to give me a hug and simultaneously rolled her eyes behind her glasses, the pair today a daring yellow, when my mother seemed to recoil. "And hello to you, too, Carole. How are you doing these days?"

My mother stared at Bev with overt suspicion. "Just fine, Bev. Why do you ask?"

Bev volleyed a smirk at my mother. "I was just wondering how you were handling the news that my poor Jesse was felled by your husband's weapon?"

*Bull's-eye.*

Bev's accusation seemed to wound my mother, and my heart twisted. It was no fun refereeing a fight between two of the most important women in my life.

But my mother's nap must have soothed her nerves. She carefully fluffed her caramel hair. "I'm not sure where you're getting your gossip these days, Bev. Truman already told me he knows Doug didn't do it. Your sources really must be slipping." My mother gave Bev a triumphant smile and nearly cackled as the dress-store owner stomped off.

"Cool it, Mom."

"I can't believe the nerve of that woman! Such wonderful hospitality in her store." My mother rolled her eyes. "Let's get out of here, Mallory."

But I insisted on staying until Garrett arrived to help Summer pick out her dress. It was one thing to sit with my mom in solidarity as she bickered with Bev, but I wasn't going to let her ire infringe on my relationship with my soon-to-be stepdaughter.

Garrett arrived mere minutes later and raised his eyebrows after he got a rather huffy greeting from Carole.

"I'll explain it all later," I whispered in his ear as he knelt down to hear.

"Oh, I think I can see what's happening." Garrett's lovely eyes moved from my mom to Bev, who was glaring from her perch by the register.

"Dad, you're here just in time." Summer had tried on three dresses, but kept coming back to the retro magenta number. She held it up and took a spin. "Don't you love it?"

"It's very you, kiddo." Garrett moved to ruffle Summer's hair.

This past spring she'd finally started to grow out the daring platinum pixie-cut that my sister had given her on a whim many summers ago, the first day we met her, in fact. Her pretty flaxen hair fell to her shoulders. She impatiently brushed her dad's hand away and fluffed her new do. "Dad, I'm too old to be called a kiddo. Come on. If you want to call someone kiddo, you and Mallory need to have one of your own. And you guys better get cracking. It's not like you have a ton of time left."

*What?!*

I felt my heart gallop for the third time in one day. I'd been meaning to broach the family expansion question with Garrett in private, then loop in Summer when we'd decided what in the heck we wanted to do. But here she was, bluntly bringing the issue to the fore, in the confident and refreshing way she always had.

Garrett to his credit no longer looked like a deer in headlights. He ruffled her hair anew, and sent her off with a laugh. "I guess that answers one question I know we both have. Apparently, Summer wouldn't mind a younger sibling someday. And if I didn't know any better, I'd swear your mother put her up to that."

I collapsed against him in a spate of laughter as Summer brought her purchase to the front of the store. Bev managed to tear her dagger eyes away from my mother and ring up the purchase.

My phone buzzed with a text from my sister.

**Out with Pia and Miles. Trying to cheer Pia up. Send Summer my regards. Sorry I can't make it!**

I pushed down the renewed strange feeling bubbling up in the corners of my mind. I was getting hitched, perhaps sooner than I knew. While my sister was having fun, fancy-free with her younger friends. It was time to celebrate the changes in my life, rather than trying to desperately hold on to what had been.

And as it turned out, Summer had just received a text of her own. She bounded away from the store counter and waved her phone around in the air as if it were a second Armistice Day. "He did it! He did it! He did it!"

"Who is he? And just what did he do?" Garrett sprang from the couch he'd been sitting on, nearly causing my mom to topple over. It was her last straw. She grabbed her purse and fumbled for the keys at the bottom of my bag and muttered something about waiting in the Butterscotch Monster. Garrett seemed torn between going after my mom to offer an apology, and awaiting Summer's explanation for her cryptic announcement.

"I was going to go to the Founder's Day dance with my friends, of course," Summer reported breathlessly. "But he asked me out!"

"Who?!" Garrett and I spoke the word in parental-like unison. I refrained from tacking on the word *jinx.*

"Preston Mitchell, of course!" Summer turned to beam at Bev, and share in her joy with her new beau's mother.

"I knew he would, sweetie. He's just wild about you." Bev bestowed a radiant smile on Summer.

"I think I'm going to be sick." Garrett whispered his assessment of the situation into my ear. His face truly was an interesting shade of split-pea-soup green. "Whatever happened to the practice of a guy asking the dad for permission to take his daughter out on a date?"

I giggled at my fiancé. "Are you serious? Just be happy Preston is a great guy. She's growing up, Garrett."

Indeed, the unmistakable electrifying look of young love, or rather young infatuation, graced Summer's face.

*Everything's changing.*

Marriage was looming, and motherhood, too, at least in the form of becoming Summer's step-mother. Rachel was making new friends, our business was expanding, and Pia was a great addition.

Bev broke into my tender and reflective thoughts. "If you stay a while, we can start looking for your dress!"

The glass doors flew open, the bells jingling harder than ever.

"I heard that, Bev. And she's not interested." Carole snaked out her hand, and nearly pulled me from the shop. I wasn't sure whether to scold her or break out into a spate of laughter.

One thing was for sure. I needed to assess all of the changes in my life, and together with my partner, Garrett, make some decisions and plans.

And somehow mediate the growing feud percolating between my mother and Bev. I couldn't really let either woman dictate my decisions. I had a feeling a different kind of war was going to break out soon. My own war of independence.

# CHAPTER SEVEN

Despite the silly, overblown spat between my mother and Bev that was ballooning out of proportion, I wanted to pay my friend Jesse a visit. He was due to be discharged from the hospital tomorrow. His stay hadn't stopped him from writing email after email with plans for the home he'd already started designing. I silently rued my mother's decision to bait him into taking on the job of designing a new abode for me, Garrett, and Summer right before his wedding to Bev. And that was before he was targeted and shot on the reenactment field.

"How's it going?" I tentatively peeked into Jesse's room. The hospital had scrounged up an extra-long bed to accommodate Jesse's mammoth frame. I loved seeing tall, lumberjack-built Jesse standing next to his fiancé, Bev, a cool foot-and-a-half shorter than him.

But Jesse looked decidedly smaller, shrunken, and weakened in his current state. Though he and Bev had both reached middle age, their vim and vigor made them appear perpetually young at heart. But today Jesse looked his actual age and then some. His injuries on the field had been no joke. He'd lost quite a bit of blood, not helped by the fact that he'd trudged up the hill carrying an already lifeless Claudia, in an attempt to save someone worse off than him.

I shook off such thoughts and entered the room with what I hoped was a cheery smile. Jesse's eyes fluttered open at the sound of my footfalls and he instantly brightened.

"Mallory! So good to see you."

I poured him a glass of water from the pitcher on his table and got down to business. Or rather, cessation of business.

"Jesse, I mean this kindly. You have a lot of recuperating to do, and I'm worried about your plan to keep your wedding date and also begin construction on my new home."

I wasn't going to be the one pushing my dear friend to the brink. Though he was doing well, he didn't need my plans, or rather Carole's, getting in his way on the path back to complete health.

"Oh, please." Jesse weakly waved a bear paw of a hand. I always startled to hear his rather high tenor voice, not what one would expect from so large a man. "Marrying my girl Bev, officially becoming Preston's parent, and having a fun new project to focus on is what's gotten me through this horrid stay in the hospital." He leaned back, winded from his passionate speech.

*Uh-oh.*

"Plus, I struck a deal with Bev. I'll finish the blueprints and apply for the permits once you and Garrett give me the A-OK on a certain design. I can pull some strings with the planning commission to get them approved right away. Then I'll talk to my best men over Skype, and they'll begin the actual construction. Your mom said you were thinking of getting married in about a month. This is totally doable."

*Double uh-oh.*

"Um, Jesse? While I appreciate virtual communication, I'm not so sure that's the best way to direct the building of a brand-new house." I wasn't game for Jesse's plan, and I was sure Garrett would have the same concerns.

"Just promise me one thing." Jesse ignored my concerns and plowed ahead. "My doctors aren't too keen on me returning to work so soon. Keep this under wraps, okay?"

I gave my friend what I hoped was a kind smile. "Jesse, are you listening to yourself? This plan is madness." I gestured to all of the wires and doo-dads hooked up to constantly monitor his condition. "My wedding can wait. Even if I wed this summer, I haven't picked an official date! This summer is flexible. And so is my housing situation. You need to chill out."

Jesse didn't take kindly to my little speech. His

expression turned grave. He reached out one of his giant bear hands and enclosed it around mine. "Please, Mallory. Let me do this."

I gulped under the laser-beam focus of his intense gaze. Though he was on the fast track to recovery, seeing him all hooked up and stationary on the hospital bed tugged at my heartstrings. Then he went for the jugular.

"I'm a medical miracle, Mallory. There aren't too many gents running around with only one-point-five kidneys. Now do me a favor and grab those blueprints I've got stashed under that chair." Jesse released my hand and pointed to a roll of papers barely nudging out from under a vinyl visitor's recliner.

I tried not to think too much about hospital germs as I knelt and pulled out the rolled-up designs. I'd humor Jesse, but I wasn't yet about to totally sign on to his scheme of building me a house from his bedside perch.

"Garrett and I did look over your emails," I admitted as I helped him spread the detailed blueprints over his swivel hospital tray. "And if, and that's a big if, we decided to go with this crazy time-crunch plan of yours, we were thinking plans A and C were the best."

Jesse nodded, a shock of iron-gray hair falling onto his forehead. I realized with a start that I'd barely ever seen him without a Pittsburgh Penguins hat firmly affixed to his head.

"And now that I've had a lot of time to think about it, too, I think plan C is the winner." Jesse held forth for a good twenty minutes, pointing out the minutiae of each line on the blueprint. "It mirrors the elaborate Italianate architecture of Thistle Park, but on a tiny scale. Summer would have her own tower. What girl wouldn't want that?"

I was convinced, and fairly sure Garrett would be, too.

"Fine." I grudgingly acquiesced. "But I'll only let you start on this if your doctor OKs it." I crossed my arms, brooking no wiggle room.

Jesse's happy visage dimmed by a thousand watts. "Oh, crumb on a cracker."

I tried to stifle a giggle at the emergence of one of his usual malaprops. He must truly be on the mend.

"You're an exacting customer, Mallory. But much easier to work with than Helene Pierce." Jesse seemed to give an inward shudder.

I frowned at his admission, not because I disagreed, but because I hadn't known him to do any work for Helene.

"You renovated stuff for that witch?"

"Oh, no. She would never deign to work with me on a construction project. And the feeling's mutual. No, I'm talking about twenty-five years ago, when I was saving up to start Flowers Restoration." Jesse seemed to peer straight into the past, his eyes taking on a faraway look. "I did some work for Helene and Richard Pierce twenty-five years ago." Jesse winced outright. "Sort of a loosely styled security job. I might have the heart of a lamb, but people didn't want to mess with a big guy like me."

It was true. Jesse couldn't hurt a fly, but his imposing build telegraphed otherwise.

He sighed with regret. "I worked for Richard in particular, up until the week he died. The Pierces were always trying to get something for nothing. Richard was chiseling me, knocking off minutes here and there to avoid paying me the agreed-upon rate. I quit the day before his accident." Jesse's hearty complexion, already weakened somewhat by his stay in the hospital, paled a degree more. "Helene never forgave me. She claimed that if I'd been there the day he died, he wouldn't have been in that accident."

Interesting. Jesse called the hit-and-run an accident. There truly were very few people on the planet who knew the truth about Richard's death, besides Helene, Truman, Tabitha, and now myself.

"You knew about the affair." I blurted out my statement before I could stop and think. Tabitha made it sound like it could have been obvious for people to observe the same dalliance she'd caught Richard in. Who would know better than his de facto bodyguard, Jesse?

But the man had a strange look on his face. "No, no affair. But that would make sense, in retrospect. The random places he advised me to take him, and an order to immediately scram. I always obeyed. His payments were fair in the beginning, and I was focused on building up a nest egg to start my current business. I didn't look too hard at Richard Pierce's dealings, if you catch my drift."

A thought struck me with such force, I wished I

had been sitting down. The last piece of the puzzle had appeared. I now knew of a motive for Helene to try to execute Jesse. Although, it would have been weird for her to carry her ire for a quarter of a century, and only act on it now. Still, she was my number one suspect to have enough genuine motive to have gone after Claudia, Jesse, and to have accidentally grazed Doug.

"Just promise me one thing, Mallory." Jesse broke me from my thoughts. "You're getting that sleuthy look in your eyes. Don't go poking around in things that don't concern you. Bev and I worry."

I laughed out loud at the now third person to warn me not to do some amateur investigating. "OK, Jesse."

But my friend wasn't done. "I can't wait to marry Bev and make it official for Preston, too. I love that kid like my own. I'm going to vow to be the best stepdad ever. And you need to think about Summer now, too, Mallory." Jesse's plea was heartfelt, and not at all a chastisement. "You need to stay safe, and stay alive, so you can be a presence in her life."

I took a serious gulp.

"You're right," I whispered. "This is about more people than just me. Of course, I want to be around for her."

I gave my exhausted friend a big hug and quietly slipped from the room as he began to doze off. While I wanted him to continue on his swift road to recovery, I wouldn't mind if his doctors forbade him from managing my quick housing project.

"*Oof.*" I ran straight into Preston Mitchell as he exited the elevator. "Sorry, Preston."

Bev's son rewarded me with a grin. "Summer told me you helped pick out her dress for the Founder's Day dance."

*She's not the only smitten one.*

Preston was a goner. His face lit up in an incandescent smile as he mentioned Garrett's daughter.

"I did. She's so excited to go to the dance with you." We made our way to Jesse's room, where Preston replicated my initial move by peeking in to find Jesse sleeping.

"I'm sorry about Cordials and Cannonballs," he stammered. "It was a great event before all of that went down on the battlefield."

"Thank you, Preston." I realized with a start that Rachel, Pia, and I hadn't heard a single scrap of praise for the event. Not that I was complaining in light of what had happened. It was enough to recall the initial joyous looks on the faces of the denizens of Port Quincy before the carnage had begun. The event would forever live in my mind like a bizarre split-screen movie, the before portion joyous and carefree, the aftermath an irrevocable shift in all of our lives.

"Something, um, is bothering me, though." Preston took off his Quincy High ball cap and ran a hand with a nervous motion through his locks.

*Uh-oh.*

"Sit down. What's up?" I didn't want to startle the boy, and he clearly had something to say. He sank into a vinyl couch three doors down from Jesse's room and looked up and down the hall before he spoke.

"I remembered something else about that day. Summer and I were so busy slinging vegan sandwiches." His bright smile returned for a moment at the memory. "I noticed about halfway through our shift that someone had left a bag of little metal balls at the foot of the table."

*Musket shot.*

"Did you tell Chief Truman? Or your mom?" I tried to keep my voice even.

Preston had the good graces to blush before he answered. "My mom is a bit of a . . . talker." He'd generously refused to label Bev as an outright gossip, but his point was made, loud and clear. "And Truman did question me, but I forgot that detail." He slapped his ball cap atop his head. "The weirdest part? When the police were done questioning everyone, hours later, Summer and I went back to the booth. Our backpacks were still under the table. But the little bag of metal balls was gone."

I had to play this right. But there was no time for finesse. "Preston, is it OK if I tell Truman what you just told me?"

I was relieved to see Preston's face relax. "Will you please?"

I nodded my promise and gave the teen a hug. He walked back to Jesse's room, his step a little lighter.

I made my way out of the McGavitt-Pierce Memorial Hospital and headed home. I was getting excited about Jesse's plans. As soon as Garrett signed off on blueprint C, we would be in business. And I didn't care whether that was in a few weeks, or later this fall. Jesse was right about one thing. Sticking around for my family was the most important thing. I realized now that we were a family, and I didn't need a ceremony to make it so.

I nearly flew to my office to dash off an email to my beau. Jesse's enthusiasm had cast a spell on me. And when I was done with the more fun aspects of my visit to the hospital, I would call Truman and tell him Preston's clue. Though the boy's revelation about the ammunition was nowhere near as fraught as the murder Tabitha had witnessed as a young teen, I didn't think it was healthy for any of the kids to be harboring secrets.

*Hm.*

The handle to my office was loose. I recoiled and realized the fixture had definitely been monkeyed with. I hated that all of the strange crimes around Port Quincy led to thoughts like the one I had next: Get a tissue to open the door, so as not to mar any potential fingerprints left behind.

I returned with a small tissue and tentatively wrapped it around the barely functioning knob. I pushed open the door and couldn't stifle the yelp I distantly heard emanate from my throat.

My beloved office was completely tossed. Chairs and loveseats lay on their sides, their legs hanging all akimbo, some broken off. My files as well as

Rachel's had been emptied all over the floor, so the space looked like a demented rendition of a winter wonderland full of fat, rectangle snowflakes. We'd gotten Pia her own desk, and the top of her workspace was strangely untouched. But she'd only been working with us a few days, and most of those were spent with her family in the wake of Claudia's murder. But the worst was yet to come.

*Holy moly.*

The distinct, solder-like smell of melted metal led me to the safe. Or what was left of it. The delicate carvings of birds, leaves, and whimsical insects gracing the original teak mantel were decimated. It looked like the perpetrator had used a hacksaw to get into the safe nested behind. I quickly assumed that the perpetrator knew the safe was behind the mantel, but not which carving to push to make the wooden panel magically swing open.

The keypad was blown to smithereens, a closely delivered shot of ammunition leaving a jagged hole in its wake. I shivered when I realized Truman had said Jesse and Claudia were shot in the same manner, a close-range shot. I reached into the tiny, charred rectangle, already knowing what I'd find. And what I wouldn't.

The veil was gone.

# CHAPTER EIGHT

"Whoever did this wanted to send a message." Truman stood in the middle of the office shaking his head in disgust. "It would have been enough to hack through the mantel and steal the veil. But this is personal."

The pretty if somewhat intentionally fusty yet cozy office space felt irrevocably violated. The acrid smell of melted metal still hung in the air.

"I can't have this." My voice sounded tinny and far away. "We're going to host a baby shower at Thistle Park in a few days. I want this to be a safe space."

"Too late for that." My sister's voice was hoarse and gravelly. Tears coursed down Rachel's cheeks. Her skill as her own makeup artist was on full display. Despite the waterworks, her gorgeous smoky eye and mascaraed lashes stayed perfectly intact.

"It's happening again." I gestured all around

me. "Whatever curse that veil brought upon Port Quincy a quarter of a century ago is back."

Truman raised one brow in response.

"Okay, fine. Not, like, a literal curse. But whoever killed Richard Pierce over the veil is back at it again. And I'm certain what happened at Cordials and Cannonballs is tied to the veil."

Truman ushered us out of the office as two techs arrived to process the scene. He led us to the safe, pristine confines of the library. "That's an interesting theory, Mallory. I only wish we were able to discern some kind of grand cosmic pattern and tie up all these loose ends, some of which, as you mentioned, are twenty-five years old."

I didn't think Truman was mocking me, but I was impatient. I keenly valued my safety, especially after my talk with Jesse. And my home and Rachel's, and our place of business, had been violated. I took the plunge.

"Fine. Let me lay it all out. Richard Pierce was killed in a hit that was cleverly disguised as a hit-and-run. The famed Betsy Ross veil was taken from his back seat, only to resurface in a hatbox at the Antique Emporium over two decades later. In the present, Claudia, Jesse, and Doug were all shot on the reenactment field. What do these incidents have in common?" I let my question hang in the air. "Helene Pierce."

Truman let out a gust of air, now clearly annoyed. "Mallory, I know there's no love lost—"

"Let me finish," I begged. "Helene, who was wearing gloves the day of Cordials and Cannon-

balls, has a motive for each crime. She fought recently with Claudia about women being allowed
on the battlefield. She will forever blame Jesse for
resigning as Richard's bodyguard the day before
he was murdered. And she knew Doug wanted to
put her in her place regarding women on the battlefield as well. And she may have known about Richard's affair all those years ago, and called in the hit
on her husband herself."

Now I had Truman's attention. "Who the heck
told you about the affair?" His hazel eyes bored
into mine.

"None of your beeswax. Although I wouldn't
mind a bit of information swapping. Do you know
who the woman was?"

Rachel let out a shaky laugh at my answer and
new query, but Truman was far from amused.

"Mallory, I order you to tell me who told you
about that. Barely anyone over two decades ago
even knew about Richard's affair."

"I have my sources."

It was the wrong thing to say.

"When will you learn to stop sleuthing!" Truman stood, his stack about to blow. He jabbed his
finger toward the wreckage down the hall. "Hello!
Earth to Mallory! Your life is in danger!"

I nearly felt like weeping. He was right. But for
once, I hadn't engaged in much initial fact-finding.
"I can't help it if people tell me things. And the
best I can do is pass something along if I think it
will help."

Truman let out a gust of air and fell back into

his chair with disgust. Whiskey sensed the tension in the room, and the cute calico kitty darted from her favorite window seat and took her exit. "There's more you're not telling me. At least I know that much."

I wasn't going to waste his time. "Preston Mitchell found a bag of what appeared to be musket shot at the foot of his and Summer's vegan food table at Cordials and Cannonballs. He didn't think it was significant until he remembered today. When he and Summer got back to the table, it was gone."

And so was Truman. He called out a gruff note of thanks as he flew out of the library, his phone already affixed to his ear.

"I guess that last bit was pretty important," Rachel drily observed.

I gave my sister a sheepish shrug, and together we made the trek to the safety of our third-floor apartment.


The next day I performed the gut-wrenching task of informing my friend Olivia that Thistle Park had been broken into. I brought my sister for backup, and together we sat facing Olivia in the suite of offices she shared with Garrett for their joint law practice.

"You don't have to have your baby shower there, Liv." I winced. "Maybe somewhere safer. Though you're running out of time." I gestured toward her giant belly.

Olivia placed her hand on her chin, pondering her options. "I don't know. The veil is gone, poor thing." She spoke of the troublesome lace as if it were a person with feelings and agency. "If the people who wanted the veil trashed the room to find it, then they won't be coming back." She swiveled her chair around to regard a large wall calendar. Nearly every cell of the grid was filled, right up until her baby's due date. Then the appointments stopped, and each rectangle was a sea of white. But the most celebratory rectangle was decked out in highlighter, designating the day of her baby shower. "I think I want to do it." Olivia's lips parted into a giant grin. "I'm sure it will still be lovely."

Rachel and I praised her decision, yet exchanged a subtle shrug. I was partially relieved that my friend had enough faith in my business that she still wanted her shower.

"She didn't see the office," Rachel muttered as we exited Olivia's office.

"She's an amazing attorney, but I'll agree with your judgment of *her* judgment on this one." Garrett exited his own office and gave me a lovely kiss. "Just be careful, ladies."

"We always are." I bade him goodbye and felt a stab of guilt. What Jesse had said about sticking around for my loved ones kept hitting home. I hoped Truman and Faith could solve the scary Tilt-A-Whirl of incidents spanning the length of twenty-five years and put the murderer away for good.

*Or murderers.*

Rachel and I made our way out into the sunshine. I cursed my decision not to bring sunglasses. But they had disappeared around Thistle Park just like a dryer mysteriously eating socks. The midday light was blinding as it struck the tiny shards of mica embedded in Main Street's sidewalks. Rachel donned a pair of Gucci shades I'd purchased for her years ago when I was an attorney as well. She opened her bag and handed me another pair of considerably less pricey sunglasses.

"Um, Rach. These were my favorite pair of glasses. Emphasis on *mine*. Ones that mysteriously disappeared at the beginning of May."

My sister answered me with a careless shrug. "I've got a big bag, Mallory. Things go in here, and you never know when they're going to resurface."

I shook my head ruefully at my sister, then ended up laughing with her. I got my sunglasses back just in time, and that was something.

"Pierces at ten o'clock. I repeat, Pierces at ten o'clock." Rachel attempted to steer me away from an outside café, but it was too late. Keith Pierce and his wife, Becca Cunningham, had spotted us walking down the sidewalk.

"Rachel. Mallory." Becca slid down her own pair of designer shades and gave us appraising once-overs. "Do sit down."

*Come again?*

My enmity with Becca was well-known. Not as flagrant as my mother and Bev's incompatibility, but not far behind. I should have held it against

Becca that she was the woman Keith was having an affair with that prompted me to cancel our wedding three summers ago. But I rightfully laid the blame for that transgression on Keith and his poor choices. No, I was not fond of Becca for other reasons. Namely, her presumptuous orders and commandeering of my time, to do her bidding. Needless to say, an impromptu invitation to lunch was setting off fervent alarm bells.

"Are you paying?" Rachel was never one to beat around the bush. She hovered over the pretty wrought-iron café chair on offer to her. I was appalled at her question, until I remembered we were dealing with Becca and Keith.

"Of course," Becca said crisply, further raising my spidey senses. She must want something, and it must be big, too. Becca was nervous, patting her pretty pouting pink lips with her napkin in an officious manner. She wore a lovely seersucker shift dress to highlight her slender frame. She was slightly taller than Keith, but somehow wore a miniscule shoe size. Today she was wearing her usual favored sky-high heels, a pair of pastel patent Louboutins with her legs strategically crossed to show off the trademark red sole. I wondered if this impromptu meeting was somehow staged, and pictured Becca following me all around town, ready to leap from behind lampposts and hedges. I giggled and awaited what would surely be some over-the-top request.

I had my answer over the first course of gaz-pacho.

"I don't want to waste your time." Becca sighed and sent a longing look at Keith. "Running out of time is what has brought us to this dire juncture."

*This had better be good.*

"I'd like for you to be our surrogate, Mallory." Becca included a sheepish Keith in her warm smile.

"Ugh! Watch it!" Keith leapt back just in time to avoid the spray of coconut LaCroix shooting out of Rachel's mouth. My sister bent double she was laughing so hard.

"This isn't a laughing matter, Rachel Shepard. Fertility, or lack thereof, never is." Becca sat back in her chair, a look of pain marring her icy good looks.

That shut Rachel up fast. She cocked her head and regarded Becca. "I'm sorry," she simply amended.

"Thank you. Now, as I was saying, Mallory— Keith and I think you're the perfect candidate." She held up her hand to quell the thousand protestations rising from my lips. "You're not getting any younger, so we need your help now. You're relatively healthy, though to be my surrogate you will need to lose at least fifteen pounds. And I know you and Garrett aren't having kids of your own, so why waste your fertility? Carrying our baby will be hard work, as I'll be monitoring your appointments and nutrition. And Keith and I will pay you handsomely, though we were hoping you'll do it gratis as a favor for dear friends."

*Oh. My. God.*

Not much rendered me speechless, but this was it. I felt my mouth open and close like a beached carp.

I finally found my voice, but it trailed out in a sibilant hiss. "I have no idea what gave you the inkling that I would want to do this." I amended my response when I took in Becca's wounded look. "I'm sorry Becca, but I need to focus on growing my own family before I help with yours at the moment." There. Nice and diplomatic, though I was internally screaming.

But Becca had an answer for everything. "You already have Summer." She gave a careless wave of her demure French tips. "Plus, Garrett's too old."

That was it. "Garrett is the same age as Keith!" My voice was now two decibels too loud, and the others dining on the patio turned to listen to my rant. Keith blanched at my assertion and ran a self-aware hand over his balding pate.

"Becca, if there will be any pregnancy in my future, it needs to be with Garrett. Though I feel for your plight, and I agree that surrogacy is a wonderful gift. It's just not one I'm entertaining at the moment."

Becca's gorgeous face, so laden with hope, deflated in a whoosh of despair. Before I could feel for her, the despair curdled into annoyance.

Becca wasn't finished. "But you're my last chance! Samantha is in Colombia. Whitney has to wait six more months after her C-section." She rattled off the names of her apparently unavailable twin and her cousin. "You were my only hope. Way to dash a girl's dreams, Mallory."

"Here's a news flash, since you're not getting the memo." Rachel loved mixing her metaphors. "Mallory's not renting out her womb to you two." She grabbed her snakeskin purse and rose from her chair. Now we had an audience.

"Best of luck!" I called out as my sister pulled me down the street. Despite being insulted, shocked, and appalled at Becca's behavior, I truly did mean it.

Becca's request produced some pretty interesting dreams that night. I was happy to see daybreak the next morning and realize I was still in charge of my own free will and my own body. It would be a busy day. Jesse was true to his word, and had gotten permission from his doctor to head up construction on the house I'd someday share with Garrett and Summer. A house that would be completed in a mere two weeks, if Jesse had anything to do with it. I had my doubts, and wanted the job done right. Garrett surprised me by persuading me to give Jesse a shot. The next day construction began on the house Garrett, Summer, and I would someday reside in.

I found myself at the hastily cleared patch of land that bridged the grounds of Thistle Park and the last few feet of Truman and Lorraine's property, where Summer and Garrett currently lived. "It's going to be awesome." I looked down at my tablet and gave Jesse a smile. He was observing the breaking of the ground for my new abode, from the comfy confines of his own couch. I'd have preferred him to be here in person and in better health, but I was starting to trust Jesse and Garrett. This would work out.

I tried to drown out the lingering protestations in my head, centered around the fact that though thorough, Jesse's plans were somewhat hastily drawn. There was also another issue that made me nervous: Jesse's promise come true of the city planning commission granting building permits in record time. I wanted this new venture to be careful and considered, not rushed and slipshod.

"I'm here to see my plans for you realized!" My mother arrived on the scene and held a bottle of sparkling grape juice aloft. No one else seemed to share my concerns. "I want to toast to your new abode!" She struggled to pull the cap from the bottle, but seconds later was pouring me a celebratory plastic goblet of sparkling juice. "Here's to a quick build and a bright future."

Garrett had a trial, and Rachel was helping Miles prepare for a catering gig. I was touched that my mom had shown up unannounced to see the house-building begin.

"I'll toast to that."

But the universe had other plans.

Half an hour into digging with giant yellow backhoes, the construction crew hit something hard and unexpected in the soft earth.

"Halt! Halt your digging!" The lead contractor,

a man I recognized from many of Jesse's projects, was capable and direct. If he ordered a stop, there must truly be an issue.

The woman running the giant piece of machinery executed a graceful leap down from the driver's seat and inspected the newly tilled earth with wonder. Jesse sat up from his perch on the couch, unable to truly see what was going on from his Skype connection.

"What the heck is that?" I peered into the gaping hole in the earth, scared that the construction workers had found a body, or worse. But it was just a peculiar and rusted piece of metal.

Jesse's usual line of business was historical restoration. His men were experts in the field, and seemed to know what to do. "I think we need to call an archeologist."

# CHAPTER NINE

"It's distillery equipment." Truman gave the verdict a mere four hours later. The lovely pink surveyor's lines and stakes for my new yard were now replaced with crime scene tape.

"Isn't that a bit excessive?" I motioned toward the yellow plastic ringing the house, or what one day would be the house.

*At this rate? Yeah, right.*

"The crime tape is necessary when we suspect a crime. And finding what's suspected to be Ebenezer Quincy's long-lost distillery equipment buried at Thistle Park is indicative of a crime."

I rolled my eyes. Truman had just named the founder of our town, a man famed for his contraband whiskey. And long-lost distillery.

*Make that a found distillery.*

"Can we have one week around here when some famous dude or lady's artifacts don't find their way to my property?"

My exasperation drew out a much-needed chuckle from Truman. The coffee and lunch I'd ordered for the new crew and the old crew from this morning arrived, and the workers noshed while the archaeologist, local history professor, and Tabitha conferred on how to run what was now an archaeological dig slash crime scene.

Tabitha and Truman were careful to avoid each other. I watched everyone's work for a good forty-five minutes, before I gave up and went inside. Work on the cottage was paused while the site was to be examined and the equipment unearthed. It was possible my backyard would be deemed a site of historical significance, and I'd never be able to build there.

As I walked through the gardens on my estate, I realized it might be for the best. Jesse was nearly apoplectic upon hearing the news via my tablet. He needed to rest, and a halt to this project was now unavoidable.

I planned on spending the day scrubbing my office of the last vestiges of the crime scene techs. There was still a good deal of polishing to do. I'd vacuumed up most of the fingerprint dust, which had not turned up any prints other than mine and Rachel's near the broken safe. The rest of the office was another matter. I regularly had families, brides, grooms, and partners in the space. The front part of the office, and the tables and smooth furniture surfaces were littered with many different prints. But I knew it was all for naught. Our savvy killer and veil absconder probably wore gloves.

Imagine my surprise to find none other than Helene Pierce, suspect numero uno, seated in a wicker chair on my back porch.

"Can I help you?" I peered behind her, half expecting another service processor to jump out of the wings with some gotcha action filed by my nemesis. Why, she may have caught wind of the distillery work in the back of the property and have come over to stake her red-taloned claim.

"May I come in?" Helene rose imperiously to her feet. Her question was anything but, and more akin to an outright order.

I stared into the woods, realizing Truman and Faith were close, yet strangely far away. I knew Truman and Faith's cell numbers by heart, but the reception was a bit spotty in the woods. I hoped clearing a few more copses of trees would alleviate the problem if I ever did get to build a new home on that land.

But for now, I wasn't sure if I could trust Helene in my B and B. We would be all alone save for my cats.

"*Arf!*" Helene's little Yorkie, Baxter, had accompanied her on this trip. I was a sucker for pets, and almost let her in. The big bad witch couldn't be so bad when she was accompanied by this little innocent fluff ball, right? Baxter blinked up at me in a beseeching manner.

*Totally not fair.*

But it was Helene's uncharacteristic, bizarre entreaty that sealed the deal. "Mallory, I need your help."

I half expected a passel of pigs to appear in front of me, flapping their wings in unison.

"Come again?"

"You heard me! Don't make me say it again." Helene's lips, swathed in their usual pearlescent coral shade, twisted into a lined and disapproving frown.

*That's more like it.*

Against my better judgment, I let Helene into Thistle Park. She sat primly in the parlor. Until she tossed back the cream sherry I'd served at her request. She was strangely sloppy in her nervousness, and the ice cubes in the cut-glass goblet hit her teeth. Her bejeweled hands shook. She was dressed as simply as I'd ever seen her, in a plain robin's-egg St. John dress and cardigan, her pantyhose with a tiny run.

It was my sign that Helene Pierce was officially losing it.

"Everything is starting again." Helene gave a fearful glance out the front window. "It's time to bury the hatchet."

*Interesting.*

This could all be an Academy Award–worthy performance, but so far, Helene seemed as flummoxed and worried about recent events as I had been.

"I lost my dear Richard over twenty years ago, and I want no more harm to be done." She absentmindedly stroked the soft, cream and tan fur of her Yorkie. "I never thought I'd see that veil again. Seeing it in your hands on Main Street? It's all tied together. It brought back vivid memories of losing him as if it were yesterday."

I reflected on Helene's love of things, and how she inextricably tied up her loss of the veil with the loss of her husband.

She seemed to consider the room we were in. "Of course, you remember that this is the house where my husband was raised. There are signs of him everywhere, in the gifts he gave his mother, Sylvia, and in some of the design choices themselves." Helene's eyes seemed to comb the room. "He was an owl aficionado. See that clock, for instance? He picked that up for Sylvia on one of our trips, that one to Japan, I believe."

I gave the pretty enamel owl I kept on a shelf in the parlor an appreciative nod. "I would think it could be hard to see reminders of a loved one you've lost." It was time to let her know that I knew. "Especially one who was murdered so uncouthly."

*Now I've got her attention.*

I didn't try to throw my knowledge of Richard's peculiar demise in Helene's face. But I wasn't entirely sure I could trust whatever game she was playing.

"Who told you that?" Her voice had dropped in volume to a barely perceptible whisper. "Never mind. I can guess." Helene sighed and grew wistful. "If only that oaf Jesse hadn't quit his protection duty for Richard the day before. I still think that may have been coordinated."

"It wasn't Truman," I quickly told her. "And if you speak ill of Jesse Flowers one more time, you're out of this house." I didn't want to further her narrative of me getting special treatment from the chief just by dint of being engaged to his son. And for the briefest nanosecond I considered letting her know I knew about Richard's affair, too. After all, I still wasn't sure Helene hadn't killed the man herself, or rather had one of her proxies do it. But it would have been too cruel of a volley, so I withheld the information.

"Fine." Helene got over her initial shock that I knew Richard had been purposely felled standing by his car, not killed in a more innocent hit-and-run. "Your knowledge of what happened just fuels my eventual point. I bet you didn't know this, though. Someone tried to help my Richard after he was run into and crushed against the driver's door."

Helene didn't mince words, though I wish in this instant she had. "Oh?" I cocked my head, unwittingly intrigued.

"Yes. The police found prints on his belt buckle and glasses case, made in his own blood. Someone touched him after the incident, but before first responders arrived. They never were able to match the mystery prints.

*Tabitha.*

I tried to keep my voice level as my heart threatened to beat out of my rib cage. I was certain Tabitha didn't know she'd left prints behind as a thirteen-year-old. She'd had the wherewithal to know how it would look, a young teen spying on the town's biggest scion as he conducted a clandestine affair. Then showing up at home with his blood all over her hands and skirt. She may have had the foresight to burn the bloody clothes, but not to wipe off prints in the moment. Her leaving them behind had been driven by a herculean act of kindness, a mere child trying to help the dying man she'd just witnessed getting hurt.

No matter. Tabitha was a straight shooter. She ran a tight ship at the historical society, and had no reason to cause anyone to take her prints.

*Uh-oh.*

Except now Truman personally doubted her report that pricey artifacts were going missing at the historical society. Right now, several acres back on my property, Truman and Tabitha were no doubt examining the distillery site, but keeping a cool, professional distance. I know my friend was hurt. Hurt that she'd lost her grandmother in cold blood just this week, and also that Truman would think so low of her, and suspect her of selling out her own place of business and one of Port Quincy's cultural treasures.

"What do you know, Mallory? I can see it in your eyes." Helene let out a low whistle, causing Baxter to sit up at attention. "Do you know who tried to help my Richard?!" A dark look crossed her face. "Or maybe the prints were left by his murderer."

I shook my head so fast that the small pair of citrine earrings I'd donned this morning for good luck in breaking ground on the new house hit the sides of my neck like small ping-pong balls. I guess I didn't have the best poker face, after all.

"I'm not sure many, if anyone at all, knows what I will tell you next." A real look of pain stole over Helene's features. "My Richard was stepping out on me, Mallory." Helene got up and poured another glug of cream sherry with shaking hands. She imbibed it in a swift gulp. "I couldn't bring myself to tell Truman. And Richard was so sly and skilled, I'm not sure even Truman knew that sordid tidbit." She shook her head. "That's my one regret. That piece of information may have helped Truman's investigation." Helene resumed her perch on a divan, looking as defeated as I'd ever seen her.

I pretended to look surprised at the knowledge of Richard's affair. My better acting job this time must have passed muster with Helene.

"There, there." I awkwardly fished for a box of tissues and handed one to my usual arch-nemesis. It was bizarre to find myself comforting Helene.

"It still stings," Helene got out in a whisper. "Even after all these years."

Now this admission almost made me snort. I was keenly aware of the hypocrisy of Helene not caring that Keith cheated on me with Becca. Why, after I canceled our wedding, Helene lobbied to get us back together, arguing that boys will be boys. But I let that annoying part of our personal history slide. It was common when dealing with Helene to find a lumpy rug left in her wake, what with all of her cavalier practices of sweeping dirty laundry, and anything she disagreed with, under it.

Helene drew in a rattled breath and seemed to

steel herself. "I ask you this with great regret. Will you investigate the death of my husband, Richard?"

I stared at Helene for a full half minute before answering. Baxter the Yorkie seemed to be awaiting my answer as well. He even gave a tiny doggie yelp. Once again, I fell for it. Helene knew I loved animals, and I was even beginning to view her decision to bring the sweet little Yorkie today as a way to ensure that I'd be on board with her cockamamie scheme.

Not that I really would lift even a finger to do so. I'd pledged to Truman, Jesse, and my fiancé not to engage in any rogue sleuthing. I would let Helene think I was looking into her husband's death, and I would not refuse any information that came my way. But I wouldn't engage in any fact-finding for her. I wondered if she really thought I could make a break in the case, or if this was just a way for her to attempt to open up an information channel from Truman to me to her. This theory was way more likely.

"Okay." I watched Helene's tense shoulders sag in relief at my apparent acquiescence to her request. "But I'm not going to be a real gumshoe for this. I guess I hear things now that I'm involved in the current investigation. And we all agree these horrible events seem linked. But I won't be asking people questions and turning this into a real mission to get new info."

But Helene had me once again. She stood, triumphant, and surveyed the kingdom she was once due to inherit. "I know you well, Mallory. Don't forget it. You can't erase the years you spent with my son, and the years I've had to work with you in Port Quincy. I know your nature. And if I'm right, your inveterate nebbiness will help solve this decades-old cold case."

And with that Helene swept from the room. Baxter seemed to give me a final doggie smile as he trotted in her wake.

*I guess she's right.*

I started to laugh with a rueful shake of my head. I'd been had by Helene again. A tiny part of me was beginning to doubt she was the killer, after all. I suppose her visit had been something of a public relations mission, as well.

"Well played, Helene, well played."

But I had one more trick up my sleeve. I hadn't promised Helene I wouldn't be relaying the information to anyone else. I slid my phone from my pocket and jabbed at the second entry on my speed dial. Truman would know every scrap of information Helene had fed to me today. I'd learned my lesson over the years. Truman would be incandescently mad if he knew I was deputizing myself in the name of Helene Pierce. This would defuse the situation.

"Unreal. But not unexpected." Truman's voice was scratchy from the poor connection. "I suppose if you don't really sniff around, there's no harm in letting Helene think you're on the case regarding Richard. Which has, officially, because of the veil, been reopened." He laughed. "And I know *everything*, Mallory. Don't you forget it. Of course, I knew that Helene was aware of Richard's affair. That silly woman thought she could get something over on me?" Truman gave another mirthless laugh, then filled me in on the news that the pieces of material in the earth were indeed part of a very, very old distillery. "Whether it's Ebenezer Quincy's famed equipment remains to be seen."

I got off the phone and ignored the little begging voice nagging my subconscious.

*Why didn't you tell him about Tabitha's observations and memories from so long ago?*

But I batted those concerns away. Truman was already suspicious of my innocent friend. I wasn't going to throw her into the fire of his laser-beam consideration. I was rewarded for my choices with a lovely knot in the pit of my stomach.

# CHAPTER TEN

After all of the murder, mayhem, and mess of June, I decided to take a break. The morning after a particularly difficult off-site wedding that Rachel and I staffed ourselves had pushed me to the brink. The show still went on, even when one was participating in a murder investigation. But I was ready for an easy Sunday. I was glad Pia had the chance to grieve with her mother and her sister, Tabitha. But I felt a frisson of guilt counting down the days until she returned to my too busy business. I knew the Battles women had had an undoubtedly difficult time burying their matriarch, Claudia. I wondered if it was too soon to pay a visit to their store.

Yet I found myself in front of the Antique Emporium on my early Sunday walk. My actions mimicked the crowd that had witnessed Helene rip the veil from my hands. I carried a coffee and a scone, and tried to enjoy the somewhat crisp air before the sun got too high.

I finished the yummy pastry as I stood before the usually pretty window display fronting one side of the Antique Emporium. Today the window art was a tad bit dusty. It was understandable. I gasped as a hand shot out with a feather duster and attacked a tidy display of brooches. June looked up from her ministrations and gave me a sweet, if somewhat sad, smile.

"Come in, come in." She mouthed the words through the glass and beckoned me into her store with a wave of her feather duster.

"Thanks." I slipped through the glass door she opened for me, the We're Closed sign still firmly in place. "I don't want to bother you before you're officially open." I gulped. "And my condolences about Claudia, once again."

June pulled away from the hug with two beads of moisture coalescing in her eyes. "I know, Mallory. And please don't feel any responsibility for what happened at Cordials and Cannonballs. It was a lovely day, up until the reenactment. And Claudia died in her element, taking an active role in getting people interested in history. She was doing what she loved best."

June's speech was so lovely and cathartic I soon found myself weeping. It was only a few minutes and a few tissues later that I realized that I'd attempted to comfort her, and it had resolved the other way around. I also realized my catharsis was accompanied by a Raffi children's song played over the speakers.

"This music." I gestured around me.

"Oh! Miri needs some low-key entertainment while I clean." June led me around the cash register to a small play yard where the adorable baby lay on her tummy, propped up on her elbows. She entertained herself by looking into a little mirror rimmed with ladybugs and flowers. She gave a sweet laugh when her foster mother came into view and promptly rolled over to her back, her little hands held up in the air as if asking to be picked up.

"I heard you're getting badgered to make a decision on having kids." June never tore her eyes away from her foster daughter and ended up picking up the baby and putting her in another carrier. "I hope I'm not too forward." June paused and set down her organic cleaner. "Wait until you're ready, Mallory. It was tough raising Tabitha and Pia without their fathers around." She gave Miri a fond pat. "It's actually easier now to be a foster mother, despite my age and still being single. I can give Miri the time and attention she needs now that my business is on track. Make sure you and Garrett create time for you and Summer first. Don't let others' expectations define you."

June took in my quivering lip and rushed to apologize. "I'm so sorry, Mallory, I stuck my foot in it, didn't I. My daughters are always telling me to stop giving advice."

But it was the opposite. Once again, June displayed her excellent emotional IQ. "It's fine. In fact, it's better than fine. This is just what I needed to hear."

June gave me another hug and her face brightened. "Oh! Those earrings you found with Bev? I unearthed the matching necklace." She ducked behind the front jewelry case, careful to hold Miri's head. "Here. They'll look lovely on you, no matter what season you and Garrett pick for your wedding. And after all that's happened with that veil, I want you to have this set free of charge."

I regarded the heavy and faceted clear crystal earrings. The necklace featured variegated beads of the same material. It would be the perfect piece, falling somewhere on the style spectrum between a subtle necklace and a statement piece.

"Thank you, June. This means so much." I reached for the necklace, my heart full. But something on my finger caught my eye.

"Oh! My ring." The pretty antique diamond ring that Garrett had procured from this very store was missing a little side stone. I gave a small laugh. "This month has been like a lesson in karmic tallies. One good thing happens, and sure enough, right after, something crummy comes up to balance it out."

"Let me see." June's eyes grew wide. "I know this piece. Garrett got it New Year's Eve day for you. Claudia actually made the sale. Well, I'm going to fix this stone, too, Mallory. The little diamond never should have fallen out."

She whisked the tasteful bauble under the counter and my heart skipped a beat. I recalled wanting to hide the ostentatious ring Keith had gotten me, with all three of its blingy, Kardashian-like carats. But I love this little ring and felt a weird emotional tear as June spirited it away.

"I'll call you as soon as it's fixed," she promised.

I nodded my thanks. The nosy gossipmongers of Port Quincy would have a field day with my suddenly naked ring finger. But I had a secret weapon in my arsenal: Bev. I'd tell her the real reason the ring was temporarily missing, and she'd set the record straight.

"Oh! There's one more thing." All of June's talk—about focusing on Garrett, Summer, and myself as a family unit first—had me thinking. I couldn't get the ethereal yet casual sundress from this store out of my mind. I would start following my gut, beginning now.

"The dress. Do you still have it?" I eagerly peered around June into the somewhat darkened depths of the store.

*Uh-oh.*

My spirits sank as June slowly shook her head. "I'm afraid not, Mallory. I sold it just yesterday."

The knowledge hit me like a sack of potatoes. I felt myself deflating, my muse gone. Then I gently mentally chastised myself. Here I was, designing my whole wedding around a dress. At least I knew that beyond our vows, the important part was the life we were building together. I could wed in any pretty dress, or even a pair of jeans. I steeled my shoulders and brushed off my surprising remorse over the sold sundress.

I headed home with a mostly full heart. June had filled my head with important considerations, and missing out on the dress had taught me an important lesson, too. I'd start listening to my heart and following my gut. In these crazy times, it was as good a compass system as any. The muse of a dress was gone. But I could still try to replicate the same casual yet magical aura for my big day.

Which I now firmly agreed should be moved up. It didn't matter if Jesse would be able to resume work on the cottage. What mattered was cementing together the family I loved. I reached home with a spring in my step. And an hour later, and after a few phone calls and texts, I'd amassed my family at Thistle Park. Truman was the only absent member, busy with his cases, of course, even on a Sunday. After a quick and heartfelt private chat with Summer and Garrett, the three of us had something to announce.

"We're moving up the wedding." Summer crowed out the news to Lorraine, my mother and Doug, and Rachel. We accepted the whoops and hollers, and all tucked in to a breakfast of bagels and cream cheese and fruit.

Garrett and I made hasty but meaningful plans for the small wedding we'd now hold the day after Independence Day. I felt lighter than ever, despite the week's events.

"We've been so silly." Garrett tenderly tipped up my chin as we stood together on the back porch.

"I know, right? What are we waiting for?" I

beamed. "This is it." We shared a sweet kiss and returned inside to celebrate with our families.

And an hour later I got another lovely surprise. Bev arrived at the house with a garment bag in tow.

"I have a present for you, Mallory." Her eyes darted to my mother and she flinched for a nanosecond. "I hope you won't think I'm being too forward."

I accepted the bag with a beating heart. My family gathered around as I unzipped the bag.

*Whoa.*

The magical sundress lay within. I felt my sharp intake of breath and all was still. The lovely moment was dimmed only by my continued preoccupation with others' expectations. I felt my head turn, unbidden, to take in my mother's reaction. I knew she resented Bev's forays into helping me plan my wedding, and our friendship in general. But she surprised me by taking my hand and helping me remove the dress from the bag. She held the garment up to my frame, tears coalescing at the corners of her eyes.

"I see what you mean. It's just perfect, Mallory." I rewarded my mother with a bone-crushing hug. And was shocked when she did the same for Bev.

"I apologize, Bev. I know you have Mallory's best interest at heart, and that's all that matters."

Our impromptu brunch party got into full swing. My heart was more full than ever. I went to bed that evening with a newfound clarity, and an appreciation for my family and friends. The same people I wanted with me when Garrett and I wed. I drifted off to sleep surrounded by my two snoozing cats. All was at peace. Things were looking up.

And the final surprise was a call the next day summoning me back to the Antique Emporium. June had repaired the lost stone in a jiffy, the turnaround time almost too good to be true. I set off for downtown, this time in the Butterscotch Monster with Rachel at my side.

"I'm thinking of shimmery emerald-green dresses, just below the knee. And peep-toe heels. Ooh! And sequined headbands. Maybe matching ankle bracelets." Rachel went on and on, dreaming and scheming up plans for color themes for my now very soon-to-be wedding.

"I'll let you and Pia decide," I said with a giggle, "since you're still my official wedding planners. And to be honest, I just want to stand before you all with Garrett and Summer and get it done."

Rachel was temporarily crushed. "C'mon, Mallory. You need to weigh in just a little bit. I saw your reaction to your dream dress. You have to have some opinion on the rest of the wedding style."

I gave my sister a grateful smile. "Honestly, that all sounds lovely. It will really accentuate the lush June season we've had, and echo all of the green from the garden."

My sister sat back on the tan bench seat, somewhat mollified. "Good! I'll order this all up."

"Oh!" I realized I hadn't told my sister. "Tabitha will be a bridesmaid, too."

I frowned at my sister's exaggerated eye roll. "Oh, come on yourself, Rach. You just witnessed Mom and Bev bury the hatchet yesterday. Don't you want to do the same with Tabitha? Especially since you're such good friends with Pia now?"

But Rachel wouldn't commit to ending her feud, one whose origins I barely even remembered. Still, my sister was willing to play ball, even if it was just a little bit. "Fine. I'm guessing Tabitha's about a size eight. I guess I'll order her a dress, too."

We exited the car and made our way to the Antique Emporium.

*Are you kidding me?!*

There in our path stood Becca Cunningham, looking a bit worse for wear than when I'd last seen her. She perked up a bit when she saw Rachel and me headed her way. But her eyes also bore a keen, hungry look.

*Here we go again.*

"Mallory! Rachel!" Becca dug her perfect French tips into the flesh of my forearm. I gently extricated myself from her grip and took a healthy step back.

"What can we do for you, Becca?" I regretted my choice of words immediately.

"You can give me some insight into that hideous woman, Helene." Becca's face clouded over with anguish. "You must have some tips for me in my current situation." She grabbed my hand and Rachel's and pulled us across the street to one of Port

Quincy's newest coffee shops. The shop smelled divine, and featured a wide variety of cold-brew coffees. I'd been meaning to check it out, but now wasn't the day. It was time to work on my boundaries.

"Becca, we have to go. We're due to pick something up at the Antique Emporium. I'm sorry, but I'll have to help you with Helene some other time."

Rachel took a different tactic. She glared at her Michael Kors watch and repeatedly offered up loud and withering, maudlin sighs. But Becca wasn't taking no for an answer.

"Helene cut off Keith's inheritance because she found out we're trying to adopt a baby."

Okay, that was a horse of a different color. Becca had succeeded in reeling me in. Rachel, too. We obediently parked ourselves at a small table, ready to help Becca do battle.

"She what?!"

Becca nodded miserably, her black pearl earrings swishing around in her perfectly dyed platinum hair. All but an inch of dark part she favored maintaining, giving her look a bit of a retro Heather Locklear flavor, circa *Melrose Place*. "She said we weren't trying hard enough." Becca made an understandably yucky face. "And that there was no way she was passing on the family wealth to someone not really part of the family."

My vision dimmed a bit as a lightning bolt of pure rage skittered across my brain.

*The nerve of that woman.*

"But any child you adopt will be your family. And if she can't get that," I added, "maybe Helene shouldn't be part of your family."

"Try telling that to Keith." Becca spat out her rejoinder. "He keeps trying to convince her. Helene puts way too much stock in her lineage as a so-called descendant of Ebenezer Quincy. But he doesn't realize one thing. He'll never change his mother's mind, or her heart. Helene has a lump of stone where everyone else has a heart."

I regretted allowing Helene to enter my home and twist me into playing some reconnaissance game.

"And with all of these crimes happening?" Becca gave a furtive glance around the coffee shop. "Keith is dredging up memories of his father's death. I think he remembers how hard it was on him to have his dad suddenly gone at the age of thirteen. And now he's clinging doubly hard to his mother When all he should be doing is clinging to *me*!"

*I still wonder what Keith knows.*

And Becca had the answers for me. "I knew Richard Pierce was killed in a car accident." Becca lowered her voice. "But Keith has always suspected there's more to the story."

Keith always was a clever one. But Rachel proved cleverer in this instance.

"Why doesn't he just get the police records about what happened to his dad?" Rachel took a healthy glug of the cold-brew-infused malt milkshake she'd ordered and closed her eyes in satisfaction.

"Rachel, you're a genius." I gave my sister an appreciative smile.

But Becca just shook her head. "C'mon, you two, don't you think he's already tried that? The records are sealed."

*Interesting, and unusual.*

I fleetingly wondered for the thousandth time in the last few days if I made the right decision concealing Tabitha's revelations about witnessing Richard's death. It must have been such a leaden burden for a young teen to carry around into adulthood. But it was Tabitha's own secret, to do with as she wished.

Still, a nagging feeling of doubt crept up between my shoulder blades like an unseasonal chill. Truman had his ways of questioning, an expertise honed over decades on the force and as chief. He might be able to tease out details and memories from Tabitha's account that neither I nor she could ever imagine. And I was denying him that opportunity, and a chance to find out what had really happened to Richard Pierce.

But there was no more time to think about it. Becca stared quizzically at me.

"This is heavy stuff, Becca. And you're definitely in the right here." I dragged my eyes from her pretty brown ones and glanced at my watch. "But Rachel and I need to head over to the Antique Emporium. My ring is being repaired, and I'd like to pick it up today." I gestured to my naked left hand.

Becca nodded sagely. "I just assumed you and Garrett broke up!" she stated in a jaunty tone.

*Of course you did.*

But Becca's presumptions knew no end. "And I'll just join you two. We can strategize about my situation after you get your ring."

And with that the three of us set off. I wouldn't be able to shake Becca today, but oh well. Even with all of my troubles and intrigues, my life really was simpler than hers, by dint of the fact that Helene Pierce was not my mother-in-law. Rachel placidly followed along, pleased as punch with her delicious turbo-charged malt shake, and giggling at my interactions with Becca.

"Hello?" I cocked my head after we entered the Antique Emporium. Little Miri was crying somewhere in the store, and unbelievably, for once June wasn't tending to the sweet baby.

"This is probably your ring." Rachel advanced toward the counter and picked up a pretty striped cream and pink bag. A pile of crumpled tissue paper lay beside it on the counter, with extra balled-up pieces on the floor. Rachel frowned. "But it looks like someone already helped themselves to the bag."

I took the little parcel from my sister. "I see what you mean." Inside the bag was a little receipt written out to me for the repair, but marked paid in full. And a pretty black velvet jewelry box with Antique Emporium scrolled across the top in metallic red script resided in the bag, too. But the box was already open, and there was no ring inside.

"Just great," I groaned. "June appears to be missing, as is my ring. And most importantly, Miri is crying in here somewhere. Let's find her, now." My voice became frantic as the three of us split up to find the baby.

"Oh, my goodness." Becca's yelp told me and my sister where to go. Miri was bawling her big brown eyes out, ensconced in a pretty antique crib with vines and roses and curlicues painted on the tan wood. "You sweet little girl. Don't worry, everything's going to be okay." Becca lifted Miri into her arms, and gave her an expert series of pats. The infant calmed and seemed to regard Becca. I wordlessly retrieved a pacifier from the crib mattress and handed it to Becca. Miri accepted her binky, blinked a few times, and fell into a blissful if not exhausted-seeming slumber. She looked at peace nestling into Becca's neck. And despite the strange circumstances we found ourselves in, Becca looked at peace, too.

"So where in the heck is June?!" Rachel turned around in a circle, taking in the various knick-knacks and endless rows of old wood wardrobes and cedar chests. I saw her take in more shallow breaths with her impending panic. "She could be anywhere."

"I don't like this." June was a doting, caring foster mama. There was no way she'd leave Miri unattended, even in a safe crib in her own store. Plus, it looked like some miscreant had already come and made off with my engagement ring. Something sinister was afoot, and I felt like we were going up against an invisible timer. The only respite was the cessation of Miri's cries. I wondered dimly how long the sweet girl had been crying.

I pushed past my sister into the final room in the back, a vestibule filled with even more heavy furniture. Most of the pieces were old china cabinets that were for sale, as well as serving as storage and display pieces for tea sets, crystal, and various other glass baubles.

In the center of the room was a gorgeous crystal chandelier, the thousands of leaded crystal pieces reminiscent of the lovely earrings June had given me. And hanging from the centerpiece of the massive light fixture was no longer its usual crystal snowflake orb. The delicate ornament had been replaced by June herself, her face a lurid shade of purple, her legs dangling lifeless beneath.

Becca hightailed it to the front of the store when she heard me scream.

"Quick! Move!" Rachel pushed a high stool past me and positioned it beneath June.

"Becca, call 911!" I hollered the order to the front of the store, hopeful Becca could hear me. "This is too short," I moaned. Even my tall sister couldn't reach the tie holding June up.

I found a bucket and a piano bench and Mac-Gyvered a somewhat sturdy tower tall enough to reach June. This time Rachel held my legs while I strained on tiptoe with a pair of rusty garden shears from one room over. I cut June down and she fell to the hard ground in a sickening, seemingly lifeless thump. The wail of first responders' vehicles advanced down the street. Becca, Rachel, and I stood as wordless sentinels when they carried June out.

# CHAPTER ELEVEN

"Thank you, girls." June's voice came out in a raspy whisper. She gave Rachel and me a tender and grateful smile. The doctors said it might be weeks for her normal voice to return. She'd been hanging from the chandelier for who knows how long. "If you hadn't gotten there when you did, I might have been a goner."

The town was all abuzz with gossip over what had happened to the antique store owner. It was a titillating, if not macabre situation. First Claudia was gunned down with a replica musket at my failed event. Then June was found hanging, by Rachel, Becca, and yours truly in her own store. Half of Port Quincy thought June had hung herself in anguish over the loss of her mother, while the other half guessed it was something more sinister.

And that was what June recollected. She touched the bandages covering the lurid bruises mottled at her throat and gave us a wince. "The last thing I can remember was packing up your ring, Mallory. I gave you a call to come pick it up. Then I fed Miri a bottle and set her in the crib while I ran to the bathroom." June took in a restorative breath and closed her eyes. Her hands fluttered up to her neck once more. "When I emerged from the bathroom, someone was lying in wait. I felt something hard connect with my face."

June had more bruises and an egg-shaped lump smack-dab in the middle of her forehead to prove it.

"My would-be killer"—June choked even more over the words—"probably strung me up then. But I can't be sure."

"We're just glad you're alive." I'd never forget the sweet advice and gentle push she'd given me to move up my wedding and make my commitment to Garrett and Summer official.

"In a sick way, maybe this was meant to be." June swiveled her gaze from my sister and me and seemed to peer out the window. "I know I talked a big game about being a better foster mother to Miri than I was a mother to Tabitha and Pia growing up. There is some truth to that." She gulped down what seemed like a painful swallow and tore her eyes back to meet mine. "But it has been hard this summer running the store and caring for an infant on top of all that's gone on."

I soothed her protestations. "This would be nearly impossible for anyone, June. Don't beat yourself up."

"I won't," June said with a weak chuckle. "Some sicko already literally took care of that."

I regretted my poor choice of words, but June didn't seem to mind. "I do think it was meant to be. Becca Cunningham happening on Miri. I let my caseworker and the judge know that Becca is temporarily looking after the baby." A serene smile lit up June's face despite her bandages and lurid bruise. "We'll see what comes of it. Hopefully something good."

Tabitha appeared in the doorway with a box of lavender tea. "I got your favorite, Mom." She gave me a hug in thanks, and hesitated in front of Rachel. "Thank you for saving my mom." Rachel gave Tabitha a hug in turn, a real one. Tabitha returned it, and I felt a whoosh of air leave my lungs.

*One grudge down, only several to go.*

It was a season of forgiveness, I supposed. First my own mother and Bev had seemed to move on from their silly enmity. And I hoped this embrace between Tabitha and Rachel was the start of a new beginning.

"Pia's getting together some more of your things at home, Mom."

We exchanged polite chitchat for a few more minutes, until June dozed off. My sister headed out to meet her boyfriend at the entrance, but I lingered to talk to Tabitha.

"I'm so sorry."

Tabitha grabbed my hands in hers. "For what? I really do owe you and your sister and Becca a debt of gratitude."

A large figure loomed in the doorway. "Mallory, Tabitha, hello." Truman looked a bit standoffish as he regarded June's eldest daughter. And Tabitha must have felt the same. She gave him an icy glare and crossed her arms against her vivid trapeze dress. "What do you want now?"

*Ouch.*

Her question for Truman was as much a warning as anything else. I'd never seen her so rude. But I guess she felt inclined to act that way, since Truman had all but accused her of selling items from her own historical society.

"I've never wanted anything but the best for you, Tabitha." Truman seemed momentarily chagrined. Tabitha answered him by shutting her mother's hospital room door in his face.

*Double ouch.*

"I can't help having to investigate her." Truman wearily gestured toward the closed door. "No one likes to be on the receiving end of that. But it's my job." A flash of empathy crossed his face. "Besides, it's got to be tough when your grandmother is newly murdered, and then your mother attempts suicide."

"Uh-uh." I shook my head. "June was attacked. Whoever did this to that poor woman wanted it to look like suicide."

Right?

Truman arched a brow. "It's early still, Mallory. And the most likely reason usually is the one that ends up being correct." He took in my frown of disagreement and changed the subject. "I'm sorry your ring got stolen. But I was so happy to hear that you and Garrett are moving up the wedding."

It was the first time I'd seen my fiancé's father since our decision. I basked in the glow of his happiness for Garrett and me, but some part of my brain was still irritated. Why couldn't he just take June at her word that she'd been attacked rather than attempting suicide? Or Tabitha's word, for that matter, that things were disappearing from the historical society?

Truman seemed to harbor a grudge against the Battles women, and it manifested in an acute case of needless suspicion. I was a bit cool with Truman as we chatted about the moved-up ceremony plans, and I knew he caught my chilly vibe. I quickly excused myself to attend to a happier visit at the hospital.

I took the elevator down two floors to the maternity unit, just in time for visiting hours to start. Olivia's last-minute baby shower was to have started right about now. But she'd canceled the event, and for good reason. She'd gone into labor in the wee hours of the morning, and delivered her son around noon.

"Mallory!" Olivia ushered me in as best she could from her perch on the hospital bed. "Come meet my little guy, Sebastian." She happily showed off her itty-bitty son. I held him briefly with the same sense of aching wonder I felt when June had first passed Miri to me.

"Toby went out to get an extra-large pizza. Hawaiian with double pineapple." Olivia seemed to swoon at the mere thought of the takeout due to arrive.

I broke the news of my sped-up nuptials. "I guess you won't get to be a bridesmaid," I told my friend. "Unless you feel up to it." Olivia clapped in excitement. "See? I knew we'd be able to turn this accident-ridden month around."

I didn't have the heart to tell her about the grisly yet fortunate discovery of June. But Olivia already knew. She picked my brain for all the lurid details, and at the end, found the silver lining yet again.

"I can't say I'm unhappy that Miri is with Becca and Keith." Olivia grew pensive. "I'm not sure if it'll all work out. Becca and Keith are not officially foster parents, but judges have made exceptions before." Her gaze grew wistful. "I chatted quite a bit with Becca in the waiting room of the OB's office this spring. She was undergoing fertility treatments, and I know how much she wants a baby."

I decided to spare Olivia the details of Becca and Keith's attempted surrogate pitch on yours truly.

"You know what would be super sweet?" Olivia's face broke out into a grin. "You might want to stop by June's place and get some of Miri's favorite things, and bring them to Becca and Keith."

I clapped a hand to my forehead. "Becca's going to need more than that! A crib, diapers, a changing table . . ." My mind went back to the flotilla of baby gifts I'd accepted today despite Olivia's shower getting canceled.

Olivia smiled again. "I don't think that will be necessary. Becca may have jumped the gun just a bit. She already has a nursery ready to go, with the drawers filled with neutral clothing, wipes, a mobile, the whole works."

*Of course, she did.*

I gave my friend a hug and set off to complete my new task.

"Oh, and Mallory?" Olivia called out one last thing as I made my way to the door. "Be a support for Becca, would you?"

"Of course!"

Becca wasn't my favorite. I'd never forget the photos sent to me detailing her initial affair with Keith while we were engaged. But we'd had a number of close calls and inadvertent adventures over the years to become somewhat, grudgingly, friendly. I returned for one last hug, grateful for Olivia's optimism.


Half an hour later I pulled into June's driveway. I had the address, and was helped by finding Pia's Nissan Versa parked at the top.

"Mallory." Pia flung open the door and gave me a hearty embrace. "You saved Mom."

"It was the least we could do." I followed her into the house. Pia was packing a pile of what looked like June's favorite things into a pretty brocade suitcase.

"Mom is still weak, but she'll enjoy having her thrillers, her own fuzzy socks and slippers, and lots and lots of lemon candy for her throat." Pia placed each item into the luggage with tender care, and patted the top closed. I couldn't help but recall the moment that seemed to have set off the deadly domino effect this month, beginning with finding the veil buried within the lining of a different suitcase.

We headed upstairs over creaky yet charming farmhouse boards to reach baby Miri's nursery. The pretty house was like a miniature, less cluttered version of the Antique Emporium, with whimsical pieces of Americana decorating the walls and small tables.

"Mom was so worried for when Miri began walking." Pia gestured to the tables topped with delicate ceramics and mirrors. "All of this would have to be put away."

But the infant's room was a soft and bright haven of yellow, green, and cream. An antique quilt hung over one wall, and I recognized a similar crib anchoring one corner of the room, just like the one we'd found the baby in yesterday.

"Let's see. She loves this rattle. And I may as well give Becca all her clothes and diapers and binkies."

We worked in companionable silence loading up board books and baby items into another suitcase. Pia finally began to grow pensive.

"Losing Grandma Claudia, then almost losing Mom, has really brought some things into clarity for me." She took a deep breath. "Did you know June has never told me who my father is?"

I dropped a pile of onesies with a start. "Um, no.

That's a pretty big deal. Not to be poking my nose into your familial business, but is it possible she doesn't know?" I recalled June alluding to the fact that it had been hard to raise the girls without either of their fathers.

But Pia shook her head. "Mom was married to Tabitha's dad, and he passed away. But I do know my mom had a relationship with my father." She rolled her eyes and left the room, returning with a grainy, yellowed photo from the local newspaper, the *Eagle Standard*. "One day, five years ago, I think she thought she could stop my badgering by telling me that this dude was the one."

The picture heralded a local chemistry professor, and there was a portrait topping his obituary. "Hm. Genes can be recessive, but you really don't look a thing like him."

Pia burst out laughing. "I know. I've even done those genealogical DNA things to see if something comes up. So far, nada."

Pia's voice grew low. "Claudia knew."

*Excuse me?*

My incredulous look said it all.

"She promised me she'd tell me on my birthday this year."

"Which is in two weeks." I knew from Pia's new-hire paperwork that we'd soon be celebrating her birthday.

"But something spooked Grandma. We'd even done a super-secret pinky swear promise when I was eighteen. And last year, when I turned twenty-four, Grandma took me out for a shot of whiskey at one of the distilleries, and reiterated her promise. But two days before she died, she wanted to push the reveal out a few years." A flicker of fear marred Pia's pretty looks. "What made Claudia so afraid to tell me? Why change her mind?" Pia showed a brief flash of anger, hurt, and disbelief in her pretty green gimlet eyes that matched her sister Tabitha's, a striking feature both girls had inherited from June.

"And why wait to tell you precisely when you turn twenty-five? Or even go against your mom's obvious wishes not to tell?"

Pia shook her head. "She's been working on Mom for years. I've caught snippets of arguments about it." A tear slipped down Pia's cheek. "I feel horrible. Claudia is gone. She was the most fun grandmother you could ever imagine. But I feel so guilty. As soon as the doctor came into the waiting room with the bad news, the first thing I thought was, now I'll never know who my father was."

I gave Pia a firm hug. "It's not the same at all, but I don't even know if my dad is on this earth still, or not."

It was true. I gave Pia the brief synopsis of my dad leaving in the dead of night with a note for our mother. Rachel and I were so astounded and bitter at his voluntary disappearance that when we later entertained the question of whether he was alive or not, we both found we didn't care. "It is a bit different, though. I still know who he was." I felt my face twist into a frown. "Or rather, who he wanted us to think he was."

My cell blared out a text from Becca, happy to receive Miri's items. I bid Pia goodbye after she helped me load the baby wares into the Butterscotch Monster.

"Thanks again, Mallory."

As I drove off, I pondered the range of emotions I'd witnessed in Pia. She was right to be angry with June that she'd withheld knowledge of Pia's paternity.

*Angry enough to string her up to the ceiling?*

I was disgusted with my mind's train of thought. Pia couldn't hurt a fly.

*Or could she?*

An icy bath, or possible awareness, danced down my spine. What if Claudia wasn't killed on the reenactment field over some tiff? What if Pia killed her because she'd backed down from revealing a much-promised secret?

I chased those thoughts away and hightailed it to Becca and Keith's house.

# CHAPTER TWELVE

The shocking structure of the McMansion that Becca and Keith had commissioned never ceased to amaze me. Cubes and right angles in maroon brick jutted off each other like a modernist cliffside. The blinding summer sun reflected off of slim and wide slices of dark glass embedded in the least likely places. The copper roof of the structure had finally gotten a bit of minty patina, seeming to cap off the whole strange Rubik's Cube of a house with an incongruous fuzzy green cap.

I loaded up Miri's things into a Radio Flyer wagon Pia had also given me and pulled the haul up to the lacquered front door. I was more used to the inside, a retro 1980s throwback homage to peach and cream and gold, this part of the house designed entirely by Helene.

But the nursery had Becca written all over it. "Ta-da!" Becca ushered me into the room, where Keith was looking surprisingly paternal. He bounced baby Miri on his knee, the little girl dissolving into a fit of giggles. I hadn't seen Keith so joyful and at ease, well, ever.

"Thank you for bringing some of Miri's things." Keith included me in his warm smile before he turned his attention back to the baby. I got a closer look at the room, a calm oasis of sage green, taupe, and silver. Little gray triangles provided a subtle pattern on one accent wall. The baby furniture was sleek Scandinavian beech, the carpet below my feet soft and perfect for tummy time.

"This was meant to be." Becca's eyes were shining as she took the infant from Keith. "I'm so sorry we had to find June in that state. But at least you and Rachel were able to save her. But I have to believe I ran into you guys for a reason, too. For this little girl, right here."

I hoped the judge and case workers agreed. I'd hate for Becca and Keith to become so attached to Miri, only for her stay to be brief.

"Nonsense. This is only a temporary affair." Helene loomed in the doorway like a bad omen come to roost.

Helene must have wrangled a spare key back from Keith. She entered the nursery, her spine ramrod straight. Her coral lips were pressed into an impossibly thin line.

"Keith, Becca, I just dropped in to give you these." She tossed two large folders onto the top of Miri's changing table. "An all-expenses-paid cruise around the Mediterranean. Your tickets, airfare voucher codes, and itinerary are all there. I thought I'd surprise you. You leave next week."

*Huh?*

Becca's eyes narrowed. "We can't go on a cruise, Helene." Her face turned sweet again as she cuddled Miri. "I mean, I'm sure some moms do, but I'm not comfortable enough at the thought of a big international trip with my baby just yet." Keith gave wordless support to his wife, standing behind her and placing his hand on her shoulder.

"You are not her mother, and she is not your baby!" Helene's voice was shrill enough to alarm Miri, even if she didn't quite understand the content of the message, which if she did, would undoubtedly make her cry as well. "Keith, I wasn't kidding. If you and Becca adopt Miri, your inheritance is gone."

I couldn't decide whether to string a score of invectives Helene's way, or pull her from the house.

But Keith for once decided to stand up to his mother. "I'll have you know I'm doing everything in my power to make Miri a Pierce."

His utterance of his famed last name made Helene flinch.

"I've hired a fleet of the best attorneys. Becca and I are taking foster and adoption classes. I'll show the court and caseworker we're the best option for this little girl."

"You wouldn't dare." Helene's face was wrought with threads of fear woven through her rage. "This baby," she spat, "won't be carrying on the lineage of being a descendant of Ebenezer Quincy!"

I'd had enough. "Oh please, Helene. Who gives a hoot? The founder of this town by all accounts was a lush who dipped into the contents of his own distillery too much. You want to keep associating with that?" A tiny trickle of an idea came to me. I recalled Pia's use of a genealogy DNA service. "You know, Helene, there are quite a few rumors around town that you're not even related to Ebenezer Quincy, as unimportant as that even is. Why don't you take a DNA test to prove it?"

A flash of real fear skittered across Helene's face, this time unmistakable. "I don't need to, Mallory," she finally sniveled. "My genealogical pedigree is impeccable. I'm the current president of the DAR. No one doubts anything."

Becca snorted. "Pedigrees are for dogs, Helene."

*Ouch. Well played.*

"I'll end this right now, Mother." Keith turned to me. "That's a great idea, Mallory. I'll take a DNA test. Then you can stop nattering on about the legend of Ebenezer Quincy coursing through your veins."

Helene was utterly quiet as she stared at her son in absolute incredulity. Then she did her best Rumpelstiltskin impression, stamping the pretty, soft carpet, the floor muting her rage. She stomped out of the house, and hopefully right out of Keith and Becca and Miri's lives.

# CHAPTER THIRTEEN

I'd nearly forgotten about my moved-up wedding. But time was moving on at a rapid pace. It would soon be July, and the town of Port Quincy would be able to come together to celebrate again, hopefully sans weapons and accidents this time. The Founder's Day festivities and dance were almost upon us. The mayor of Port Quincy had tripled security for the event in light of what had happened at Cordials and Cannonballs. I just hoped the denizens of Port Quincy wouldn't be too spooked to attend, and that when they did, they had a safe and fun celebration.

And the day would soon be here when I'd wed Garrett, whether I was ready for it or not. Fortunately, Rachel had taken my plea to heart and she and Pia were running the whole thing. The ceremony would be short and sweet, and the guest list for the reception very small.

Bev and Jesse's wedding was another matter. Right after Jesse's shooting, I'd emailed each invitee to their wedding and reception to tell them the nuptials were on hold pending Jesse's recovery. And although Jesse had been home with Bev last week, and had even made the trek to the construction-turned-archaeology site that was to be the location of my new cottage, it looked like Garrett and I would actually beat them down the aisle.

I left Bev's store with a spring in my step. She'd had the ethereal sundress steamed and pressed, and the garment looked good as new. I completed my next task as well, picking up the wedding rings at Fournier's jewelry shop. My left ring finger still felt a bit funny without the antique piece I'd been wearing since New Year's Day, but there would be a new band to take its place after the wedding.

I swung the small jewelry bag in my hand as I started to walk back to Thistle Park in the radiant sunshine. I wouldn't be able to put the jewelry in my destroyed safe, but it was no matter. All that mattered was that things were finally looking up. Becca and Keith were making progress convincing the caseworkers and the judge in charge of Miri's case that they should be her forever parents. June was home from the hospital, and Jesse couldn't wait to wrap up the issue with the distillery and commence work on the cottage. All would be well. That is if we could all stay out of trouble, and stay alive, until July.

"Mallory!" A familiar voice called out behind

me on the sidewalk. It was Horace Overright, the Smithsonian archivist.

*What is he still doing here?*

I'd last seen the little man the day he'd inadvertently revealed the location of the safe and the Betsy Ross veil to Helene. He seemed to have read my thoughts, or at least the quizzical look I'm sure was on my face.

"I've been enjoying the charms of Port Quincy so much that I decided to stay an extra week. I even convinced the Smithsonian that the veil might turn up." His cheerful face fell into a frown. "But that's not looking likely, is it?"

I shook my head and we fell into a pleasant walk together.

"Where are you headed?" We'd reached the end of downtown, and were staring down a giant hill paved with yellow bricks. It was time to part with the pleasant, if enigmatic, man.

"Well," he began a bit sheepishly, "I was actually hoping to tag along. If you're headed to Thistle Park, that is." He rushed on. "I heard that your builders discovered some distillery equipment that was possibly owned by Ebenezer Quincy. I must confess I'm dying to see it!"

Horace leapt lightly on the balls of his feet, his worn Vans bouncing on the pavement. I winced at the choice of his words, *confess* and *dying*. But I had no reason to deny his request. He was a consummate history geek, much like Tabitha and my stepdad. This would be fun.

"Well, sure. There are a lot of people digging, under the supervision of the archaeologist, and the police are there, too. I'm sure they'd be happy to have your expertise."

We settled into our walk in amiable silence again. Especially the part that featured the upswing of the valley, which peaked at Thistle Park. We were both huffing and puffing a bit as we ascended to the top.

"Being here in Port Quincy has dredged up a lot of memories," Horace began in a confessional tone. "I was in town when Richard Pierce was in that accident, you know."

*Come again?!*

"And I just remembered something that the police maybe should hear all these years later."

I nearly stopped on the sidewalk, frozen with a weird mix of excitement and trepidation.

"I was in town to re-authenticate the Betsy Ross veil. There had been some rumblings that the veil was a fake, and that the one purchased by the Pierces in the 1950s from Sotheby's had been swapped out. I came up to authenticate it again, and leave. I didn't even know Richard was in an accident until I returned to the Smithsonian. I left for D.C. that day, you see. But before I left, I saw the most peculiar sight. A young woman, a child basically, covered in blood."

*Oh. My. God.*

He was referencing a young Tabitha. I had no doubt. Still, I willed my beating heart to calm down. I remembered my evidence class back in law school. Most people struggled with the most basic and distinctive details when recalling a suspect. Tall people became short, while portly suspects became slim, and the old become young again. What were the chances Horace could accurately describe a blood-covered Tabitha?

"That's very interesting." I kept my voice level. "I'm sure Truman would like to hear it. Although he is very busy, and that case is twenty-five years old. Why, it was an accident, right? So I guess that strange sight you saw was something else." I gulped and waded in. "Do you remember what the girl looked like? Shoot, this was twenty-five years ago. Could it have even been an older person, or a male?"

Horace shook his head. "Oh, no. I vividly remember. This girl was tall, but you could tell she was youngish somehow, too. I think she had on a jean skirt? And though it was an accident, if she was there at the scene, she could probably shed light on what happened. I know Helene would want to know."

*Drat.*

His details were matching Tabitha's exactly.

"And the girl had blond hair," he continued.

I let out a relieved sigh. Tabitha had always had red hair, whether natural or dyed.

"Or maybe a bit reddish? That part I can't remember."

My recent relief dissipated again. I began to construct a crazy plan. I'd just keep Horace away from Truman so he couldn't tell him of the specter of a girl he'd seen covered in blood the day Richard was murdered. Easy-peasy.

*Yeah, right.*

If Truman ascertained that Horace was talking about Tabitha, it would be all over. Truman's current distrust of Tabitha would color his judgment of her split-second decision when she was just a teen, a decision she'd made to conceal that she'd been at the crime scene. Truman might conflate the whole thing and charge Tabitha with the murder of Richard Pierce. It wouldn't be a fair assessment, that much I knew, and I was determined not to let it happen.

We finally reached Thistle Park, and grabbed some Gatorade before we made the second leg of the journey wending our way through the gardens and paths into the woods. We made it through a cloud of mosquitoes to the little glen of trees that had been cleared for construction, the site now a busy hive of activity.

"This is fantastic!" Horace rubbed his hands together. "I'm supposed to check out of my hotel tonight. Do you mind if I stay at your B and B for the next few days?"

I shrugged, then turned my mouth up in a smile. "Of course, Horace. I'd be happy to have you."

*All the better to keep my eye out to make sure you're not talking to Truman.*

"Check out my finds!" Summer abandoned her work with a little chisel and toothbrush to show me a tiny piece of metal. I marveled at her patience to sift through the earth on a volunteer basis, when I spotted another enticing draw for her. Preston appeared at her side, and the two teens talked animatedly about what the archaeologists had taught them about digging. Horace engaged the two in an animated conversation, and I walked around the cordoned-off plot of earth for a closer look.

Ten minutes in, a Quincy College anthropology major made quite the find. "What the heck is this?" The tall, freckled kid started pushing at a large metal pot.

"Hold up, Hudson." The chief archeologist rushed over to snap photos of the find. She finally got the metal receptacle out of the earth and tore off the intact lid with a flourish. And gave a gasp. A plastic rectangle was within the metal pot.

"Correct me if I'm wrong, but that shouldn't be there, right?" I watched in awe as the archaeologist continued her work documenting the unearthing of the object. She held it up triumphantly, if not a bit dejectedly. It was a cassette tape, the kind that hadn't been used much at all since the advent of CDs and MP3 technology.

"It looks like a mixtape," the woman said with a combination of disappointment and wonder. "Alanis Morissette, Live, P. Diddy."

*An artifact maybe from the late 1990s?*

"Now that's a biscuit of a different bonnet." Jesse ambled over, his movements labored and slow. I was happy to hear his malaprops, if it meant he was truly on the mend. And he seemed happy that once this site was fully unearthed, there was a chance he could commence building the new cottage.

Summer wrinkled her elfin nose. "What's a mixtape?" I felt a motherly wave of love wash over me. She was getting a bit of a tan, the rest of her face catching up to her freckles. I found myself wanting to deliver a nagging reminder about sunscreen, reminiscent of my mother, Carole.

Preston jumped in. "It's like the playlist I made for you."

Summer turned all swoony. I was glad Garrett was at work. If he'd just witnessed his daughter's heightened crush on Preston, he'd probably want to die and be buried right there under the distillery equipment.

I felt protective and bittersweet toward Summer's getting older, too. I knew I would never replace Adrienne, Summer's mom, with whom Summer now had a renewed and blossoming relationship. But I couldn't wait to form an official family unit in a mere few days.

"This is now officially a crime scene." Truman popped the bubble of my warm and fuzzy reverie. He gestured to the lurid yellow-and-black tape announcing it as so.

"What do you mean?"

Truman explained. "The archaeologists are making the tentative determination that the distillery equipment was moved and interred as recently as twenty or so years ago."

This was both good and bad news. The good was that this land wasn't the original site of the distillery, and when the dig wrapped up, Jesse could build the house. The bad was that this was now a place where someone had moved and stashed the distillery, and Truman and Faith would need to find out why.

"I'm beginning to think this place is something of a landfill." I pointed to an edge of fabric peeking out from the earth just beyond my toe. It appeared to be a dirty, moldy cream. Truman called the archaeologist over again, and in minutes, she'd freed up an ancient Chanel wallet. Well, not *ancient* ancient, but circa 1980s or 1990s.

I was one of the lucky few, along with Horace and Truman, who got to see the archaeologist gently tease open the wallet and peer within. Truman donned gloves and took over when we saw there was a stash of plastic cards, and even some moldering cash within. The chief carefully shimmied out a slim Pennsylvania driver's license covered in grime.

*Holy moly.*

There, looking back at us, was a smirking, haughty, quarter-century-younger Helene Pierce.

# CHAPTER FOURTEEN

"Leave it to me, Nancy Drew." Truman took a swig of sweet tea and placed the sweaty glass back on the table with a satisfied sigh. It had been four hours since we'd found the wallet at the distillery site. There was no way I was going to miss Truman's grilling of Helene if I could help it.

I'd had time to drive Horace's things over to the B and B and officially check him in, take a shower, and start prepping for a breakfast tomorrow, which would be a bit fancier than usual, now that I had a weekday guest.

And in that time Truman had readied his strategy to question Helene about just how her wallet with its 1990s license had ended up buried with what was likely Ebenezer Quincy's famed distillery.

I craned my head up the back stairs to make sure Horace wasn't snooping. When Truman arrived, the two engaged in heated conversation. I'd dipped onto the back porch to see what it was about. But they were only discussing the relative merits of the Washington Nationals and Pittsburgh Pirates, not a young Tabitha covered in Richard Pierce's blood. And soon after that, Horace had retired to his room. Last I'd heard, he'd given in to a spate of heavy snores behind his equally heavy door.

"This is all moot, Mallory." Truman glanced at his watch. "I left a message for Helene to meet me at the station in an hour. I think she'll comply, but with her attorney in tow. No matter. She'll rush in to clear her name and incriminate herself in the process anyway. The poor thing can't help herself." Truman broke out into an anticipatory grin.

"Fine. But play along with me. I at least want to know if my theories are correct." I placed most of the cut fruit for a breakfast salad in a pretty crystal bowl to chill overnight in the fridge. But I set aside two smaller bowls to entice Truman to share his motive, means, and opportunity ideas with me.

"The wallet makes it pretty clear that Helene moved the distillery equipment to this property." I fished around in my bowl for a purple grape.

Truman batted away my first point before he viciously consumed a chunk of honeydew melon. "That spindly lady didn't move that equipment herself."

"True. She probably had her cadre of minions do it." Helene often did employ various fleets of people to carry out her projects, some more nefarious than others. "But I think she oversaw the project. I bet she stole the artifacts and buried them at

Thistle Park to bolster her erroneous claims of being a descendant of Ebenezer Quincy." I remembered Keith's promise and let out a giggle. "Keith is actually putting that to rest. He did one of those genealogical DNA tests. I bet it'll show a very different story than the one Helene wants to tell."

Truman laughed. "Keith should worry about getting murdered." We both turned momentarily somber.

"Now back to my theory. What Helene wants, Helene gets. And if she moved a whole colonial-era distillery, there would be people paid off long enough ago, and cushily enough, to keep quiet."

Truman gave a nod. "If that's true, and they exist, we'll find them. But riddle me this, Mallory. Let's say Helene moved the equipment there in the 1990s. There's a chance she didn't want it to be found for some reason we're not thinking of. And if so, it would have been when she and Keith were trying to fleece Sylvia out of her land to build a housing development at Thistle Park."

I frowned. It was true. But we were still missing something.

"Or," I began, liking this scenario the least, "Helene was framed. She definitely wasn't listening to a mixtape featuring P. Diddy in the 1990s. Maybe the person who really moved the equipment owned that tape and accidentally dropped it into that metal pot or kettle." The theory sounded unlikely, even to my ears.

But Truman was no longer listening. He was

reading an email on his phone, and he looked up with a triumphant, if wolfish, grin. "Bingo."

I had a feeling this wasn't about Helene.

"We got the IP address report from the artifacts sold from the historical society on eBay. And it looks like your dear friend Tabitha was listing the items she was supposed to be curating for the town of Port Quincy from her very own personal laptop."

Truman gave me a slightly pitying look and continued. "I may have to put my questioning of Helene on hold, Mallory. I have bigger fish to fry with Tabitha Battles."

I sat wordlessly after Truman left, my fruit salad uneaten. It was no matter, as I was no longer hungry, but rather fighting off a feeling of nausea.

*Truman is out to get Tabitha.*

My hackles had officially reached DEFCON 1.


I was relieved the next morning to observe the Founder's Day celebration churning along at full speed, with nary a hiccup or dead body. Rachel, Pia, and I worked flawlessly to make sure the event went well. The extra security hired by the mayor had been a concern in the back of my mind. I didn't want festival-goers to feel like they were in a police state, yet I wanted them to trust that the horrible incident at Cordials and Cannonballs would not reoccur. I needn't have worried. Everyone was having a grand time under a cloudless sky, thankfully and safely devoid of even a bit of fog.

Unfortunately, Helene still walked, a free woman. Or rather, she minced and strutted in her kitten heels and Anne Klein dress. A cloud hovered around me all day as I watched Tabitha man her booth for the historical society. She was still a free woman, too, but I knew Truman had probably rounded her up for an extensive and grill-worthy voluntary question session. Tabitha offered smiles and brochures to passersby, but the smiles didn't reach her eyes. She spent an inordinate amount of time on her cell phone, and I wanted to warn her to stop, as the little device could become evidence.

*But if she's innocent, you don't have to worry.*

The thought soothed me enough to return to my tasks. I wondered if Tabitha had kept her questioning at the police station from Pia. It wouldn't be hard to do. Tabitha rented a little house near the Monongahela River, while Pia was living with June this summer. The youngest Battles daughter still wore an air of sadness, but was smiling again at the end of the day.

And the highlight of it all came as I chaperoned the Founder's Day dance with Garrett. Summer hadn't been too thrilled when she found out her dad would be watching her dance with Preston.

"Mallory!" Summer dropped Preston's hand as she entered the Community Center, where the dance was held. She gave me a little spin in her magenta throwback bubble dress.

"You look lovely, kiddo." I included Preston in my praise. "And you're quite handsome, Preston." Bev's son blushed.

"Son, I wanted to have a word with you."

*Slow your roll, Garrett.*

My fiancé had moved toward his daughter's date, his cross-examination game-face at the ready. Preston took a step back and gulped so hard his Adam's apple was on full display.

"Daaad." Summer managed to stretch the one syllable word into about five. "Leave him alone."

Summer was in luck, while I was not. A kerfuffle was breaking out behind her in line.

"I said, get off of me! Give me a chance to come in on my own steam."

It was Tabitha, taking tickets for the dance. Or she was, before Faith appeared to read her her Miranda rights. Tabitha convinced Faith that there was no need to cuff her, but she still had to submit to Faith leading her out to a police car for all of Port Quincy to see.

The dance was abuzz about Tabitha's arrest. Summer and Preston cut a rug under the watchful eyes of Garrett. Everyone had a wonderful time. The event would do a lot of good soothing people's minds after Cordials and Cannonballs. But I couldn't enjoy a single second of it.

# CHAPTER FIFTEEN

The next morning dawned clear and calm. The lovely weather seemed almost mocking, as if my dear friend hadn't been unfairly arrested and thrown unceremoniously in the Port Quincy jail. There was the evidence Truman had presented as incontrovertible. I wasn't sure how the IP information had gotten onto Tabitha's laptop. Wasn't it possible the information was merely tracking that she'd just found the items on eBay and reported them, rather than uploading them for sale herself? My mind spun and whirred, trying to make sense of how Truman had botched Tabitha's arrest and charge. There was no way my friend did what he'd said she had.

I supposed it would all shake out. There was nothing else I could do about it, anyway. I headed over to June's house to bring a contract for attorney's services. Garrett had recommended a skilled and fair defense attorney for Tabitha, and June had agreed to pay the retainer. I was happy to help, but it felt like a joyless mission.

"Hello, Mallory. I wish we were meeting for different reasons." June ushered me into the home I'd just visited Pia in to gather the items for Miri.

June seemed to have the baby on her mind, too. "I saw Miri a few hours ago. She is so happy and content and thriving with Becca and Keith." Her face fell and a teardrop quivered at the end of her nose. She nabbed a tissue from her sideboard and dabbed at her face. "I feel like I didn't do such a great job with Tabitha and Pia."

"Of course, you did," I soothed. "Pia is the most wonderful addition to our team that my sister and I could ever imagine. And Tabitha didn't do what Truman is accusing her of, I'm certain. She has been a shining light in this town, teaching and educating and curating history. She was also one of my first friends here. She's gracious and kind and smart, and she couldn't have done what Truman said."

Hearing the litany of her daughters' positive attributes only further agitated June.

"Then where did I go wrong? Why was Tabitha selling items from the historical society?"

*Uh-oh.*

For some reason, it was extremely important to me that June consider her daughter innocent.

*Because she is.*

But even my dear Garrett had startled me last night at the dance by discussing in low tones Tabitha's best possible defenses, with a focus on the assumption that she had indeed smuggled out and sold the items she should have been curating and protecting.

Truman must have gotten to June. And she'd had enough troubles lately as it was. The thick scarf wound around June's neck slipped down, and I was treated to a mottled array of bruises the colors and shapes of camouflage fabric. The poor woman's voice was still raspy from her time under the chandelier. I shivered at all that had befallen the house of Battles. It wasn't fair. Claudia was gone, someone had attempted to murder June, and now Tabitha was in the clink for unrelated and erroneous charges.

June began to pace around her combination farmhouse-kitchen and dining room. She gesticulated as she went, threatening to knock the myriad ceramic figurines and ornaments from the shelves and sideboard. "I haven't always made the best decisions." She seemed to size me up before she went on. "I'm honestly embarrassed about the identity of Pia's father. I never told her who the guy is. I thought if I forbid her to know about him, she'd drop it." She gave a mirthless laugh and chastised herself. "Parenting one-oh-one, June. That move was guaranteed to create an obsession. I've held off far too long. I'll let Pia know soon enough."

It was a start, but it also omitted the part about how she'd tried to pass off one of her professors as Pia's real dad. But I wasn't about to bring that up.

"And imagine my surprise when I learned that

Tabitha and my own mother were working together in cahoots to fleece the town of Port Quincy."

*Come again?!*

June nodded at my surprise, then shook her head with disgust. "Claudia tried to sell some colonial weapons to Quincy College. Thank goodness, their archivist and your stepfather refused. They'd recently been donated to the historical society."

*Uh-oh.*

Doug's own words two weeks ago corroborated this story. I recalled him telling me, Rachel, and Pia about how he and the archivist at Quincy College had given Claudia a pass.

"But what if Claudia was just working alone? Did Tabitha necessarily have to be involved?" I didn't want to speak ill of the dead, but I would be okay with this whole nefarious plan having been Claudia's work, with no input from Tabitha.

"But who gave her the weapons? It must've been Tabitha." June nearly moaned and proceeded to rip her damp tissue into shreds. "My once-sweet girl and my very own mother, working together, just not in a way I can be proud about. And I'm sorry about your ring." June looked like she was about to vomit. Her voice dropped to an even raspier whisper. "I think she took it when she did this to me."

*Oh, heck no.*

*June. Listen to yourself. Did you just insinuate that Tabitha knocked you out and tried to hang you?!*

*This conversation has jumped the shark.*

June stilled her nervous hands and willed herself to drag her now-rheumy eyes to meet mine.

"Something happened when Tabitha was thirteen."

*No, no, no!*

"The day that horrible man, Richard Pierce, died in a car accident? I found some of Tabitha's things covered in massive amounts of blood." June had turned a sickening shade of green. "And then when she thought I'd gone to sleep, she carried the whole lot out to the grill and burned them into charcoal."

I decided to break the promise I'd made to Tabitha, if only to convince her own mother she wasn't some kind of bad seed. "What if she just tried to help him after his accident?"

June looked up sharply and considered my question. "I guess that's possible. But why hide that? Why burn the clothes?" June sighed once more, a rattling, sad sound. "The person who hit me at the Antique Emporium swung like a lefty."

Her case against her daughter was nearly complete. Tabitha, of course, was left-handed.

"Please tell me you didn't tell Truman about Tabitha's bloody clothes."

But June's stricken look gave me the answer. "I had to, Mallory. I guess I didn't do a good enough job protecting my daughters when they were little, and I'm trying to do the right thing now."

I left June to her sorrows, and toted out the last of Miri's baby things at her behest. If Tabitha didn't even have her own mother in her corner, it would be very hard to prove her innocence. Innocence that no one apparently believed in except me.

Imagine my surprise when my mother answered the door at Keith and Becca's house.

"Surprise, Mallory!" My mother spun around in a circle to show off her decorating work. Painters swarmed the peach monstrosity of a great room, obliterating all vestiges of Helene. The gold, sea-foam, and seashell furniture had been spirited away, replaced by buttery suede and leather couches in shades of hunter green and slate.

*Wow.*

Keith must finally be over Helene if he was will-ing to cover up her stamp on his and Becca's house. All around us rollers flew up walls to trans-form them into a chic navy, gray, and cream can-vas.

"All of this is with Miri in mind, too," my mother gushed. She showed off a new coffee table with a sleek padded leather edge to keep the baby safe when she started toddling. The immense gas fire-place had a new, padded grate, and I realized all of the paint should have been giving me a headache, but wasn't. I mentioned it to Carole, and she ex-plained the lack of paint smells.

"I used no-VOC paint for Miri, too. No chemi-cals, no headaches."

I was glad my mom was getting all of her baby-related practice with Miri instead of demanding a grandchild from me. If only Helene were more accepting of her own new grandchild.

But thinking of the sour dowager empress of Port Quincy always seemed to drag her out from under her rock. The pretty lacquer doors jiggled open, and in walked Helene. She carried a large flower arrangement designed to match her version of the interior, a muted blend of peach roses and mums and cream lilies. The vase and flowers crashed to the ground. And Helene began to scream.

"What is this abomination of a room?! No one consulted me!"

Becca's gorgeous and giant Maine Coon, Pickles, stretched in his cat condo and then leapt from its top level to approach Helene. The big guy gave a loud growl, clearly not up to taking her shenanigans today. And neither was my mother, who held her own.

"Sorry Helene, but I take orders from the owners, not you." My mother tossed a grateful look at the stairs, which I realized with a start she must have had her contractors fill in, the open staircase now transformed into a regular set of steps, probably also as a safety measure for Miri. Down came Keith and Becca.

"Settle down, Mother, or you'll wake my baby." Keith proudly used the possessive pronoun for Miri. He nearly sent Helene into a tailspin.

"Get this woman out of the house!" Helene instead chose to order Keith and my mother to do her bidding.

But Keith wasn't done. "I had Dad's accident records unsealed, Mother. And instead of hearing it from you, I got to read too many decades too late that Dad was targeted and smashed against his own driver's-side door, not in an accident. Dad was murdered in an apparent cold-blooded hit."

A pin could have dropped. The painters even stopped rolling up the walls to see where this was going. Becca placed a soothing hand on her husband's arm, and he in turn clasped it close.

"I was just trying to protect you." Helene's voice was a whisper laden with sincerity, the truest I'd ever seen her. But it was too little, too late.

"I knew a lot, Mom." Keith's voice was pitying. "I knew about Dad's affair."

"What?!" Real alarm crossed Helene's face. "You knew her?"

But Keith just shook his head. "Not by sight or name, no. But I knew he was stepping out on our family. Isn't that enough?"

Miri's initial stirrings of wakefulness were transmitted over a monitor in the kitchen. Helene stiffened as her wails began. Becca started up the steps.

"You will not add her to the family, Keith."

"It's too late, Mom. Too late for you, but the best decision ever for me. Miri is my family now, and you are not. Now give me your key."

It was the only time I was treated to Helene's retreat without her putting up a fight. She handed over a key on a silver chain, wiped a tear from her eye, and swept from the house.

# CHAPTER SIXTEEN

"I guess it's official. I won't get to be one of your bridesmaids, after all." Tabitha offered me a rueful smile and smoothed down her prison-issue jumpsuit. I appreciated her stab at humor, but couldn't bring myself to laugh. It was the day I was due to get married, and here I was in jail with one of my best friends. I hadn't told anyone I was planning on dropping in on Tabitha. I'd high-tailed it over after picking up my marriage license, hoping I could stop for a brief visit, unnoticed by my family. They wouldn't think it very auspicious to spend even a minute in a jail on the day one was going to wed.

"Don't worry, Tabitha. Rachel will save your crazy green dress and matching ankle bracelet to wear when you get out."

*If you get out.*

I knew we were both thinking the same thing.

Tabitha's case was looking increasingly dire and airtight.

"Too bad you and Pia are the only people in this whole darn town who know I'm innocent." Tabitha gave my hand a grateful squeeze.

I was saddened to notice she hadn't included her mother, June, in the tiny list of two. But also heartened that she'd said that we knew she was innocent, not merely that we just believed it, too.

"And although I do believe Grandma Claudia was trying to broker the sale of certain items, I'm almost positive she didn't steal them. Not for the usual reason, at any rate." Tabitha rose to pace around her miniscule cell. "But Truman doesn't even want to hear new information that could help with his other investigations."

"Like what?" I had been a good girl this month, not directly sleuthing and soliciting information around town. But I still knew a lot.

"Horace Overright is a very distinctive man. I saw him on the sidewalk just minutes before the car barreled into Richard. I think he may have run him down, Mallory."

A chill danced down my back.

*It does fit.*

"Horace said he saw you back then with blood all over you. If he was there minutes before the attack, then just after, it could be him. Plus, who would want the Betsy Ross veil more than him?"

And the man was currently residing in my B and B and residence. Great.

"What are you waiting for! Tell Truman!" I sprang to press the button to summon the guard. I happened to know my soon-to-be father-in-law was getting ready at his house. But Tabitha could get her info in the record right now.

"Like I said, he's not interested in anything I have to say now that I've been all but convicted in his mind." Tabitha nearly came to tears with her frustration. "And I've meditated a lot in here, too. I can think of one more detail, but it's still a smidge hazy. When I went to help Richard, I thought that the veil was gone." She paused. "But in the back seat, I swore I saw a bat of some kind. Softball, maybe."

"Time's up." Faith appeared at the door, and did a little tsk. "Really, Mallory? Here on your wedding day?"

I stood and gave Tabitha a bone-crushing hug. "For good friends, I'd do anything."

I got home to Thistle Park with room to spare. It was bizarre showing up for a wedding with nothing to do. Oh yeah, except pledge my love and affection and commitment to the best man I'd ever known, and his equally amazing daughter. I broke into a grin as I donned the magic sundress that had served as my wedding muse.

I missed my engagement ring, but soon would have another, a different and lovely symbol on my left hand.

It would be the smallest wedding to take place

at Thistle Park, save for Keith and Becca's, which had been a teeny affair with Rachel officiating, Pickles the cat, the bride and groom, and yours truly.

"You look gorgeous." Rachel walked in a circle around me. Her retro taffeta jade dress swished and rustled. "No veil, but I love your clip."

It was best that I had not worn a veil. Not after all of the events of the newly finished month of June. I'd never look at another bridal veil the same way again after the apparent curse of the Betsy Ross veil had befallen me, my family, and friends. My hair was half held back with a demure pearl clip. And I'd chosen to don some lovely emerald earrings Garrett had given me, to tie in Rachel's bridesmaid dress, rather than the heavy crystal ones June had gifted me.

"It's showtime." Rachel nudged me to the back door of the kitchen, where my mother and stepfather stood.

"I've never been prouder," my mother whispered as she took one arm. Doug was a sweet and blubbering mess, who couldn't get a single word out. He grasped my other arm, and we were ready.

"Let's do this."

Rachel preceded me out the kitchen door, down the back-porch steps, and toward the simple unadorned trellis. I seemed to float down the steps on the arms of my parents, my path a clear one to reach Garrett and Summer at the trellis.

Garrett wiped away a spate of tears and took me in his arms when I finally reached him. And together we were wed by our favorite judge, a small group of onlookers cheering as we finished our short and simple ceremony. And together, hand in hand, Garrett and Summer and I made our way down the path to the garden. We danced the night away amidst the fireflies, noshing on sangria punch, five kinds of cookies, and vegan sandwiches requested by Summer. It was the wedding I never knew I'd dreamed of, and it was just perfect.

Garrett and I were the last ones in the yard, holding on to each other under a limitless black bowl of twinkling stars. He swept me up in his arms and carried me over the threshold of the kitchen. "I'll see you in a few minutes." He left me after delivering a smoldering kiss, and headed up the back stairs to the honeymoon suite.

I spun in a dreamy circle and poured two glasses of water to take upstairs. A cell phone buzzed on the kitchen table. I reflexively picked up the phone, swiping to light its screen. Only then did I realize the phone belonged to Pia. We had the same phone, with similar floral cases. I made to turn it off, when the screen that popped up revealed information too intriguing to ignore.

Pia's genealogical DNA results had been cued up for her perusal. And her closest relative was someone I knew. The DNA lab predicted that this person was Pia's half brother. It wasn't the answer she'd sought about her father, but it got her the answer just the same. There next to Pia's name on a digital tree resided her half brother, with what were probably his own newly released results. Pia's brother was Keith, making Richard Pierce her father.

I stood motionless in the dark kitchen. The news was more shocking to me than when Luke Skywalker found out about Darth Vader.

Footfalls raced down the back stairs. Garrett swept me up in his arms once more.

"I just can't wait, Mallory." He took Pia's phone from my hand and slid it onto the kitchen table. I didn't give it a second thought.

Amidst gales of my own laughter, my husband carried me up the steps to begin our married life together.

# CHAPTER SEVENTEEN

I awoke in Garrett's arms, my favorite place to be. I tenderly turned my gaze to him as he peacefully dozed. I rose from the bed and donned my robe, part of a surprisingly tasteful gift from my sister to wear on my wedding night. I slipped from the honeymoon suite after sending a look of love back at Garrett.

And promptly had the bejesus scared out of me in the hallway.

"Mallory." Rachel appeared an inch from me.

"Hey! Way to creep up on me." I gave my sister's arm a playful punch.

"Oh, stop. I've been dithering in front of your door for half an hour, deciding whether it would be totally rude to wake the newly married couple."

*This had better be good.*

Rachel gestured toward an open door down the hall. "Horace is gone."

*Okay. Not good.*

"Like, take a stroll in the dewy morning air gone, or *gone* gone?" I was already tearing down the hall to see for myself.

"The latter."

Every scrap of Horace's things had been removed. Guests were free to come and go, of course, and he'd paid in full. But it was a cold way to leave. He'd joined in on the wedding festivities, and I thought I'd at least get to say goodbye.

"Let's check the office," I suggested. "I don't like the feel of this."

Rachel nodded, and we set off. As we reached the top of the stairs, the honeymoon door cracked open. I trotted back for my first morning married kiss.

"Hurry back, love." Garrett planted a scorcher on my lips.

A few minutes later, Rachel and I turned in slow circles in the office. We'd finally set it right after the room had been tossed, with some new chairs and couches.

"It seems okay," I muttered. "And it's funny. Helene said her late husband favored owls. I never realized how many owl pieces came with the house, and how it's all Richard's doing."

*Richard.*

How could I have forgotten?!

I filled Rachel in on Pia's father's true identity. She let out an expletive not to be repeated.

"Oh, my goodness, Pia's phone! It doesn't seem like she has a pass code. I should have secured it." A wave of fear coursed through me.

Rachel and I raced to the kitchen. It was too late. The phone was gone.

*Uh-oh.*

The information about Pia's paternity in the wrong hands could be disastrous. Rachel and I discussed the ramifications as we took one more slow inspection around the house. In the parlor, my sister picked up the little owl statue Helene had remarked upon, and slowly tossed it in the air, catching it again and again.

"Watch it with that, Rach."

Of course, after my admonition, the piece fell to the hardwood floor, the pretty Japanese ceramic bird bursting into a thousand shards.

"Oopsies." Rachel blushed and moved to sweep up the mess with the nearby chimney tools stashed near the fireplace. "What is this?"

A sheaf of papers had resided within the owl.

"Whoa."

One was weathered and delicate, with spidery, barely perceptible faded brown ink scrawled across it. I'd seen it before, on a digital photo Tabitha had held up for me. It was Betsy Claypoole's—née Ross— receipt for the veil.

"And these?" Rachel thrust the other papers into my hands. I shook more ceramic shards from the documents and took a closer look.

"It's an amended will. Made out just a month before Richard died." My eyes nearly bugged out of my head. "He knew June was pregnant with Pia. Dear God, he left half of Thistle Park to June's un-born child."

Rachel and I stood stock-still.

I wasn't sure about the rules of succession and newfound, amended wills anymore. But I did know what Richard had wanted. Half of Thistle Park should go to Pia as rightfully hers.

"Helene." It came out in a whisper. "Rach, she probably knew. She finally figured out who Richard's mistress was, and was afraid June would tell Pia about her father's identity. Helene tried to kill June." It made sense. "And Claudia, too, for that matter, since she'd promised to tell Pia in just a week, on her twenty-fifth birthday."

"Let's go." Rachel moved to confront Helene this very instant.

"Give me just a few more hours." I wiggled my eyebrows and ran back up to Garrett.

Yes, the new revelations were dire. But some things could wait.

# CHAPTER EIGHTEEN

"**D**on't be ridiculous." Helene attempted to push her front door closed, but Rachel stuck a bejeweled, high-heeled sneaker in the jamb to stop her.

Perhaps announcing that we knew she'd tried to murder June in addition to killing Claudia hadn't been the most persuasive gambit to gain entry. I tried another tactic.

"We found an amendment to Richard's will, Helene. One leaving Thistle Park to the child he conceived with his mistress. Meaning Pia, June's daughter."

*That got her attention.*

"You're making it up." Helene's voice was a fearful hiss.

"Here it is." I handed Helene a thin stack of papers.

She perused them and then promptly began

tearing them into smaller and smaller chunks. "You'll never prove any of this."

"Oh, puh-lease. Like we wouldn't have just given you a copy, not the original." Rachel breezed past a stunned Helene and held the door open for me. I was nervous entering my enemy's home, especially now that I knew she'd killed Claudia and probably had attempted to kill June, as well as Jesse. My original hunch about the silly white gloves she'd worn to Cordials and Cannonballs had been correct.

"You still blame Jesse for Richard's death since he'd quit his security detail for Richard," I added. "That's why you tried to take him out, too, when you had the chance in the fog. But your real target was Claudia. You must have known that she was going to tell Pia that Richard was her father, as soon as she turned twenty-five."

"I did know that," Helene conceded with a bitter twist of her mouth. "And while I begged Claudia not to reveal her knowledge, I'm no killer, you idiot."

Perhaps Helene's preoccupation and bullying about women on the battlefield had just been a proxy war of intimidation designed to make Claudia think twice about telling Pia the truth.

"Then you tried to kill June, but failed. Or maybe you had one of your minions do it. I'm not even sure when you figured out who Richard's mistress was."

Helene grew still. "I always suspected. But it was

when she showed up at the funeral, in the back, already with child, that I knew for sure." Her face fell, her spirit totally dejected.

"And you framed Tabitha to get her out of the way," Rachel added. "She was close to the scene when Richard was killed, and you might have even thought she knew."

"Good one, Rach."

I worked in one last theory. "It's totally possible you killed Richard, too, Helene. You claim to have not known right away that he was with June, but you did know he was having an affair. Did you gun down your own husband in cold blood, then take off with the veil?"

Helene opened her mouth once more, but our uninvited guest answered for her.

"Getting closer, Mallory, but not quite."

A slim hand with a gun whipped around the corner of the front door. A hand wearing my purloined engagement ring.

"Into the woods, ladies. All of you. *Now.*"

June Battles gave us a triumphant smile and brought up the rear of our death march into the woods.

# CHAPTER NINETEEN

*Duh.*

It irritated me that my last day on earth would be the one after I wed the love of my life. And after I'd finally fit all of the chess pieces together in my head. Of course, the perpetrator was June. In retrospect, it fit.

Rachel gave me a desperate glance back, and was rewarded with June's hand lashing out to turn her around.

"Ouch! Lay off of me!" Rachel glared at June.

But the accomplished murderess just laughed. "Rachel, as if you haven't noticed, I'm quite skilled with a gun. It doesn't matter if it's a modern piece, or a historical replica. And when I'm done with all of you three, it'll look like the two Shepard sisters tried to take out Helene Pierce, but that there was a shootout. The town will mourn all of your deaths, that's for sure. But I won't. I'll get to keep going on."

"You framed your own daughter." I tried to keep the anger from my voice. "You're lucky Tabitha didn't know the person having the affair with Richard all those years was none other than her dear mother."

June shrugged, unfazed. "It was so easy to steal items from my daughter's place of work, then take her laptop when she was having lunch or dinner, and list the stuff on eBay." June snickered. "It was even easier to steal items, present them to Claudia as newly found or acquired treasures, and watch her try to sell them here in Port Quincy."

"You were trying to get your own mother and daughter in trouble and out of the way." I shook my head. "You are a sick woman."

"You mean I'm a genius," June amended. "And I had to punish Claudia. She started selling items she knew were mine from Richard, as punishment for not telling Pia about him. She stashed those suitcases downstairs, when I told her not to sell them and to put them away for safekeeping. It's not Pia's fault she brought those hatboxes up, and you found the veil. But I wasn't worried. I knew I'd steal it back."

"You tossed our office and broke into the safe."

It made sense now. It was also the reason why Pia's desk had remained remarkably unscathed.

"But can I ask why you're wearing my engagement ring?" I shivered. I didn't want the piece of jewelry back, now that it had resided on this psychopath's finger. But I still wanted to know.

"This is the ring Richard gave to me," June conceded. "Claudia sold it out of spite. She just happened to sell it to Garrett."

"But the real reason you had to kill your mother was because she promised to tell Pia about her father."

June nodded. "If you must know, that horrible man valued Keith more than my daughter. He made out a trust for me as an enticement not to tell Pia of her identity until she turned twenty-five. A random number that was really oriented toward keeping Keith in the dark, so that his precious son didn't think badly about his father."

I wasn't about to tell June about Richard bequeathing half of Thistle Park to Pia.

"And you tried to frame me for stealing the distillery." Helene finally spoke up. "You put it on my property and stole my wallet to bury it there."

It was my turn to volley a theory. "You cruel, cruel woman." A wave of anger crested and crashed within me. "You killed Richard yourself, stole the veil, and let your poor daughter Tabitha carry the knowledge and secret that she'd been on the scene. A secret that weighed on her for years."

June signed. "That I did regret." She turned to Helene. "You always win, Helene. Richard had proposed with this ring, and promised to wed me wearing the Betsy Ross veil. At the last second, he chickened out. He didn't want to leave you and Keith. He chose your family over mine. He had to go."

"Just like it's time for you to go, June."

Horace Overright, knight in shining suspender armor, whipped around a thick tree trunk.

June took one look at him and burst into laughter. "You sniveling little fool—argh!"

June fell to the forest floor as Horace sprayed an inordinate amount of mace into her face. June wildly shot out at us, hoping to catch us even in her newly blinded state. She stopped her game when Baxter the fearless Yorkie sunk his tiny little teeth into her ankle. The little fellow must have followed us into the woods.

"Ouch! Get him off of me!" June grabbed her ankle and Baxter moved to her face, coating her with wet doggie kisses in apology for the bites.

We used Helene's stretchy coral belt to tie June to a tree, and waited, exhausted, for the police to arrive. I closed my eyes and sent thanks skyward.

I would live another day to spend with my husband and stepdaughter, my family and friends. It was a great day to be alive.

# EPILOGUE

Three months later, Garrett and I returned from our honeymoon. We were still in the honeymoon phase, though. We'd waited for the dust to settle from June's numerous confessions and revelations and had taken a little trip with Summer to Montreal, a healthy distance in time from the melee that had happened in June and July.

When we returned, I was able to thank Horace in person for rescuing us. He'd returned to Port Quincy one last time to personally take possession of the famous veil. He'd had a hunch that June must have been behind the murder of Richard Pierce and the original theft of the veil. He'd been tailing her and followed her to Helene's house. I was relieved to witness Truman handing over the two pieces of the Betsy Ross veil, hidden once again in June's store, to Horace for safekeeping at the Smithsonian.

Jesse was nearly finished with our cottage in the

woods. He'd taken his time and had properly healed, wed Bev, and started his own married life. Pia and Tabitha were still processing the realization that their mother had murdered Richard Pierce, her own mother Claudia, and had faked her own attempted murder in order to frame her daughters.

Pia had been hesitant to accept my offer of half the property at Thistle Park as her father had wanted. But as soon as the little cottage was complete, she was due to move into the third-floor apartment with Rachel. The three of us fell into an easy rhythm, planning weddings and hanging out during our off hours.

Today my family and friends were gathered to celebrate the official formation of another new little family. Keith and Becca had formally adopted Miri, now a crawling nine-month-old.

I moved through my house with smiles for everyone, including Helene. She'd made her amends and apologies, and it was in her arms that Miri now resided, giggling and practicing her clapping. She gave the little girl a kiss on the cheek and sent me a wink.

I brushed away a tear. I still felt like celebrating my own family each and every day. I'd been silly to obsess over what time was perfect for my nuptials. As the party wound down, I joined Garrett and Summer on the back porch to take in the stars, my heart unbelievably full.

# RECIPES

## Chocolate Almond Cookies

2 cups flour
½ cup cocoa
½ teaspoon salt
1 teaspoon almond extract
½ cup coconut oil
½ cup white sugar
½ cup brown sugar
1 cup chopped almonds

Preheat oven to 350 degrees. Sift together flour, cocoa, and salt. Add almond extract and coconut oil, both sugars, and cream together. Form dough into small, teaspoon-sized balls. Roll in chopped almonds. Bake for fifteen to twenty minutes.

## Sweet Cherry Whiskey

2 ounces whiskey
1 teaspoon honey
3 maraschino cherries
Ice

Combine whiskey and honey. Shake. Pour over ice. Garnish with cherries.

## Sparkling Berry Sangria

1 bottle sparkling rosé wine, chilled
1 liter ginger ale
1 cup mixed raspberries and blueberries

Combine ingredients in a large punch bowl. Serve by the ladle-full.